Wicked and Wild

A BAD THINGS NOVEL

New York Times and *USA Today* Bestselling Author

CYNTHIA EDEN

CHAPTER ONE

"My, what *big* teeth you have..." The feminine voice drifted from the darkness. He jerked against the chains that held him, an instinctive response to that sensual purr of sound. "Would those be the better to *eat* your enemies?"

A snarl built in his throat. It vibrated against the thick collar that had been sealed around his neck.

"And, oh, my...what giant claws you have," she continued, her voice sliding over him as she hid in the dark, just beyond his view.

His claws scraped across the stone floor. He'd already gouged deep slash marks into the stone, cutting in desperation over and over again.

"Let me guess. Those claws—are those so that you can rip your enemies apart? The better to slice and dice?"

He opened his mouth. Flames didn't shoot out. The collar stopped the flames, but tendrils of smoke escaped.

Husky, throaty laughter reached him. A taunt. "Oh, what wonderful flames I bet you have. The better to roast anyone who gets in your way?"

He strained against the chains that held him captive. She was so close. He could smell her.

Some sweet, flowery scent that didn't belong in the dungeon. When had she been placed in the cell next to him? He didn't remember her arriving, but since he'd been trapped in the form of his beast, he'd been losing time.

He'd been losing his fucking mind.

A shifter wasn't meant to stay this way. If you stayed as a beast too long—particularly in the form he carried—you would lose your humanity. The man died. The monster reigned. His monster was very, very close to taking over. And when the beast did, even those chains wouldn't hold him. The only way to stop him?

Kill the beast *and* the man.

A soft sigh reached him. "No response? Well, it's not like I truly expected a dragon to talk with me. Though that would certainly have livened up my night."

Come closer! Inside, he was shouting those words. But from the beast's mouth, only a growl emerged.

Still...footsteps shuffled forward. She'd been hiding in the very far corner of her cell, beyond the area he could see because of the damn bars and stone walls around them. But she advanced slowly, as if she had all of the time in the world. The sweet scent—what was that? Roses? Lilacs? He had no fucking clue. The scent drifted to him, and the beast greedily inhaled. He'd been in that prison for so long, only smelling waste, rats. Death.

His mystery woman smelled like hope.

Impossible, of course, because he had no hope. And soon, his captors would be forced to end him. If he couldn't transform back before the rising of the full moon, there would be no stopping the beast. *So they'll kill me before the full moon can reach the top of the sky.*

"Oh, wow, what very, very thick and *big* scales you have." Her voice was a little louder now. Definitely mocking. She thought it was funny to mock a beast? Her hand curled around the bars between their cells. "What are those used for? So that no one can ever touch your cold, cold heart?"

He lunged at her—or, rather, he lunged as far as the chains would allow. About a foot.

She laughed. Actually laughed in the face of a snarling dragon. Her laugh was kind of like...a cackle.

Shit. No, don't be—

"Hello, dragon." She smiled at him. She was fully visible now, as she stood with her face close to the bars. An absolutely perfect face. Oval, with porcelain skin that looked as if it had never been marred by anything in her long life. Her lips were full and sexy. Cherry red. Her eyes were chocolate and framed by the thickest lashes he'd ever seen. Her long hair—deep, dark black—tumbled over her shoulders. She was dressed in a pale blue dress, one that clung tightly to her curves. One that made it seem as if she should be attending some fancy ball and not be trapped in the darkest dungeon to ever exist.

He recognized her on sight. There was only one woman this particularly beautiful—unforgettably, hauntingly so—who would be trapped in a cell. After all, this was a paranormal prison. A place reserved for the worst of the worst.

And he was looking at someone who was *evil*. To her very core.

Only she had the face of an absolute angel.

Her gaze swept over him. No fear showed on her face. He didn't know if she was capable of feeling fear. According to the stories, she didn't feel anything.

Valerie Storm.

The most wicked of all the witches. Not that all witches were bad. Some were quite good. Valerie had missed that whole *good* memo.

"Shifter, shifter, shifter...you seem to be having yourself a very bad day."

Not a day. Not a week. Try a month. He'd been in that cursed form for nearly a month. *When the full moon rises again, I'll be dead.*

She shook her head. Made a *tut-tut-tut* sound that grated on his nerves. "Got stuck, didn't you? You changed into your strongest beast, and I'm betting you were having a serious rage moment when you did so. Shifters. You always let your emotions rule you. That's a flaw."

He blew smoke at her.

She just laughed. "I'm sure that would have been *way* more intimidating if you'd actually been able to spew a flicker of fire my way. But, well, since you're collared, you're kind of like a really big, really sad, puppy."

The hell he was.

His claws scraped against the stone.

She winced at the grating sound. "Please, stop that. Especially when I'm here, offering to help you."

Bullshit. The baddest witch on the block didn't help anyone. She killed. She cursed. She left hell in her wake.

She...she was batting her long lashes at him. "I know shifter secrets." Now her voice was a bit sing-songy.

He realized the stories he'd heard about her were true. The dark magic she used had destroyed her mind. He was staring at one crazy witch. She crooked her index finger at him, as if urging him closer to her. Of course, he couldn't get closer because of the *fucking chains*.

"The council could have helped you. They could have used their magic to turn you back into a man."

No, impossible. The high council—a witch council—had been adamant that there was nothing they could do. They'd poked him. Prodded him. Tried their spells. Nothing had worked.

"Don't believe me? What? Does the big, bad beast think I'm a liar?"

Hell, yes. He snarled.

Tears gleamed in her eyes. "I'm hurt."

What?

Her head sagged forward. Her long hair shielded her face. "Everyone thinks I'm evil. That I don't feel. But I do. I—"

She was cackling again. Her head shot up, and her beautiful features were lit with mirth. "Too much fun. Beast, you are making my night. Yes, I'm a liar. Don't forget that. Not ever."

Why was he being forced to be cell buddies with Valerie Storm?

Her smile faded. "Want to know why the council didn't help you?"

He wanted to know why she was still talking to him.

"It's because they don't believe in cheating death. You see, death is coming for you. He's almost taken your human side. *That's* why you can't shift. The part of you that was a man—that part is at death's door right now. The council doesn't want to fight death. You can't fight death with their *good,* white magic. You have to fight evil...with evil." She grinned at him, revealing dimples. Dimples, seriously? "Luckily for you, I'm the most evil witch you'll ever meet. I'm Valerie, Valerie Storm. You know, in case you haven't heard of me."

He'd heard. In great detail.

"I can turn you back into a man. I can do what those other witches were too afraid to do. I don't mind using dark magic. In fact, it's rather my drug of choice."

He wasn't scraping the stone with his claws any longer. She held his attention completely.

"But it's not like I'm the type to do things out of the goodness of my heart." Her hand rose and pressed to her chest, drawing his attention to— well, her high, firm breasts. "Some would say I don't even have a heart."

Plenty of people said that. Maybe the whole world.

"So if you want my help, we have to make a deal."

Not like he had any options. If he didn't change back, he'd die. That meant all of his people would be without a leader. They'd fall to his enemies. Their deaths would be on him.

"I'm pretty, right?" She was batting her lashes again. The crazy witch. "And I'm smart. Like, wicked smart. I'm also funny. And I think I have a really great laugh."

She did *not*.

"I'm kind of the total package."

If the package was a ball of hellfire.

"So, truly, I'm your best choice for a mate."

Wait—what? More smoke escaped from his mouth.

She waved the tendrils away. "Okay, you need to work on that. I don't like smoke to the face. No one does."

He clamped his gaping mouth full of razor sharp teeth *closed*.

"You're a shifter. Um, obviously. And you guys mate for life. Your mates are the most important thing to you, right? You'd do anything to protect the woman you were bonded with?"

Yes...

"I want to mate with you."

He was in freaking dragon form—

"Don't look at me like that. I'm not being pervy. I'm not suggesting some weird dragon sex. I'll give you a little of my blood. You give me a little of yours, and presto, we have a link."

Mostly right. They'd have a *temporary* bond. The bond wouldn't become permanent until they had sex, and that could only happen when he was in human form. He wasn't just any shifter. He was royal. The most powerful shifter out there, and the rules for him were different.

"So if you want me to change you back, you have to bond with me first. Come on," Valerie wheedled. "What's a few drops of blood between friends?"

They weren't friends. No one was friends with her. She killed her friends.

"Here. I'll make it easy for you." In a move too fast to see, she'd slashed her arm. Not some deep, gaping wound. Just a little cut near her wrist. Had she used her fingernails? Did the witch have a knife hidden on her? What was her deal?

She shoved her wrist though the bars. "Just stretch that dragon body and neck of yours. Take a little lick."

If he did that...

He'd be tied to her.

Temporarily. He didn't have to ever have sex with the woman. And, he could go back to human form. Providing she wasn't just bullshitting him. *But it wouldn't be to her advantage to lie.* Not right then. She'd either change him back or she wouldn't.

She wiggled her fingers at him. "I'm waiting."

He didn't want to die in that cell. He *wouldn't* die in that cell.

He stretched. Stretched hard against those chains. His tongue snaked out. Caught a drop of her blood. Blood that tasted ridiculously sweet, like candy. Blood that—

Her hand moved—lightning fast—and she *was* holding some kind of knife. A knife that penetrated his scales, so he knew the blade had to be magic. *How had she gotten a knife in her cell?* She brought the knife up to her mouth, and her little pink tongue delicately lapped up a drop of blood on its tip. "Someone tastes spicy."

Deep inside, he could feel a change. Like a door had just closed.

Death's door?

"Okay." She sighed. "This may hurt a bit. But, whatever, maybe you're in to that." And her stretching fingers—just the tips—touched his head. A tingle began when she touched him. She was chanting, and a faint, blue light slid from her hand to him. The blue light grew. Grew. And it *burned.*

It fucking burned!

He didn't just snarl. He roared. He bellowed. He—

Broke the chains. Tore them from the wall. The collar that had circled his neck shattered.

She kept touching him. Her eyes were closed as she chanted.

His scales vanished. His body hunched, and his head shoved harder against her fingertips. Bones popped and snapped. His breath heaved in and out. He opened his mouth, ready to let fire spew out and—

"Valerie!" Her name tore from him.

He could speak. He wasn't a beast anymore. He was a man.

"Well, hello, stranger." Her smile winked at him, but her face was paler than before. Her dark gaze dipped over his naked body. "My," she licked her lower lip. "What a big—"

"Trust me, it's better for the pleasure."

She laughed. Cackled. And *why* was he starting to find that horrible sound to be oddly cute?

"Griffin Bastien," he growled his name. Yes, he could speak like a man again, but he was still on the deep, growly edge. His voice was often like that.

Her eyes widened. "I do think I know that name."

He stared down at his arms. His fingers. No claws, not anymore. No scales.

"You're the king of the shifters."

His gaze slid back to her.

Her dimples were winking, but dark shadows now lined her eyes.

"Figured you had to be," she murmured. "That's why I knew we had to do a blood link. Not just anyone can turn into a dragon."

No, not just anyone could.

"Is it true?" Valerie asked, only sounding vaguely curious. "Can you also shift into the form of a wolf?"

He could shift into three different beast forms. That was why he was the damn king.

When he'd turned back into a man and that crazy blue light of hers had been sliding everywhere, she'd shattered his chains and his collar. Or maybe he'd shattered them, Griffin wasn't sure. Didn't really matter. Slowly, deliberately, he stalked toward her.

She didn't back away from the bars. Valerie just waited for him. Studied him.

"You're much more handsome as a man. Nice jaw. All hard and square and clenched."

His jaw clenched harder.

"And I like your eyes. I think they are as green as your dragon scales were."

He was sure his eyes were glowing with fury right then.

"Lots of muscles. Great body. Got to ask, do you work out?"

"*Stop.*" She was trying to drive him mad.

His witch shrugged. *His.* Because, yes, they were mated. *Temporarily.* He could feel the connection inside. A pull toward her. He wanted to put his mouth on her lips. Those blood red lips. Wanted to taste her. Wanted to fuck her.

Not the way he should be reacting to Ms. Wicked.

"Why did you want to mate me?" Griffin demanded. "Were you really so hard up that you'd take a dragon?"

She didn't flinch. Just sighed. "You'll find out why. Soon enough."

Hardly a good answer.

She glanced over her shoulder. No one was in the corridor beyond their cells, but he could hear the approach of guards. Nibbling her lower lip, she peered back at him. "Is it true?"

Was what true? She'd lost him again. "Did you use dark magic to save me?" Griffin demanded.

"Yes, and that's why I can barely stand up." One hand pulled away from the bars, and she waved vaguely in the air. "You're welcome."

Griffin stiffened. He...hadn't thanked her. The spell had obviously taken a physical toll on her. She was using her grip on the bars to stand upright. "I didn't think witches *could* work spells down here. Aren't these cells supposed to be magic proof?"

"*White* magic proof. And they're pretty good at stopping dark magic, too. But I worked around their system." She winked. "They thought I'd try to break out. That's where they focused their magical guards. Instead, I just pushed the magic into you. I'm sneaky like that."

She was quite mad like that.

And he was...oddly fascinated by her. *Wrong*. Absolutely.

"You didn't tell me if it was true," Valerie muttered, frowning at him.

He was stark naked and talking to an infuriatingly sexy woman. "Because I don't know the question."

A furrow appeared between her brows. "If your mate dies, is it true that you go mad?"

Now he stiffened.

The footsteps of the guards were very close.

"I'll take that as a yes," she whispered. "Okay, here's the deal. You're really, *really* going to have to hurry. The fire is going to be really hot."

What? *"What?"* Griffin roared.

But the guards were already in her cell. Four men. They seized her. Too rough. Too hard.

He snarled at them, "Get your fucking hands *off* her!"

They didn't.

He grabbed for the bars that separated his cell from hers.

The guards were dragging her from the dungeon. She waved to Griffin. "Hope to see you soon. Like, *really* soon, okay?"

His chains were broken at his feet. Rage blasted through him. The bars he gripped began to bend.

My mate. He wouldn't have chosen her. No way would he have chosen Valerie Storm as his mate, but he hadn't been given an option. She'd linked them, and now he could *feel* her, inside. A flame of dark magic within him.

She was being taken away. Forced away from him. His beast stirred. Growled.

You couldn't separate a shifter from his mate. Whether he'd chosen her or not...*you can't separate us!*

The bars broke. He lunged into her cell. The guards had foolishly left her cell door open. He rushed right out, claws bursting from his fingertips.

He wasn't going to lose his witch.

Not when he'd just *gotten* her.

CHAPTER TWO

"Oh, wow, that's a lot of wood." Valerie Storm tugged at the ropes that bound her wrists. No give. Of course. They were enchanted ropes. Witch proof. Well, *bad* witch proof. That fact totally and completely sucked, by the way.

The jerk guards brought out more wood. Put it around her feet. A crowd had gathered to watch the festivities. Because everyone loved to watch a good show, right? She smiled at them. Did they think she was going to beg? To plead? To scream?

She wasn't. Well, she *might* scream. Valerie would leave that one to fate.

"Guilty!" The one word blasted through the air.

Valerie rolled her eyes. Could the scene get more Salem-esque? Only the difference here was that witches were burning other witches. "This is not the way it's supposed to work! We're on the same side, remember? Us against the mortals?"

"You're not one of us." Ah, it was the council leader who'd just spoken. Genevieve Remonde. Her blonde hair was in a stylish pixie cut that framed her heart-shaped face. Her pale blue eyes gleamed as she pointed to Valerie. "You chose the wrong path. Dark magic isn't to be used. It's forbidden."

Blah, blah, blah. Like she hadn't heard this talk a time or twenty. Valerie narrowed her eyes on the woman who'd once been her absolute best friend. It sucked when your BFF went all righteous. "If you'd helped me," she said, voice low, "I wouldn't have gone down this path."

Did Genevieve flinch? Hard to say.

"You did what was forbidden." Genevieve crossed her arms over her chest. "Your crimes are many..."

A man stepped forward. Tall, muscled, with hair the same blond as Genevieve's. Prince Charming handsome. He unrolled a scroll.

"Here we go," Valerie muttered.

"You were found dancing on the grave of your recent kill," Devon Vesiux called out, his voice echoing and quieting the murmurs in the crowd—a crowd primarily composed of witches, but also consisting of a few shifters and even some vamps. "You showed no remorse for the crime. In fact, you were laughing."

Yes, she had been. Valerie shrugged or tried to shrug. The bindings were too tight for much movement. "If you think that vamp didn't have it coming, you're dead wrong."

The nearby vamps hissed at her. She hissed back. Since when was the witch council all chummy with the undead?

Valerie decided to defend herself. Why not? The defense would buy her a little more time. "For the record, he deserved to have his head lopped off. I was just dancing because well...there was a *tiny* chance he might have been one of those all-powerful creatures you hear about in legend. You know—creatures like *moi*? I thought he might rise again, and when he didn't, I danced."

More hisses.

"You are guilty," Devon boomed, "of practicing black magic. You've killed dozens of humans."

Dozens? That seemed like a lot. But her memory was a bit foggy. That happened after the first one hundred years of life.

"You've attacked shifters..."

She had. They'd deserved it, too.

"Drained vampires."

Wasn't that only fair? They drained humans, too.

"And you're working to overthrow your own kind!" This last was bellowed from Devon with a particularly angry intensity.

Silence.

All eyes were on her.

Valerie smiled. "Guilty," she purred. Her chin lifted. "I am working to overthrow this stupid council." A council that mostly consisted of Genevieve and her goody-goody lover Devon. "Because your rules bore me." Now her gaze darted to the crowd. "And you want to know why they have me up here? *Bound* by magic rope so I can't cast a spell? It's because they fear me. They know I'm the prophesized witch. The all-powerful one who will rule over every witch in this realm. I'm the one who should be leading, not Genevieve. She knows it. She's felt my power growing every single day." Valerie turned a pitying look on

Genevieve. "Soon you won't be able to stop me. You know it. That's why you're trying to play your end game now."

It was the reason why Genevieve was trying to light her up before Valerie could reach her full potential.

Genevieve snatched a flaming torch from the hand of a nearby witch guard. "You will never rule the witches. We will *never* submit to someone like you." She touched the flames to the wood around Valerie's feet. "You die tonight!"

Smoke hit her first, and Valerie was reminded of her dragon. All smoke, no flames. Only there *were* flames this time. The wood began crackling. The flames started dancing. Orange and gold. Quite angry. They lapped at her feet. Rose to her thighs. She clamped her legs together and wondered just where in the hot hell her dragon was—

"No!" A truly phenomenal roar reached her. And then he was there. Her big, bad beast. He leapt right through the flames. Grabbed her. His green eyes *blazed* as he ripped apart the magical bindings. *Oh, yes, thank you!* And in a flash, he had her out of the fire. He held her in his arms, rather protectively. What a strong shifter.

At first, there was just stunned silence from the onlookers around them. Those righteous bastards who'd come to watch a woman burn had been rendered speechless. Her fingers twitched. She'd love to send some fire back at them. *Payback.*

"*Griffin...*" His name emerged from the crowd as a whisper. Then a swell of sound let her hear them say...

"*The king of all shifters is back!*"

"*He's a man again.*"

"*Griffin!*" A cry of triumph. Relief.

Then... "*Why the hell did he just save her?*"

Valerie smirked. Why, indeed.

Genevieve ran toward them. Devon, as always, was right at her side. "What are you doing?" Genevieve cried. "Let her go! Put her back in the fire!"

"No, thank you," Valerie demurred. She realized Genevieve would look absolutely gorgeous with a snake's tongue. Fitting because—

"You *don't* burn her," Griffin rasped.

Valerie nodded as she looped her arm around his neck. "No, you don't."

The crowd was closing in. Lots of shock appeared on lots of faces.

"How are you back, Griffin?" Devon asked, staring at the other man in wonder.

Well, she could kind of understand the wonderment. Griffin was pretty sexy. And he was still naked. Valerie's eyes narrowed. She didn't want everyone gawking at *her* mate. She wiggled her fingers, and clothes appeared on his body. "You're welcome," she murmured.

Griffin's head turned. His eyes were still unnaturally bright. Helluva sexy. "I just saved you."

He had.

"*You're* welcome," Griffin told her flatly.

Her lips wanted to twitch.

"*Put her down!*" Genevieve's face was blood red. "The council administered a punishment! Valerie Storm is to die for her crimes! She is—"

"One law triumphs all of your council rules." Griffin's voice was arctic cold. Crazy, scary cold. Sexy cold. "Mating law. No *witch* council can ever kill a shifter's mate."

Boom! Valerie mouthed that little exclamation when Genevieve's suddenly bowl-shaped eyes flew to her. *That's right. Guess who got mated in your dungeon?* It took all of her willpower not to sing out those very words.

Never let it be said that Valerie Storm could not think fast. And, yes, she'd known about the shifter mating rule.

"No one can kill a shifter's mate," Griffin continued grimly, "not without starting a war with my whole nation."

Pale blue flutters of light danced in the air around Genevieve. Uh, oh, someone was angry. Please, if Genevieve thought those little lights were supposed to be something intimidating...

Valerie smiled. She wiggled her fingers again. Giant, cavernous cracks appeared in the earth, separating her and Griffin from everyone else.

Cries of fright filled the air when smoke started to rise from those cracks.

One witch called, "She's summoning beasts from hell!"

Valerie barely contained another eye roll. And these people thought she was the crazy one?

"What have you done?" Devon demanded. He stared at Griffin in growing horror. "We had a deal. *What have you done?*"

A deal? Bull. Devon had thrown Griffin in the darkest pit he could find. "You should have helped him when you had the chance. Just like you should have helped Tomas." *No, don't let the rage erupt, not now.* She was too weak. The cracks in the earth were all just for show. Valerie had seriously depleted her powers when she'd worked her mojo on Griffin. "Since you didn't, I stepped in. I'm a great helper like that."

"This cannot be!" Devon was still in denial. "She has to...live?"

"We're mated, so, yes," Valerie replied, rather enjoying being held by her beast. "*She* has to live." So that meant...*Watch out, witches.*

"Banishment." Genevieve had a broad smile on her face. "You cannot stay in this realm, Valerie. You cannot live among humans. Not with the evil in your soul."

Seriously? Harping much?

"You mated to a shifter. You have to *live* with a shifter."

Valerie stiffened. "You can put me down now," she instructed Griffin. Because this development wasn't part of the plan.

"You take her to your realm, and she can *only* leave with the aid of shifter, isn't that how it works?" Genevieve pressed Griffin.

"Yes." Griffin's reply was soft.

Valerie tried to jump out of his arms. He just tightened his hold on her. His strength wasn't so sexy any longer.

And Devon was smiling, too. She didn't like his cold smile. "Banishment," he agreed.

No, no. "Hold on—"

"We can't kill a shifter's mate, but we can banish a witch. And once you are in the land of the shifters..." Genevieve laughed. It was a stupid, musical sound. "You'll never come back."

Griffin moved his head in the slightest of nods.

Oh, no. No. He'd *better* not be—

"Agreed," Griffin promised.

This wasn't happening! She'd helped him! Given him clothes! She'd—

"You will never get away from me," he whispered to Valerie.

Her head turned. She stared into his incredible green eyes.

And she knew that she'd just traded one fiery hell for another. "Shit—" Valerie began.

But her curse was cut off by the howl of a fierce wind. Genevieve and Devon had their hands up, they were chanting, and a door had just opened. A bright, glowing door.

Griffin's whole body suddenly seemed too hot. She knew *he'd* been the one to open the doorway. A portal, really. Genevieve and Devon were just chanting because they were putting up a magic blockade to make sure she didn't just pop herself out of that place right the hell then. If she'd known this messed-up situation would occur, Valerie would have tried vanishing sooner. Unfortunately, it was too late now.

"It's not going to be that easy," Valerie warned her foes. Griffin's hold was freaking unbreakable. "I will find a way back. And when I do..."

"Go play with the beasts." Genevieve's face twisted with fury. "I hope they rip you apart."

Such a sweet BFF. "Hey, Genny, how about you go screw—"

Griffin leapt through the portal. Pain burned through Valerie, tearing through her body. Witches *weren't* supposed to travel to a shifter's land. At least, not this way. She screamed, the scream she hadn't given when the fire lapped at her legs. She screamed and screamed as the pain hit her and then she heard—

"I'll take care of you. It's okay."

The hell it was! She was going to *kill* her ungrateful beast at the very first opportunity. A shifter would go mad without his mate, but she wasn't a shifter. And a wicked witch would be just fine without an asshole dragon at her side for all eternity.

First mistake, beast...you just became my enemy.

CHAPTER THREE

She'd been sleeping for a very, very long time.

Griffin frowned at the woman in his bed. She was breathing fine, nice and easy. There were no injuries on her body. He'd checked, not in a sleazy way, but just to make sure she hadn't gotten burned when she'd been tied to the stake. He hadn't stripped her gown off, but he'd lifted the now tattered and soot-covered material to look at her legs. Amazingly, she wasn't burned at all.

She was just out cold.

He sat on the edge of the bed. His hand lifted, and he brushed back a heavy lock of her dark hair. She didn't look evil when she slept. Her lashes were long and thick, casting shadows over her cheeks and—

Her hand flew up, grabbing his wrist. Grabbing it *hard*. "I hope you weren't about to play Snow White with me."

"What?"

"Because I don't need a kiss from my true love to wake up." Her lashes snapped open. Her fury was plain to see. "What I do need is for you to tell me that I am *not* in the realm of shifters."

That was funny. Most people didn't even know shifters were real. They were. Plenty of shifters lived right in the midst of humans. Bear shifters and panther shifters seemed to love mingling with them. Very few shifters—mostly the ancients and the very young—still preferred to stay in a separate realm. This realm was where they'd all started, though. Where they'd stayed safe in times of persecution. It was—

"I better not be in that hellhole," Valerie fumed.

It *wasn't* a hellhole. It was his home. For the next month, it would be her home, too.

Witches didn't have their own realm. That was why when they got persecuted, they tended to get their asses kicked. No good place to hide. They had to blend with the humans as best they could.

"Griffin!" Her hold tightened on his wrist.

He leaned over her. Felt her tense. Smiled. "You're in that hellhole."

"Argh!" She released his hand. Tried to surge out of the bed.

His hands curled around her shoulders, and he pushed her right back down. "Easy there, Val. I need to make sure you're okay."

Her brows shot up. "Val? Who the hell is Val? My name is Val-uh-ree."

He wouldn't smile at her. Okay, maybe he did. A bit. "You've been out for over ten hours."

Now she gave a little eye roll. "That kind of happens when you're taken through some kind of creepy dimensional portal. The fairies made it for you, didn't they? I know they bred with you shifters about a thousand years ago, and bam—after some hot sexing, the fey gave shifters their very own magical land."

Yes, they had. Only he was surprised she knew that part of his history.

"But here's the thing," Valerie continued grimly. "Fairies and witches are *enemies*. Like the sworn forever kind of enemies, so that means I wasn't supposed to come through your portal. You're lucky you didn't kill me on that road trip!"

He'd leaned over her. Valerie's mouth was just inches from his. "I knew you weren't going to die."

"How?"

"Because you're my *mate*," Griffin said those words with a low growl. He didn't like being tricked and the woman had definitely tricked him. "As long as we're mated, you won't die when you travel into or out of this realm. Witch or no witch."

"Hmmm." Her expression immediately became completely calm. "That's an interesting tidbit. Thank you for sharing it with me."

Griffin got the feeling he'd just made some sort of massive mistake.

"Are you going to kiss me?" Valerie asked. A totally casual question. She tossed it out the same, easy way someone else would ask about the time. "Because you keep looking at my mouth."

He—shit! He had been looking at her mouth. Jaw locking, Griffin gritted, "We need some rules."

She shook her head, sending her sleek, dark hair sliding over his pillow. "I don't like rules." Valerie sounded regretful. "I'm sorry, haven't you heard that about me? I'm a rule breaker."

"Not in this realm, you're not."

She just smiled. Her dimples flashed.

She was really incredibly beautiful. It was a pity that her beauty only went skin deep.

"*My* realm," Griffin stressed. "My rules."

She didn't try to break out of his hold. She just lay on the bed, staring up at him. "So you really are the big, bad king of all the beasts?"

Yes, he was. Grimly, he nodded.

"And I saved you." She batted her lashes. "I bet everyone here will just love me."

Doubtful. Not if they'd all heard the stories about her. And when it came to Valerie Storm, *everyone* knew the stories.

Her tongue slid over her lower lip. "You're doing it again."

She had a sexy little pink tongue.

"Staring at my mouth. I really do think you want to kiss me. Since we're mates, go ahead. I give you permission."

She—*no*. Snarling, he shot away from the bed. "We're *temporary* mates."

Valerie sat up, slowly. Her gaze raked around the room. Frowned at the sparse furnishings. "I kind of expected more from a king." She bit her lower lip.

His gaze went right to her mouth.

The woman was *playing* with her mouth deliberately, making him look, he knew it. His gaze flew back up to her face—

Valerie winked at him. "Gotcha."

Griffin growled.

"Okay, fair warning. I think that growly thing you do is oddly hot." She shrugged. "I'm wired a little differently than most witches, sorry. I know my kind is supposed to be all cold and you know, *not* into the wild beast thing, but I think it's a major turn on."

Was she screwing with him?

Or actually being honest?

No, no way. Valerie Storm wasn't honest. She was a liar and a trickster and a killer straight to her core.

She waved her hand at him. "Can we get back to the *temporary* thing that you mentioned? Because I was pretty sure we were in this mating thing forever. You know, in it to win it and all that."

He had no idea what she meant—what were they going to win?

She reached down to touch her gown. Sighed at the damage. Then Valerie just ripped away the torn fabric, making the dress end right at mid-thigh.

Gorgeous legs. Sexy. Long. He could imagine them wrapped around—

"I think I see a little fang. What's that about?"

It was about him getting turned on, dammit. He needed to get away from the witch. The bond—*temporary though it was*—had already started to mess with his head. And his body.

"I'm of royal blood," Griffin announced.

Her hands immediately flew to her chest—super dramatic.

He forced his back teeth to unclench. "I'm the oldest damn shifter in the world. I can shift into three beasts, I am the strongest shifter you'll ever meet, I am—"

"Awesome. Yes, I get it. You're spectacular. That's one of the reasons I wanted to mate with you." She rose. Stood near the side of the bed. "I'm spectacular, too."

She was...smaller than he'd expected. Maybe five-foot-five? Five-foot-six? She seemed to have so much power and strength, but she was actually...delicate.

Fragile?

He retreated a step. No, Valerie *wasn't* fragile. She *was* screwing with his mind. He needed to get back to his rules. Pronto. "You'll be here for a month."

"Here? In shifter paradise?"

"At the end of the month, our *temporary* bond will end, and you'll go back to the witches."

Valerie pursed her lips. Probably just so he'd look at her mouth again. "Did you *miss* the part where they banished me? Or, um, maybe where they were trying to *burn* me?"

His hands fisted. When he'd seen her trapped in those flames, a rage unlike anything he'd ever known had burst to life inside of him. He'd tossed witches and vampires out of his way as he barreled to her. Nothing—no one—would have stopped him from saving her. "One month," Griffin said, not letting emotion enter his words. "Then you will leave. Our bond will end."

She didn't speak. She also *didn't* look happy. "I've never heard of a mating bond just going poof like that."

"Ours will."

"Because you're all extra special and royal? With three beasts inside?"

Because he hadn't fully mated her. Because for him, mating truly would be forever. His

dragon—the strongest of the beasts he carried—
would recognize his mate. And then there would
never be any parting from her.

"I *felt* the connection when I took your blood."
Valerie squared her shoulders. "We're mated. If
we weren't, you would have let me die in the fire."

"We're *temporarily*—"

She held up a small hand. "Stop using that
word, or I might help you shift into a fourth beast.
I think you'd make an awesome snake right now."

She wouldn't.

Oh, wait, wicked witch. She *would*. Or at
least, she'd try. "You're gonna find that most of
your magic won't work here."

Valerie paled. "That will make me...helpless."

"Think of it as...human."

She lunged forward. Locked her arms around
him. At her touch, heat seemed to burn all the way
through his body. "You don't know the enemies I
have, shifter king. I'll *die* without my magic."

The hell she would. Not on his watch. "No one
will hurt you here. My word is law, and until the
next month is up, you're mine."

The last came out far more possessively than
he'd intended. But—she was.

Her face softened, went all sweet and
innocent. "You promise to keep me safe?"

He opened his mouth, *almost* ready to
promise her any—

Oh, hell, no. Griffin smiled at her. Flashed
some fang. "Rule one."

"What?"

"Rule one is no lying. No pretending to be
something you're not." She was definitely not

sweet and innocent. "You're the most feared witch on the planet. Everyone knows your heart is as cold as ice."

She let him go. "Right. Everyone knows that. Common knowledge."

"Rule two. Don't even try your magic. Not so much as a spark of fire. Just pretend you're on vacation. Relax for the next month. Take in the sights."

"You have got to be kidding me."

"Rule three..."

"How many rules do you have?"

A sharp knock sounded at the door. "Griffin!" A strong, male voice boomed. "Your people are still waiting!"

Dammit. He hadn't finished his rules. But his people had to come first.

"They're in the courtyard!" That voice continued. "And they won't leave. Not until they all see you with their own eyes."

Griffin sighed. Then he locked his hand around her wrist. "You're coming with me." He hauled her toward the door. Yanked it open.

His senior guardsman turned toward him, a wide smile instantly crossing Warren's face. Warren LaTroix had been at his side for centuries. There was no shifter he trusted more than the blond, dark-eyed wolf.

Warren's smile froze, though, when his gaze darted to Valerie. "You, um, you're bringing her with you?" His stare slid down her body. Seemed to linger on Valerie's exposed legs.

Griffin immediately moved in front of her. He had to bite back the snarl of *"Mine"* that rose to his lips. "They need to know she's under my protection."

"That's sweet," Valerie said from behind him. "Like white knight kind of sweet."

His head was throbbing. Without another word, he marched forward, making Valerie advance with him. Warren rushed to follow them.

"Oh." Valerie's exclamation as they hurried through the stone corridors was less than thrilled. "This is very, um, medieval castle-like, isn't it?"

Yes, it was.

He turned to the left. Shoved open two wooden doors that were hidden in an archway. He strode onto the balcony—

Cheers erupted from the people gathered down below. His people. Griffin smiled at them.

Valerie slid to his side.

The cheers began to dwindle. Whispers replaced the enthusiastic yells. The shifters below them had incredible sight. They'd be able to discern Valerie's features perfectly. And since shifters also had incredible hearing, Griffin could easily make out—

"Tell me that's not..."

"Why is she here?"

"Isn't that the wicked one? I thought she burned!"

"Hello, people!" Valerie called out in an amazingly cheery voice. "Yes, the stories you've heard—no doubt, over the last ten hours while I slept like the dead—are all true! I did save the life of your big, bad beast Griffin."

No more whispers. No more cheers. Nothing.

"I know, I know," Valerie continued in her perky voice, "you're grateful. I accept your gratitude."

He pulled her closer. Put his mouth right at her ear. "Woman, are you mad?"

She shivered. He realized his tongue had accidentally licked the shell of her ear. Oh, who was he kidding? The lick had been deliberate.

Valerie tilted her head back to stare up at him. "A little bit mad, yes. But being sane is boring."

She was certainly not boring. She was also doing that lip lick thing—

Warren cleared his throat. "They're waiting."

Right. Shit. He focused on his people once more. "Valerie Storm is under my protection! No one here will harm her, not unless you want to face my fury."

"Oh, that's good," Valerie praised him in a husky voice. "But maybe you should add something a little bloodier like... 'Not unless you want me to rip your head from your shoulders'—I think that works."

He slanted her a glance.

"Too much?" she asked, seeming genuinely puzzled.

Griffin could only shake his head. He'd given the warning. No one ever, *ever* disobeyed his orders.

For the next month, he was stuck with Valerie. No one would harm her. She'd be safe.

And he would make absolutely certain she followed all of his rules. If she didn't, he'd lock up the witch.

Simple.

CHAPTER FOUR

Valerie had never met a rule she liked. So as she strolled through the streets of what she thought of as shifter land, Valerie was hoping to find some delightful trouble.

Instead, she found people who...hurried away from her. Who wouldn't look her in the eyes. Who acted as if she were the devil himself.

She wasn't, of course. The man who had that particular distinction was a fellow named Lucas Thorne. An ex-lover that she hadn't seen in *ages*. She wondered what he was up to right then. Maybe she could use some help from the devil...

"Don't let her fool you. She's only pretty on the outside."

Valerie's shoulders stiffened at that overly loud whisper. Her head turned to the right, and she found a group of shifters staring at her. They appeared young, maybe around twenty or so, but, of course, it was hard to tell the true age of a shifter. A blonde female was in the middle of the circle, her lips curled in a grin. Derision twisted her features as she gave her all into working that mean smile.

"Don't let her touch you," a redheaded male added in another too dramatic whisper. *"She'll turn you into a frog."*

She was certainly tempted to do so.

"Course, that would be an improvement for *you*, Rio!" The redhead slapped the back of another shifter, a tall, gangly fellow with too-long, black hair.

The gangly guy stumbled at the hit—one that had obviously been injected with supernatural strength—and he fell, hitting his knees too hard on the ground.

The others in that little group laughed.

"How old are you all?" Valerie snapped at them, as she put her hands on her hips. They were acting like infants.

The blonde female tossed back her hair. "I'll be twenty next month."

Old enough to know better.

"How old are you, *witch?*" The blonde's gaze raked Valerie. "Because you look positively ancient."

Oh, hells, no. The girl had *not* just said that.

The youth on the ground tried to rise, but the blonde gave a little jerk of her chin, and the redheaded goon kicked the fellow once more, sending him crashing into the dirt. The blonde smirked the whole time.

"I don't like mean children." Valerie's voice rang out, loud and echoing. Her special talent.

The group stopped laughing.

She sauntered toward them. Took her time, enjoyed the moment. And enjoyed the absolute hell she was about to wreck. Griffin had said her powers wouldn't work in this realm. Why not test and see if he was right?

Her hands stretched at her sides, wiggling a bit, and, yes, she felt the surge of power. She glanced down and saw the sparks dancing from her fingertips. "Do you know what happens to mean children?"

"We're not kids!" The blonde called. Ah, the leader. Such a waste of potential. "I told you, I'll be twenty soon!"

Good for her. Definitely old enough to know better. Valerie stopped walking. She lifted her hands, knowing they'd all see the sparks. "Do I look like I give a shit what you are?"

A few of them were backing away. Smart. But it wasn't time to run yet.

"What happens to mean *children*..." She let her smile stretch, knowing the term would infuriate the group. "I take away the things they value *most*."

Silence.

"Like..." Valerie cocked her head. "Beautiful, long blonde hair...hair that doesn't have to be...there." A wave of her finger.

And suddenly...half of that long blonde hair was on the ground.

The blonde started screaming.

Valerie snapped her fingers. The hair instantly returned, mostly because it had only been an illusion spell. She kicked ass at illusions. Always had. The blonde was frantically running her hands through her precious locks. "You should be careful," Valerie warned her. "It's easy to be pretty on the *outside*. But things on the *outside* are never what you think. And in an instant, everything can change."

The blonde raced away. All of them were rushing away. Except for the kid on the ground. He was staring at Valerie, gazing at her with something like awe on his face.

People didn't usually look at her that way. They stared at her in horror, gazed at her in terror, but awe? That was new. She glanced over her shoulder, making sure no one else was lurking there.

Nope. Just her.

"You are amazing."

She looked back at the boy. Maybe she preened a little bit. "You're right." But then she noticed her fingers weren't sparking any longer. *Uh, oh.* Maybe magic *didn't* work so well here. At least not for anything other than simple spells.

She started to whirl away, but...something was nagging at her. Sighing, long and loudly, she glanced at the boy. "Why are you still on the ground?"

He gulped, his Adam's apple bobbing, and then he shot to his feet. "I, um, I don't know."

"You're a shifter. That means you're supposed to be all badass." She waved her fingers into the air. *No sparks.* Dammit. "Why'd you let them push you around?"

His cheeks turned crimson. "I can't shift."

"Come again?"

"I, um, I can't shift, ma'am."

He'd just ma'amed her. Oh, the horror. "Why can't you shift? I mean, you *are* a shifter, aren't you?"

A quick nod. "Griffin is giving me until my nineteenth birthday, but if I don't change by then, I'll have to leave."

"When is your nineteenth birthday?"

"In three months."

Her eyes narrowed. "And if you don't shift, where will you go?"

Another bob of his Adam's apple. "To live with humans."

She could practically smell the fear rolling off him. And she didn't even have a shifter's nose. Though, to be fair, she *did* have enhanced senses, courtesy of a spell she'd worked on herself. "Griffin would turn you away from your home, just because you don't sprout fur?"

"Yes."

That was a big, giant black mark for the big, bad beast. "What's your name? Rio? Is that what they called you?"

He nodded. "M-my mom had me here, then left for Rio. She never came back."

What the actual fuck? Sparks started to dance from her fingers again. Better. Maybe she just needed the right energy to rev herself up. Rage had always been her favorite fuel. *Mental note— dark emotions and power work like a charm in the land of the shifters.*

Rio backed up a step. "They...they think maybe she mated with a human, and that's why I'm just...this."

Her gaze swept over him.

"I'm useless," he whispered. "Not as strong as the others. I don't fit in, I—"

"I don't have room for pity." Her voice was cold. Biting.

He flinched.

"I don't have room for sob stories." Her arctic voice rose. "I don't have room for the weak in my life."

His whole body was shaking now.

She pointed her sparking fingers at him. "And if you are going to be my newest henchman, you don't have room for those things, either."

"I—what?"

Now she walked around him, studying Rio from head to toe. "I am in need of a new henchman."

"Wh-what's a henchman?"

Spirits save her... "Do you not get any TV or books in this wretched place? Come on, Rio...think mad scientists, think bad guys. They *always* have henchmen to help do their evil bidding." She returned to stand in front of him. "I think we've established that I'm evil."

He just frowned.

"I *am* the queen of evil." Valerie was pretty sure she'd once owned a T-shirt that said that very thing. "And *you* are my henchman. From now on, you will go where I go. You will fight at my side. You will stand between me and danger."

"I...will?" His eyes were huge. "Why...why me?"

"Because only someone very special can be my henchman. Someone who has power buried deep inside." She touched his chest, right over his heart. "You have that. I don't give a shit what the shifter punks say. I see you. I know what you are."

"And I'm...?"

Another smile. A pleased one this time because she'd just seen his shoulders straighten a little. "You're my henchman."

His lips curved in a faint smile.

"Where do you live, henchman?"

And he was suddenly back to flushing dark red. "Um, I, um, the baker down the road lets me stay in the back—"

"That's why you smell like pastries. Excellent. Go get your things. While you're packing up, steal me some pastries, and then head toward the castle." Griffin's home base. "You'll have a room there as long as I'm in shifter land."

"Shifter what?"

"Valerie!" The bellow was absolutely deafening.

Wonderful. Her mate was calling. "I really like chocolate. Get something chocolatey for me, and you'll win bonus henchman points." He just stared at her. She shooed him. "Go." She didn't want the kid watching what was about to go down. It wasn't going to be pretty.

She turned away from Rio. Saw the very angry looking king of the beasts heading her way. His hands were clenched at his sides. His eyes were shooting green fire, and Valerie couldn't remember if she'd ever seen a jaw clenched so tightly.

"You attacked one of *my* people?" he roared.

Shifters began to fill the streets. Same old, same old. Folks always loved to see a good fight.

"You *dared?*" Griffin snarled.

"I dare lots of things." She put her hands on her hips. Lifted her chin. "Is this about the blonde? Because I can assure you..." Dammit, her lips wanted to twitch, but she still had to say, "I never touched a hair on her head."

His eyes widened. Then he was bounding forward. He was—

"Don't you touch her!"

Rio had just jumped in front of Valerie. And the young shifter had his hands up. Weak fists, but fists still the same.

Griffin's jaw dropped.

"I'll stand between you and danger," Rio swore, looking back at Valerie quickly. "It's what a henchman does."

Oh, my. She blinked a few times. When she focused again, Griffin was towering over her henchman.

"What in the hell are you doing, Rio?" Griffin wanted to know.

"Protecting Valerie. You can't hurt her. I won't let you."

"She's my fucking mate, kid. Of course, I won't hurt her. But she doesn't get to terrorize the shifters in this place, either. She doesn't get—"

"It's all right, Rio." Valerie kept her voice calm. Her heart was racing way too fast. The boy had stood up for her at the first sign of trouble. Definite henchman bonus points. "I need to talk with Griffin. Go over some *rules*."

Griffin growled.

She gave him a gracious smile. "I have rules, too, and I think he needs to know about them."

Griffin's thick brows climbed.

"I think you were supposed to be retrieving pastries," she reminded Rio pointedly. "Chocolate just doesn't conjure itself." Unfortunately.

Nodding and appearing extremely relieved that he would not, in fact, have to tangle with Griffin in a battle to the death, Rio hurried away. Griffin stared after the fellow with a bemused expression on his face. "Henchman?"

Everyone was still watching. She hated having so many eyes on her. Despite the stories, she wasn't an exhibitionist. "Let's go somewhere else," she said, feeling weariness tug at her. It *had* been a big twenty-four hours. "Somewhere private."

And, surprising her, Griffin took her hand. He laced his fingers with hers. And they just walked away. Strolled past the gawking people with their avid stares. He led her away from the town and it was so strange...it was almost, *almost* like they were a real couple. Or something. And it was—

"As soon as we are alone," Griffin rasped, "your sweet ass is going to be mine."

Well, that was certainly promising.

***

The stream flowed against the bed of rocks, and the faint sound of the water normally soothed Griffin. This was *his* damn spot. The place where he came to in order to regroup. To center himself. To calm down. Only he didn't feel calm. Not even a little bit. Probably because of *her*.

"This is quite lovely," Valerie murmured. "Very scenic."

She'd kicked off her shoes. The shoes he'd had his staff pick out for her. He'd ordered them to give her pretty much anything she wanted. He'd been *good* to the woman. He'd turned his back just for a moment so that he could tend to shifter business and bam—she'd been up to no good.

Valerie waded into the water. She laughed. Cackled. "It's so cold. Icy." She looked down. "And I think I see tiny fish." She was still smiling.

Fuck, but the woman was gorgeous. "Valerie."

"Um?" She closed her eyes. Tipped back her head. Spread her arms at her side. Just seemed to be enjoying the moment of nature.

"Valerie, did you make Lucinda's hair fall out?"

"Who's Lucinda?"

He stalked closer to her. She could slip on the rocks nearby, and he didn't want her to fall. "Lucinda is a cat shifter. Nineteen, niece to my *friend* Warren LaTroix and—"

"My memory is coming back." She lowered her arms. Opened her eyes. Gave a nod, but said, "No, I did *not* make her hair fall out."

"She said—"

"I just made it *look* as if her hair had fallen out. A wee payback spell. She was being rather unkind at the time, and if she was going to worry so much about what people looked like on the outside, I thought it was only fair that I play around with *her* outside appearance."

"That wasn't quite fair. You're a witch. She's a shifter. She's—"

"I have rules." She straightened her shoulders. Angled her chin up at him. "You think you're the only one who gets to throw out a list?"

He cocked his head. "I didn't get to provide you with my full list."

"Joy. I can't wait to hear the others."

His lips wanted to curl again. He wasn't the type to laugh often, and smiling wasn't usually his thing. On good days, most of his friends would call him grim. A dangerous bastard—that was his description. But when he was with his witch...

Something seemed to change.

"Before you launch into what I am sure is a very, very long list of incredibly boring rules," Valerie continued, moving closer, "let me tell you mine. K? I only have three total." She tried to climb out of the stream.

Her foot slipped on the rocks. Before she could fall, he was there. Grabbing her, scooping her into his arms, and holding her tight.

She smiled at him. "I do love shifter reflexes."

He loved her smile.

Wait, no, shit, he *didn't*. He would not be blinded by dimples. Griffin let her go—on solid ground. Then he backed up, crossed his arms over his chest, and worked up a good glower.

She sighed. "Rule one...I don't like bullies."

His brow furrowed.

"Goldilocks? She isn't some sweet, innocent thing. She was the ring leader. They were mocking *my* henchman."

What the hell was she talking about?

"Rio," she said, rolling out the R. "They shoved him down. They were making fun of him. So the kid can't shift. So what?"

In the shifter world, not being able to shift was a big fucking deal.

She pointed at him. Looked very *un*pleased. "And you're going to just kick him out into the cold, cruel world on his next birthday? I thought better of you."

She had? "Why?"

"Because you're king! You're supposed to take care of your people."

"I *do* take care of them. I'm not the one working illusion spells and making them have near breakdowns!"

Her lips curled, but her gaze hardened. "You lied to me."

Now he was the one to stiffen.

"You said magic wouldn't work here. It does. Or at least, it worked a little."

He stalked back toward her. No smiles. Only coldness filling him. "You will *not* work more magic in this place. That is an unbreakable rule. You do it, and—"

"What?" She fluttered her lashes. "You'll send me away like you're planning to do to poor Rio? I'm starting to sense a pattern. Something you don't like—or someone—and bam, that person gets kicked out of shifter paradise." She sniffed. "Though I don't really consider it paradise."

He stepped closer. "Valerie..."

Her hand flew up and pressed to his chest. Seemed to burn right through his skin.

"I have a month here. You already told me that. So I doubt you'll try to kick me out before the month ends, and our *temporary* mating goes bye-bye."

She was right. "I don't have to kick you out. I can just lock you up."

He heard the faint catch of her breath. "What?"

"I have a dungeon in my castle. Instead of walking around, enjoying the sunshine, I will put you in that pit."

She paled.

Griffin...didn't like himself.

"That's not very nice," Valerie said. Disappointment filled her dark eyes. "I thought you might be one of the nice guys."

"You're supposed to be the most wicked witch to walk the earth! I don't think being *nice* will work with you." So he was trying to be a hard ass. But her delectable lower lip was trembling. And her shoulders had slumped. And he just—he felt like shit.

This could be a trick. It's probably a trick. She gets off on tricking people. So he kept his voice flat and ordered sternly, "No magic. You do another spell on my people, and you'll be locked up for the next month. And I'm going to tell my guardsmen that very fact. If they see you so much as sparking your fingers, they'll toss you in the dungeon."

"That's *not* a nice way to treat your mate."

"You used me, Valerie. You knew what I was, who I was, and you worked that to your advantage when we met. You could have healed me without the mating bond—"

"Then I would have died," she spat at him, real anger flaring. For a moment, her hair blew around her face. Only...there was no wind.

He opened his mouth to tell her *no* magic—

Then he realized she might not even be aware of what she was doing.

The air around him had heated. *Her rage.*

Deep inside, he felt his dragon stir.

"I wanted to live," Valerie continued hotly, "so excuse the hell out of me for thinking on my feet. I saved your ass, and, as payment, you want to toss me away? Lock me up? I thought you might be different. But you're just another asshole." Her hair stopped blowing.

Her hand fell away from his chest.

He...missed her touch.

His dragon seethed.

"Don't you dare glare at me." She put her hands on her hips. "I'm not the type to be intimidated. You think you're the worst foe I've ever come across? Not even close. Though I do think you're the most *ungrateful* man I've ever met."

"Valerie—"

"Rule one. *My* rule one. I don't tolerate bullies. I spent the first eighteen years of my life being pushed around and punched nearly every damn day, and that shit *never* will be tolerated by me."

He opened his mouth and nearly roared, "Who *hurt* you?"

"Don't act like you care." She shook back her glorious mane of hair. "Rule two...I control my own life. No one tells me what to do. I am an unstoppable force."

"*Who hurt you?*" He was still stuck on that. And his claws had come out. An instinctive response because he wanted to rip the skin off whoever the bastard had been.

"Rule three...try to listen, would you? Because I don't want to repeat this again."

He put his hands on her shoulders, pulling her against him. "*Who hurt you?*"

"Rule three...If you hurt me, then I hurt you back. Only I will hurt you a *dozen* times worse. So think about that, remember that, before you ever toss me into a dungeon." She smiled. Only it wasn't her sensual, dimple winking smile. It was a shark's smile. "And to answer the question you *keep* asking...the people who hurt me are dead. I took care of them myself. Like I said, you hurt me, and I hurt you back times twelve."

He should step away from her. Back the hell up.

Only everything in him wanted to get closer. She was dangerous, she was infuriating, and she might be crazy but...He wanted her. "If you hadn't killed them, I would have."

She blinked. "What?"

He had no fucking clue. Griffin was starting to think he might be going crazy, too. Before he could stop himself, before he could think, his mouth crashed down on hers.

CHAPTER FIVE

The shifter was kissing her.

Shock kept Valerie immobile for all of two seconds, and then her body, well, it reacted. It sort of *burned*. In a very good way. Not the whole set-on-fire-at-a-stake way.

Heat filled her. Desire pulsed in her blood. Her hands flew up, wrapped around his arms, and held tight. Her mouth opened beneath his. His tongue swept past her lips. She tasted him. Realized that she *loved* his flavor. Rich, masculine. And the guy could kiss.

Her bare toes were practically curling against the grass.

Her breasts were aching, her nipples tight, and her body arched toward him. His arousal was apparent, heavy and thick, and it pushed against her.

Valerie enjoyed sex. She liked pleasure. Who didn't? And she had the feeling Griffin Bastien could give her a great deal of pleasure.

If he wasn't, you know, such a bastard.

He pulled her even closer. Kissed her harder. Made her want him a bit more. A lot more. Her heart thundered in her chest. Her nails scraped over his arms. She—

He let her go. Backed up a step. "*Witch*."

Her breath was coming too fast. She didn't try to speak. Instead, she just waved her hand, as if to say...*Um, yeah. Established that.*

"You're trying to bewitch me."

No, she hadn't been. "*You* kissed *me*."

His eyes were on her mouth. Doing that glowing/burning thing that she thought meant he wanted her. Badly. "Mistake."

Her spine straightened. "Do mistakes usually make you feel that good?" Yes, her voice was husky. So what?

"Can't happen again."

"Then tell that to *yourself*. You were the one getting all grabby and kissy."

"Our mating *will* end in a month."

"I've heard that story before."

"We will *not* kiss again."

Seriously, someone was protesting too much. "Stop acting like that wasn't the best kiss of your life."

His mouth opened. Closed. He...didn't deny it.

And had his cheeks just flushed?

"Oh, baby..." Now she purred at him. "If you think *that* was great, I have so much more to show you."

"*Rule four.*"

She shook her head. When had they gotten to his rules? Valerie was pretty sure *she'd* been the one spouting rules.

"No kissing," Griffin gritted out.

That was just...mean. "No kissing at all? Or just no you kissing me? Can I kiss other shifters?"

She needed clarification, right away. "Like sexy ones that I might—"

He growled. Took a fast step toward her. Seemed to catch himself. "You do *not* kiss another shifter."

"But I can kiss you?"

His eyes were on her mouth. She knew longing when she saw it. Griffin was so messed up. Valerie gave a sigh. "Why do you keep yourself from having what you want?"

"Because I *don't* want you forever."

That hurt. But like every other hurt she'd ever suffered, she didn't cry out. Didn't flinch. Didn't let him see the pain.

"No kissing," Griffin said, but his voice was halting. He stared at her, frowning. And then he actually did manage to surprise her. "I...I'm sorry."

"Sorry for what? Having stupid rules? Being ungrateful to the woman who saved your life? Or just being an all-around asshole?"

"Val—"

"Stop. You're giving me a headache." Where was her henchman with the chocolate? "And don't you have things to do? I mean, you're the *king* here. Other kings I've dated have needed to complete actual work. They didn't just hang out by streams all day."

A line grew between his brows. "You've dated other kings?"

"Dude. I'm awesome. Men have literally *killed* to be with me." Which made his rejection all the more insulting. "Go do some kingly crap, okay? I want to be on my own for a while."

"You...won't work magic."

She turned her back on him. Of course, she'd do magic. She'd do whatever the hell she wanted. "Maybe you should pass the word about *my* rules to your people. If they don't break my rules, then I won't break the shifters."

"That isn't the way it works."

"No?" She didn't look at him. Mostly because she wanted to make sure her face didn't give away any of her emotions. "That's how it works for me. You heard my rules. I heard yours—"

"I haven't said them all."

She almost laughed. "Then I'll catch them tonight at dinner." It was a dismissal. Obviously.

Only the guy didn't go anywhere. "Did I hurt you?" Griffin spoke haltingly.

"If you did, I'll get you back, times twelve," she promised.

"Valerie—"

"But how could you have hurt me?" Valerie continued as her hair began to blow. "You don't mean anything to me. So you don't want to kiss me again. Big deal. It's your loss. And for the record, I never asked to be with you *forever*." Forever was far too long. Especially since she had plans.

She was going to rule the witches. Destroy their stupid council. Maybe she'd even take over the whole world. Totally just depended on her mood. She didn't have time to stay forever in shifter land. Valerie didn't *want* to stay there.

"I never said I didn't want to kiss you," Griffin muttered.

He was *still* lingering.

"Sometimes, it's just best not to take what we want."

Now she laughed. Valerie glanced over her shoulder at him. "Who told you that bunch of crap? Life is fickle, and pain is inevitable. So if you can take something you want in this world—you do. You grab it tight, and you enjoy the hell out of that ride." Because, sooner or later, the ride would end.

A bitter truth that Valerie had learned when she'd been young.

***

Griffin gazed out of the window, looking for a long, sleek mane of black hair. Valerie hadn't come back to the castle yet, and, soon, night would be falling.

He shouldn't have left her alone at the stream.

"So, yes, I've asked you the same question five times now, and I've gotten *no* response," Warren announced. He waved his fingers in front of Griffin's face. "I was joking before when I asked if she'd enchanted you, but now I'm starting to legitimately worry."

Griffin grabbed his friend's hand. Shoved it down. "She could get hurt in the woods."

Warren's mouth parted. It seemed to take him a moment to actually form words. Then he managed, "She's *wicked*. As in, the most feared witch, ever. Her own people were getting ready to burn her. They don't burn their own kind on a whim. If the stories are true, she's murdered without hesitation. Valerie Storm has tortured, stolen, and laughed while she did it all."

But I think I hurt her feelings today.

"Tell me, again, very, very slowly, how you wound up mated to her."

Griffin's gaze darted to the window once more. If she wasn't back in the next five minutes, he'd hunt her. "We were in the dungeon together."

"And everyone knows that dungeons are incredibly romantic." This sarcastic as hell comment didn't come from Warren. Instead, it came from the bear shifter currently lounging near the door. Elliott Urso gave Griffin a broad smile. "All of those chains, the darkness, and, of course, let's not forget the delicious smell of death."

"I was trapped in dragon form," Griffin snapped. "Valerie said she could help me. For a price."

Warren whistled. "A mating. Conniving witch. She knew if she was mated to a shifter—the *king* of shifters—she wouldn't be put to death."

"Very smart," Elliott noted. His golden eyes gleamed, and he sounded admiring. "Good to know she's as smart as she is sexy. Caught a glimpse of her earlier today. The stories about her beauty are not exaggerations."

Griffin exhaled very, very slowly. Then he turned to face the bear. "Don't even think it."

"What? You said it was a *temporary* mating. That means, one day, Valerie will be on the market again."

The hell she would.

But, wait. She *would*. And that was what he wanted. Didn't he?

"So if you just don't fuck her, if the bond doesn't get sealed by the flesh, then you're good to go." Warren clapped his hand on Griffin's shoulder. "That's nice and easy. I mean, hell, who would want to screw someone so evil?"

Elliott raised his hand.

Griffin lunged toward him.

***

The raven whispered into Valerie's ear.

"So if you just don't fuck her, if the bond doesn't get sealed by the flesh, then you're good to go."

She smiled and stroked the raven's head. "Well, well, well, my new friend. You just hit the jackpot."

The raven preened.

"Um..." Rio cleared his throat. "That's not a shifter, Ms. Valerie. That's just a bird."

The raven gave a low, angry *caw*. "This is *not* just a bird. He's my new familiar." And she'd found him at just the right time. Valerie had been sitting at the stream, her feet in the icy water, and, okay, embarrassingly enough, she'd been *moping,* when she'd heard the raven's pain-filled cry.

The poor little fellow had broken his wing.

She'd used a *tiny* bit of magic to heal him.

After all, she was a rule breaker.

"Go see what else you can learn, darling." She gave the raven a bit of seed. She'd picked it up just for him in town. She'd be sure to keep some handy as a reward for future tidbits of gossip that he brought her. "Find me later."

He whispered again to her.

Valerie laughed. "Really? I must meet the bear shifter at the first opportunity." She extended her arm. The raven flew away. She brushed off her hand and turned to find Rio staring at her with confusion clear on his young face. *So much work to be done with that one.*

He scratched his neck. "You act like it was talking to you—"

"He. Not it. And he prefers the name Edgar." What a fun new familiar.

Rio blinked at her.

She smiled back at him. "Edgar *was* speaking to me." Her index finger covered her lips, to let him know that she was imparting a secret. "Don't tell, but I can talk to animals."

"Can *all* witches do that?"

Her hand fell. "Certainly not." Now she was insulted. "Only the very baddest." It was one of the forbidden powers. And if anything was forbidden, she just had to do it.

"I-I won't tell." He grabbed his bag. "And you promise, when you leave, we'll go together? I won't...I won't be alone out there?"

She looped her arm through his. "Henchman, you will never be alone again. Besides, being with the humans is not nearly as bad as you seem to think. I actually quite enjoy them. And they are going to love you."

He gave her a quick, nervous smile. "Really?"

"Of course. You're strong, have supernatural reflexes, you're brave—"

"I—no, I'm not."

He didn't think he was. They'd deal with that later. "You've got potential. I can see it practically glowing inside of you." Those words were truer than he probably realized. A secret for another day. "You have all of this without the incredibly unfortunate side effect of sprouting fur and howling at the moon. You, Rio, are what's called a winner."

"I want to be a winner."

"Of course, you—"

"*Valerie!*"

She sighed. "That man seems to always be bellowing my name."

"Griffin sounds upset," Rio mumbled.

"Good. I'm rather upset with him myself."

"*Valerie!*" Another roar.

"Oh, for goodness sake!" And she *hated* goodness. Valerie raised her voice as she called, "We both know you have supernatural senses, Griffin! You can find me easily."

There was pounding close by. As if something was rushing through the woods. Coming right at her.

Rio moved in front of Valerie.

"Just focus," Valerie called out, knowing that Griffin was closing in. "And you'll find me right—"

He burst out of the trees.

She peeked over Rio's shoulder. "Here."

Griffin's breath heaved in and out of his lungs. Was it her imagination, or did he look a little bigger? More muscled in the shoulders and chest? He'd been big before, but now he was—

"You should be home." He pointed at Valerie. No, maybe he was pointing at Rio. Hard to tell.

Griffin stepped forward.

Rio's trembling body stiffened. That kid had heart. Hopefully, no one would ever rip it from his chest. She shouldn't mention to him that very fate had befallen a previous henchman. But Valerie had very kindly put the heart *back* in the djinn's chest.

"Valerie…" Griffin seemed to struggle for patience. She knew exactly how he felt. *The struggle is real.* "You said we'd talk at dinner."

She had? Valerie totally didn't remember that promise.

"Darkness is coming. The beasts roam free at night. It's not safe for you to be out," Griffin added.

"It's not? But I thought you told everyone I was off limits."

"Some of these shifters are…troubled. Too young. If they can't control their beasts, you could get hurt."

"Maybe you should have told me *that* part before." Was he lying to her? Hard to say. She couldn't get a good read on him.

"He's telling the truth," Rio whispered. As if a whisper would do anything. Griffin would hear him perfectly no matter how low Rio pitched his voice. "When the moon comes out, shifters will shed their skins. And since a lot of them, um, don't like you—"

Their loss.

Face glum, Rio told her, "You should probably go back to the castle."

This just sucked. She'd been told not to use magic, but the shifters got to use their claws and fangs? How was that fair?

"Come, Valerie." Now Griffin sounded too pompous. Probably because he'd gotten his way. "Time to go home."

The castle wasn't her home. It was just her resting spot for the next month. But she wasn't in the mood to argue. She was saving her energy for something bigger. "Let's go, Rio. We need to make sure you've got a good room." She sashayed around Griffin. Gave him the side-eye as she passed him. "You *have* given orders that Rio will be given some kind of deluxe suite, right? Because my henchman deserves the best."

"He...you..." Griffin wasn't pompous any longer. He squeezed the bridge of his nose. "Fine. Whatever you want. Let's just get out of these damn woods."

"Griffin's beast is pushing him," Rio said in his too loud whisper. "He probably wants to run wild and free, too."

Griffin glared at him. "Get to the castle, kid. Go find Elliott. He'll make sure you have a good room. Just tell him I gave the okay."

Rio shook his head. "I *won't* leave Valerie unprotected."

That kid...adorable!

Griffin's eyes became green slits. "She's not unprotected. She's got me."

Rio still didn't move. Valerie almost rubbed her hands in glee. Such promise. Great potential.

But she didn't want to see that potential ripped to shreds right in front of her, so she patted Rio on the arm. "I'm fine." Always. "We'll talk tomorrow. Get settled now. Get dinner. Multiple portions, you got me?" He looked far too thin. "We'll plot in the morning."

Rio marched away, but kept glancing back, as if looking for a threat.

She wiggled her fingers at him.

Griffin caught her wiggling fingers. "What in the hell are you doing?"

She tried to ignore the fact that when he touched her, she felt a hot surge of awareness. A tingle that she might enjoy too much. "I'm making friends with the locals."

"Why are you moving him into *my* castle? It's his turn with the baker. He's supposed to stay there for the next month."

"Turn?" She played with that word in her mind. "Why don't I like that?"

"I give Rio a turn with different shifters, trying to let him learn trades, trying to help him find a family that fits with him."

Rio was gone. "How long have you been doing this?"

Griffin didn't answer.

So she knew. "His whole life? And he never found anyone that he...fit with?"

"He can't shift. It makes it hard to bond with the others."

"No, I think it makes it hard for those jackass others to look past the surface."

"Valerie..."

"He fits me. He's going to stay close to me, and when I leave, I'll be taking the henchman with me."

Silence.

She started walking, and Griffin immediately fell into step beside her. He wasn't talking, but she could practically hear the guy thinking. Trying to figure her out. Trying to understand why she was taking the boy.

Griffin didn't get it. Sometimes, you didn't need a reason. Sometimes, you just had to act.

Finally, he mumbled, "You...stayed in the woods a long time."

"I like the woods. There weren't any big, bad wolves to bother me, so Little Red was just fine."

His hand brushed hers. Valerie swallowed.

"You think I'm a wolf?" Griffin asked.

"Aren't you?" She didn't look at him. When they'd been in the dungeon together, she'd asked him about being a wolf. He hadn't answered her. Still, a witch had her suspicions. "I know you can shift into the form of a dragon. But I'm guessing your other two forms are something pretty fierce, too. A wolf makes sense. Not that it really matters. Seeing as how you and I aren't going to be besties or anything."

"You're angry."

Give the man a cookie. "And you're not too fast on the uptake." She stopped walking. Spun to face him. "I thought you didn't want to be around me. If that's the case, why come looking for me? I could have gotten back to the castle just fine on my own."

"I told you, I was worried."

"Bullshit. You gave the order I wasn't to be hurt, and I don't buy for a second that the shifters here would go against your order."

Darkness had begun to stretch across the sky. Did he know that the dark made her more powerful? Probably not. She certainly wasn't going to tell him.

"I don't want you hurt. Not in any way."

He sounded as if he meant those words. Interesting. Considering now, she looped her arm through his.

Griffin immediately stiffened. "What are you doing?"

"Walking. You wanted me to walk, didn't you?"

"Your...arm."

Someone needed to work on making full sentences. "It's wrapped with yours. You know, so I don't fall or anything. It's getting dark, and I can't see in the dark as well as you can." Total lie. "If I stumble, I thought you'd help steady me. Seeing as how you don't want me to get hurt and all."

He kept walking with her. His arm was very tense and strong.

She slanted him a glance from the corner of her eye. "Are you bigger? Or is that my imagination?"

"I was worried, like I said. So my body may have changed a bit."

He *was* bigger. "It's nice of you to worry."

"I thought we'd established I wasn't nice."

He was many different things. "Where will I sleep tonight?"

"At my home."

Right. The big, medieval castle. The drafty castle, though it did have all of the comforts of a modern home. "I figured that, but where will *you* be sleeping?"

He kept walking.

"I want to sleep with you," Valerie told him.

He stumbled. She steadied him.

"Bad idea," he said. "Very, very bad."

"I have to confess something to you." She didn't like doing it, but oh, well. "I'm a screamer."

He swore.

"Oh, wait, not *that* kind of screamer. The sex kind? Is that what you think?" She stopped walking. Then considered the matter. "Actually, yes, I am that kind of screamer. If the pleasure is good enough."

"*Valerie...*"

"But I can also scream at night, when I'm dreaming, in a manner unrelated to sex. Quite powerfully. Quite...terrifyingly, I've been told."

"By lovers?"

She didn't answer him. Instead, Valerie explained, "I may also occasionally do a wee bit of summoning in my sleep."

"What? What in the hell does that even mean?"

"It means when you play with dark magic, there's a price. When I'm asleep, sometimes, I pay that price in my dreams." She'd thought about this all day. "So if you really want to make sure I don't hurt your precious shifters, you'd better bunk down in the bed with me. And if I start screaming or levitating or opening the gateway to hell, you can wake me up."

He shook his head. Over and over.

"I take it that's a yes? We're on for sleeping together?" Valerie pushed.

He swore.

She gave his hand a soft stroke. "Excellent. Can we start walking again? I find I'm quite famished."

He didn't start walking. "All I have to do is wake you up? And you'll stop whatever the hell you're doing?"

"Maybe." She gave an encouraging nod. "We'll cross our fingers on that one, shall we?"

"You're bluffing."

Her heart slammed into her ribs.

He leaned closer to her. Lowered his head. For an instant, Valerie thought he might kiss her again. Instead, he whispered, "Your heart is racing, and your breath is hitching. You're lying, sweetheart, and I can tell."

No, he couldn't.

"You'll be sleeping on your own tonight. I'll give orders that *no one* is to enter your room. Your games aren't going to work on me."

She wasn't playing a game. He'd see that truth for himself.

When the screams started.

CHAPTER SIX

Her scream pierced the night. Utterly terrified. Heart-wrenching.

Griffin jerked away from his position near the great fireplace, his gaze immediately shooting for the door. Valerie had warned him that she would scream. And he'd warned his guards to stay the hell away from her room if she did.

"I give you five minutes." Elliott stood just a few feet away, an amber liquid in the glass he held so casually. "And then you're breaking down the door to get to her."

Her scream had died away.

"It's a trick," Warren snapped. "She is obviously trying to play some mind game with you, Griffin. She warned you about the screams because she thought you'd stay with her. When you didn't, well, she just decided to use those lungs of hers to make some drama. She *thinks* you'll come rushing to the rescue."

Elliott lifted his whiskey in a little salute. "Because he will."

Griffin snatched the glass from the guy and drained it in one gulp. He barely felt the fire in his throat.

Another scream. Longer than before. Louder.

Griffin threw the glass into the fireplace. It shattered. He stormed for the door.

Warren blocked his path. The shifter held up his hands. "Take a breath. *Think* about this. She's playing with you. Do you really think, even for a second, that a woman like her would have nightmares? She *is* the nightmare."

"Get the fuck out of my way."

Warren locked his jaw. "I'm trying to help. The witch is tricking you—"

"A woman who looks like her would never have to trick me into her bedroom," Elliott offered. "I'd be at her door begging for entrance."

Griffin turned his head. Glared at the bear. "I told you at dinner—when you were practically drooling on her—*stay the fuck away.*"

Elliott shrugged. "I can't help it. I like beautiful women. If that's a sin, call me guilty. It's not my fault that she's freaking gorgeous."

Another scream. Screw this. The sound of Valerie's fear was making his dragon claw at Griffin's insides. He didn't like her screams. Not one fucking bit.

Griffin shoved Warren out of the way and—

"Help her!" Rio was in the doorway, body shaking. Two guards were at his sides. "She's screaming. I tried to get to her—*it's what a henchman does!*—but they wouldn't let me near her room. She needs help. She needs—"

The very castle itself seemed to tremble. And the temperature in the place...rose.

"Uh, oh," Elliott murmured. "That can't be good."

Griffin glanced up just in time to see a long crack run the length of the ceiling.

Valerie was in the room above him.

"I'm thinking she may not have been lying about the summoning part you mentioned," Elliott added, some of the humor leaving his voice.

No, she *may* not have been lying.

"Uh," Warren cleared his throat as the crack deepened. "Maybe go wake up Sleeping Beauty?"

Griffin bounded out of the room. He rushed past gaping guards—

"Help her!" Rio's plea followed him.

Griffin raced up the stairs. He didn't slow when he saw the room he'd given her. Two very nervous and sweaty shifter guards—a dark-haired male and a blonde female—were stationed at her door. When they saw him, they immediate stepped aside.

And Griffin kicked in her door. *"Valerie!"*

She was in bed. The covers twisted around her—

Around her naked body.

He whirled back to face the guards. "Stay out. I've got her." He didn't want the male seeing her body because...

She's mine.

Griffin shook his head. "I've got her," he announced again. Then he slammed the door shut. He hurried to Valerie's side, jumping over the widening crack in the stone floor. The woman was going to destroy his whole castle. "Wake up!"

She didn't. She did start to levitate.

Shit. Shit. He hadn't known witches could actually do that—"*Valerie!*" He grabbed her. Pulled her into his arms.

Her breath rushed out of her in a hard exclamation. She shuddered. And then her long lashes lifted. Her eyes were so dark and deep, and her red lips curled into a sleepy smile as she whispered, "Hello, beast."

Her body was naked. Soft. Silken. Pressed to his.

She stretched against him, moving like a cat, and her hands twined around his neck. "I think I was dreaming about you," Valerie murmured.

His cock was at full attention. A beautiful, naked woman was holding him tight—of course, his body was at attention. He even found his head lowering toward those tempting lips of hers—

No. Griffin cleared his throat. "Sweetheart, you were having a nightmare."

A furrow appeared between her brows. "Are you sure?"

He just stared at her.

She blinked. Glanced around. So did he. And Griffin realized the giant crack in the floor was gone, as if it had never been there.

"Did I scream?" Valerie asked.

"A lot."

"Oh." She nibbled on her lower lip. "Did I scream anyone's name in particular?"

What?

"Right. Of course, I didn't." She kept her body pressed to his. "Did you run in to save me?"

He...had. "I ran in to keep you quiet."

Valerie batted her very long lashes. "Same thing."

His cock was about to burst through his pants. Her scent was freaking making him drunk. How did she smell so good? He wanted to put his mouth on the curve of her throat. Wanted to get more of her scent, wanted to lap at her—

He didn't.

Griffin put her down on the mattress. Pulled the covers *up* to her throat. "Don't scream again." He turned on his heel.

"I will." Her voice was almost cheery. "I have bad dreams. Terrible, terrible dreams."

Griffin whirled toward her, eyes narrowed in suspicion. "You were working magic. I *told* you what would happen if you did that."

She shrugged. The covers immediately fell, exposing her chest. Exposing the most perfect breasts he'd ever seen in his life. High, firm, round. With dusky nipples that were tight, and he knew she'd taste like heaven on his tongue. He knew—

"You can't punish me for something I never meant to do. The magic happened when I was unconscious. I couldn't control it. Surely there is some leeway in your rules for things I can't control." She made no move to lift up the covers, but her gaze slid over him. He saw the flare of satisfaction on her face. "Surely you understand about...reactions...that can't be controlled. You seem to be having one right now."

His dick shoved toward her.

Griffin sucked in a deep breath. He took a step toward the bed.

Her smile curled her lips.

He pulled in another breath. Stepped forward again.

"Griffin—" Valerie began, voice breathy.

He grabbed the covers and pulled them up to her chin.

She frowned at him. "Are you a prude?"

"Keep. The. Covers. *Up.*"

A long-suffering sigh came from her. "I thought shifters were comfortable with nudity. I mean, you are the ones constantly ripping out of your clothes. That's not a witch thing."

"The covers—"

"Oh, all right! I'll keep them up!" She slapped a hand to her chest, holding the covers in place. "Happy?"

Not even a little. He'd be happy if he were balls deep in—

"My, my...what are you thinking right now?"

He closed his eyes. "Stay in this room tonight. Don't work any magic. Don't—"

"Don't leave me alone." Her voice was different. Softer. Huskier. Almost pleading.

Griffin opened his eyes and peered at her.

"It will happen again if you leave me. I can't stop the demons in my head when I'm asleep. I can't control them. The power leaks out of me."

Was she lying? Did the woman even know how to tell the truth?

"If you leave, then you'll just have to rush back in and stop my screams." She slid over in the bed. Patted the mattress next to her. "So why not just stay here? If I start to scream, you can just shake my shoulder. Or kiss me. You know, whatever works for you."

He would *not* smile at her.

"Come on." Now she lifted one brow. "You're not really scared of me, are you?"

"I'm not scared of anything."

"Of course, not. You're the big, bad king of shifters. The roughest and the toughest. How could you fear anything? Especially little old me." She slid down, moving so that her head was on the pillow. "There's plenty of room for two in this massive bed."

Sure there was. "It's my bed. It has to be big."

Her lips parted, but she didn't immediately reply, and he knew he'd just caught her by surprise. After a moment, when he could practically hear the gears grinding in her head, she said, "You gave me your bedroom? Your bed?"

He had. "You're my mate. Where else would you sleep?"

She smiled. "Where, indeed." Her hand stroked over the empty pillow that rested near her. "You have to be tired. I mean, you were trapped as a dragon for weeks, weren't you? And then a wonderfully kind and incredibly gifted witch came along to free you. Now that you're back home—safe and sound—you must want to crash." Her gaze dipped down his body. "Well, you obviously want to fuck first, but you're being very weird about that..."

"We are *not* fucking."

"Your loss. And I mean that with absolute honesty. I would have changed your world."

He believed her.

"One day, you'll practically beg to have me." She looked at her nails. "We'll have to see how *I* feel then."

His temples were throbbing. And his dick was aching. Griffin glanced at the door.

"Are you truly afraid of me? Afraid of little old Valerie? Surely you don't believe all of the stories you've heard about me. I mean, haven't I been incredibly helpful to you? If it wasn't for me, you would have been put to death. Or at least, the witches would have tried to kill you. Don't know if they would have succeeded before you burned your way through the council." Now she let out a wistful sigh. "Wish I could have seen that."

He slid into the bed with her. Felt Valerie's start of surprise. He inhaled her absolutely intoxicating scent and managed, "Told you already, I'm not afraid of anything."

"Right. No fear. None."

"And you did help me." Truth. So maybe he owed her this. And that was why he was staying. Because he owed her and not because— "What are you doing?" She'd just slid against him. Thrown one silken leg over his thigh. Put her arm over his stomach and moved her delicate fingers over his heart. He still wore clothing, but he could feel the heat of her touch all the way through the fabric.

Her head angled on his shoulder. Her breath blew lightly over his neck.

"Valerie." Every muscle in his body was rock hard with tension. "What are you doing?" he snapped again.

"Snuggling. I thought that was obvious." He was pretty sure he felt her rub her nose against him. "You're warm. I like that."

He should tell her to get on her side of the bed. He should.

But he liked how she felt against him.

His left hand clenched the bed sheets.

"I'm glad I saved you," she murmured, her voice huskier.

His gaze was directed straight up, on the ceiling, and his lips curved a bit at her words. "Don't you mean that you're glad you saved yourself? That was all part of your plan, wasn't it? Save me, then I save you."

"Seems equal to me."

His head turned. He stared down at the top of her dark head. And Griffin tried to ignore the odd thought that she felt *right* against him. "Are you truly as wicked as they say?"

Her head tipped back. Her dark eyes stared up at him. "Yes."

Right.

"They weren't going to save you." Her gaze seemed sad.

"The witches on the council said they *couldn't—*"

"That was a lie. They could. They were just afraid."

Now he was interested. "What did they fear?"

"To save a man trapped within a beast—to do something like that requires a very big sacrifice."

His brows lifted.

"You have to give up a little bit of your soul to work magic like that." Her finger tapped against his chest. "Do you feel me...inside? Because that's what I did. I gave you a part of myself so that you'd be strong enough to come back."

Impossible.

Wasn't it?

"If I scream, wake me up." She yawned. "Or, if you decide to let that amazing cock of yours guide you..." Her witch cackle—an oddly sexy sound now. "Wake me up. I wouldn't want to miss a thing."

A few moments later, he felt her body go lax against his. Her breathing was nice and even. Relaxed. Instead of pushing her away then, he pulled her even closer. He looped his right arm around her body and turned so that she was cradled against him. The truth of the matter was that he did owe his maddening witch. He owed her a great deal.

Unfortunately, he feared it was a price he'd never be able to repay.

His lips pressed to her forehead. *Sleep well, witch. If any bad dreams come, I'll be here.*

***

She waited until her shifter slept. She faked her own unconscious state, letting her muscles go limp, keeping her breathing all nice and deep. He kissed her forehead, and the move surprised her so much that she almost stiffened.

Almost.

But Valerie didn't break character. She waited...

Soon he slept.

Then she smiled. Her plan had worked. She had the shifter right where she wanted him. Her fingers slid up, moving carefully to *his* temple. *What do you dream of, my beast?*

The spell was an old one. Incredibly easy. It let her peek inside his mind and allowed her to see...

Fire. Raging out of control. Burning the castle they were in. Rushing toward the two men she'd met at dinner. The arrogant Warren. The flirtatious Elliott. They burned, and they screamed, and the fire still raged from the dragon.

From the dragon...from Griffin.

The fire swept out, destroying everything in its path. The dragon raged and burned, and as he did, his pain and madness echoed in his roars. There was no stopping the beast. No safety. Only death.

Only flames. Only...

"Wake up." Valerie's voice was trembling. Griffin's body was so hard and tight against hers. He'd barely drifted to sleep, and the shifter had immediately fallen into a nightmare. One of the worst she'd ever seen.

At her order, though, his gaze flew open. He gave a hard jerk. "What—Valerie?"

"You were snoring," she lied.

His head turned on the pillow. They gazed into each other's eyes. His breath came a little too fast.

"Don't do it again," she ordered.

Then she closed her eyes. It was a long time before she slept.

Because in Griffin's dream, he'd burned her, too.

CHAPTER SEVEN

Silken skin. Soft moans.

He woke to that paradise.

She was all around him, holding him as tightly as he was holding her. Her moans drove him wild. He kissed her, thrusting his tongue past her lips, loving her taste. He could live forever off her sweet taste. His cock shoved toward her, heavy and hard. He'd pinned her beneath him on the bed. Her legs were spread, open, waiting, and if he could just ditch his pants he'd—

Griffin stiffened. His mouth tore from hers. "Valerie?"

She smiled up at him and appeared way too perfect in the morning light. "Good morning to you. My, my, someone does have an awesome way of starting the day."

He'd—dammit, he was still—helplessly, his hips pushed against her.

She arched up against him. Her hands were on his shoulders, her delicate nails digging into his skin, and he sure as all hell loved that bite. His claws wanted to burst from his fingertips because his beast was so close to the surface. Close to what he wanted most—

His mate.

"Dangerous," he barely managed the one word. Valerie had no idea what danger she tempted.

But she just licked her lower lip, as if still tasting him, and said, "I enjoy danger."

He kissed her again. Harder. Rougher. He caught her moans with his mouth. He should pull the hell away. He should but...

He was kissing his way down her neck. Licking. Lightly biting, and her breath came faster and harder. He heard the drumbeat of her heart—and his. They were both on the edge.

Down, down his mouth trailed over her. He caught one tight nipple in his mouth. Licked. Sucked.

She nearly came off the bed. "*Griffin!*"

He loved the way she said his name. With such stark hunger and raw need. Had anyone ever wanted him this much? Had he ever wanted *anyone* this way? And she was his mate. Why not keep her, permanently? Why not keep—

Fists pounded on the door. "Griffin!" Warren's bellow. "Griffin, we have company."

He lifted his head, only so he could snarl his rage at the door. He didn't want company. He wanted Valerie. He wanted to keep kissing, licking, and tasting. He wanted to explore every single inch of her. He wanted—

"The company is of the prodigal variety," Warren snapped. "You get what I'm saying?"

Warren's words slowly penetrated the fog of lust surrounding Griffin. His hands flattened on the bed, and he lifted his head, dragging his mouth off her tight nipple. His gaze met Valerie's.

Spots of pink color stained her cheeks. Her pupils were wide, making her eyes even darker. Her breath came quickly in pants.

"Give me a minute," Griffin snarled.

Valerie instantly frowned. "I need longer than a minute." She shook her head. "I don't know what kind of lovers you're used to, but I enjoy a whole lot of pleasure. Not some one minute deal."

His chest ached—no, it felt warm. And he smiled at her.

She blinked. "What are you doing?"

"I have to leave."

"*Now?*" Real anger in that word. Before he could speak, she'd shoved him—not hard enough to make him move, but hard enough that he got her fury. "You are such a tease!"

Warren's footsteps hurried away.

"I didn't..." Griffin huffed out a breath. He tried to take his gaze off her. Tried to cool the heat in his blood. Absolutely failed. "I woke up and..." Again, his words trailed away.

"For the record, you kissed me. You always start shit." She jumped from the bed. Glowered like a queen. "Here's the deal. Never start shit again, unless you're finishing it. I don't do teases." Then she spun and marched into the bathroom. Valerie slammed the door so hard he was surprised the thing didn't fall off its hinges.

He wanted to go after her. When the shower roared on, he wanted to join her under the spray of water. He wanted to give her so much pleasure that she screamed. Louder than she'd screamed with her nightmare. He wanted her body to tremble. He wanted...

Her to need him as much as he needed her.

But sex between them—it would create too many problems. He *knew* that. Now, he also knew that when it came to Valerie, he had a major weak spot. Because when he'd woken, his beast had been in control. A beast that craved her.

Griffin jumped from the bed. Changed his clothes. Tried to look like he was calm and collected as he hurried for the door but...Griffin stopped.

Fuck it. He whirled and rushed to the bathroom. Yanked open the door.

She turned toward him. Naked. With water streaming down her beautiful body. Valerie was the most gorgeous thing he'd ever seen.

And she is mine.

He had to protect what was his. That meant he had to see the visitor. Right the hell then. "We'll talk later."

Her eyes narrowed. "I don't like you right now."

His jaw locked. "I need you to stay in this room today."

Surprise flashed on her face. "You're kidding me."

No, he wasn't. "I'll return and get you as soon as I can." As soon as the visitor was gone.

"Wait, let me be sure I understand. You're not asking, are you? You're *locking* me in the room?

He was. Yes.

He turned away.

"I'm going to give you horns!" Valerie called out. "So when they grow from your head today, just know they are a gift from me."

His hands flew to his head. Touched only hair. He glanced over his shoulder. "*No. Magic.*"

She yanked off the water. "Right. That rule. How could I have forgotten? And, oh, wait, what did you say you'd do if I broke your rule?" She didn't bother to dry off. Instead, she stalked right toward him and left a trail of water in her wake. "I think you said...*you'd lock me up!*"

Shit. Griffin clenched his hands into fists so he wouldn't touch her. "I don't want the visitor to see you."

She shook her head.

"It's...for your protection. I want you safe. Out of sight. If it's who I think it is, then he's not a friend."

Her wet hair slid over her shoulders.

Cursing, Griffin grabbed a towel and wrapped it around her body.

"You are always covering me," she muttered.

His hands lingered. "He doesn't like witches. I don't want him near you, so that's why I asked you to stay in this room."

She laughed. Gods, when had her cackle turned so cute? "You didn't ask. You ordered. Why don't you *try* asking me instead?"

He forced his clenched jaw to unlock. "Will you...please...stay in this room?"

Her smile was brilliant. "Of course!"

Really?

"Just let me know when your frenemy is gone, will you? I have some things I need to do today."

It was truly that easy?

He wanted to believe her but...

She had a nasty habit of trickery. So did he. "What things?"

"I want to conquer your people. Get them to swear undying loyalty to me. You know, the usual."

He wasn't so sure that Valerie was lying. Griffin forced his hands to release her. He turned away. Began to walk—

"Who is this man who hates witches?"

He hesitated.

"Must be a shifter. I mean, if he's here, he has to be, right?"

He did. He was.

"So who is he?"

She deserved to know. "My brother." But he didn't tell her more. He'd already left his bastard of a brother waiting too long. And when Carmichael waited, trouble started.

***

Griffin found Carmichael in the throne room. Typical. His younger brother had always been after the things that Griffin possessed. The guy was eyeing the throne with a bit too much hunger in his green eyes. Eyes exactly like Griffin's. "What in the hell are you doing here?" Griffin demanded.

Carmichael turned to face him. Both Warren and Elliott were also in the throne room, and their hard gazes were locked on their guest. A very unwanted guest.

"I heard a vicious rumor..." Carmichael smiled. His brown hair was brushed back from his high forehead. "The rumor was that you were trapped as a dragon. Everyone feared you'd be put down."

Griffin kept his steps slow and certain as he walked past his brother—and then sat on the throne.

Carmichael's handsome features tightened, for just the briefest of moments.

"You thought I was out of the picture? Is that it? That I was imprisoned, so you could help yourself to the title of king?" His fingers tapped against the stone arm of the throne. Deep claw marks cut into the stone.

Carmichael shrugged. "I am the next in line."

A problem. One that Griffin had been aware of for a very long time. "I'm not trapped any longer. No need for your concern."

Carmichael closed in on him. "The beasts you carry are too strong for you. It's only a matter of time before they overwhelm you. You've gone too long without a mate. There is no one to center you, no one to help you fight the darkness that closes in—"

"He has a mate," Elliott snapped. "So just back the fuck off." He headed for Griffin's right side.

Warren moved to position himself at Griffin's left.

Surprise flashed on Carmichael's face. "Mate? You took a mate?" His claws burst out. Long, thick, black. His eyes shined too brightly. "Who the hell would mate you?"

The throne room doors banged open.

A sweet, seductive scent filled Griffin's nose. He shook his head because this absolutely could not be. He'd *asked* Valerie to stay in her room. He'd asked *nicely*. Even said please, for shit's sake.

Yet there she was. Wearing a beautiful, red dress. Skin tight. Where in the hell had she even gotten that dress? Her dark hair trailed over her shoulders. Her red lips gleamed. She walked with a sensual grace that practically had his mouth watering.

And Carmichael gazed at her as if he'd just been given the best treat in the entire world. "Who are you?" he bounded toward her, reaching for her hand.

Oh, the, hell no.

A warning snarl broke from Griffin.

Valerie smiled. As sweet as you please. "I'm Griffin's mate."

Carmichael's hold tightened on her. "You?" His nostrils flared. "You're no shifter."

"Aren't you the observant one? I'm a witch."

Carmichael jerked her toward him.

That was the bastard's first and last mistake.

Griffin leapt out of the throne. As he shot into the air, his beast took over. Not the dragon—luckily for them all—but his wolf. The wolf tore through skin and bones, erupting as he dove at Carmichael. The beast hit Carmichael, sending the fellow tumbling to the floor. Then the wolf positioned himself between Carmichael and Valerie.

Valerie. My mate.

She must be terrified. She must be shaking. She must be—

Her fingers sank into his fur as she gave him a nice, long stroke. "Aren't you a gorgeous wolf?"

He turned his head. Bared his teeth at her.

Valerie smiled back. "Are you protecting me? That is so nice."

He wasn't *nice*.

Carmichael was rising to his feet.

Griffin shifted back into human form, barely feeling the bones snap and pop. His rage was a living, breathing monster, and he kept seeing Carmichael jerking Valerie's delicate arm. "You don't touch her." The words came out as a rumble. He wasn't quite back to speaking as a man, not yet.

"You changed *fast,* brother." Carmichael straightened his shirt. "Too bloody fast." The faintest hint of an English accent slid into his words. Testament to his own loss of control. "How did you do that?"

Valerie wrapped her arm around Griffin's waist. She also waved her fingers in the air, and clothes immediately appeared on his body.

Griffin stiffened. *I told her no magic.* But at least he'd just figured out the mystery of her red dress. The woman had conjured it.

"Freaking witch." Carmichael's face darkened with his fury. "You mated her? After what happened to our family?" His claws became even sharper. "After all of the years you told me that witches were our enemies?"

At any moment, Griffin expected his brother to lunge at Valerie. The guy didn't get it. In order to hurt Valerie, Carmichael would have to get past him first. "Stand the hell down."

Carmichael had brought up his claws. "You can't stay with her. There is no way I'll let this happen."

"Why the hate?" Valerie asked in her husky voice. "What have I ever done to you?"

Oh, hell. Sweetheart, don't ask—

"Your kind killed our parents. That's what the fuck you did to me." Carmichael's canines had elongated. "So as far as I'm concerned, the only good witch...*is a dead witch.*"

***

That little meet and greet had not gone well. Valerie stood on the ramparts—actual freaking castle ramparts because she was in the Twilight Zone—and she watched from her stone perch as Carmichael was escorted out. Warren gripped one of Carmichael's arms. Elliott held the other.

She leaned forward. Where would he go? Would he be kicked out of the castle? Forced to live in the woods or town? Or kicked out of the entire shifter land theme park? As someone who'd been banished, she didn't like the idea that the guy might lose his home. Sure, he was an asshole but...

"What in the hell were you thinking?"

Valerie jumped and gave a little scream. She stumbled a bit and had an absolutely horrible flash of herself tumbling over the castle's high edge and slamming down into the earth below. Luckily, a hard, strong hand grabbed her arm. Steadied her.

Then whipped her around.

"I said *'please'* for shit's sake! You were supposed to stay in our room!"

Our room. That sounded promising. "I was going to stay there." She'd thought about it. "But then I realized that your frenemy was my frenemy."

"He is not—ahh!" A bellow of pure frustration. Griffin let her go. Paced the ramparts.

She pushed her hands behind her back. That way, he couldn't see her nervous finger twisting. "You said he was your enemy. You seemed worried. I thought it might be a good idea to present a united front."

He stopped pacing. "Carmichael hates witches."

"Yes, I got that." When it had looked as if he'd like to use his claws to cut off her head. Right then and there. "Because of your parents."

His back was to her. His angry, stiff back.

Valerie swallowed and asked, "What did a witch do to them?"

"Killed them. Just like my brother said."

She wanted more details. But prying seemed incredibly wrong. She didn't usually worry about things like that. This time, though, she did. And she found herself just saying, "I'm sorry."

He whipped toward her. "What?"

Her tongue swiped over her lower lip. "I'm sorry. That your parents were killed. That you lost them." Her fingers twisted tighter behind her back. "How old were you?"

"A kid," he snapped. "I found their bodies. Their burned remains. A witch said she'd help them. Help my father control the beasts inside.

She didn't. She just trapped my mother with him, and she made them both burn. I tried to help them, but I wasn't strong enough."

Was it any wonder that Griffin had nightmares about fire? About killing the ones close to him? She crept forward. One step. Two.

He seemed to tense more with every step that she took. "What are you doing now?"

Determinedly, Valerie kept advancing. When she was close enough, she threw her arms around him.

"*Valerie?*"

"I'm hugging you. Because I want you to feel better." And as she hugged him, Valerie worked the tiniest of spells. A little pull spell. *Pulling the pain from you...letting it come to me.*

He jerked away from her. "What in the hell was that?"

"I told you, it was a hug. I was—"

"*Pulling the pain from you,*" he repeated, as if puzzled, "*letting it come to me.*"

Her jaw dropped. Almost hit the dirty ramparts. She had to close her mouth, fast, and school her features. He'd heard her? Impossible. She'd just done the spell in her own mind. Because she was that awesome. She didn't have to whisper out loud. She could do things nice and silently. All-powerful witches spun spells that way. But if he'd picked up on her thoughts...if he'd felt the spell...

Suspicion hardened his already amazing jaw. "You were working magic on me."

Fear pounded through her. So thick and heavy that she almost couldn't breathe. "How did you hear that?"

His eyes were green slits. "You worked more magic! I've told you again and again...*no magic* here. The people in this place have never had good experiences with witches! The more magic you work, the more they'll resent you. Don't you see that? I don't want them fearing you. Hating you. For the month that you're here, I want you to fit in."

"I've never fit in." Not any place.

His thick lashes flickered.

He'd...he'd been trying to help her? Protect her? In his weird way. Almost sweet. Almost...

"Why the hell would you want to take my pain away?" Griffin demanded.

She pressed her lips together. Valerie wasn't exactly sure why she'd wanted to do that. Her gaze slid from his. She looked down below. She could see Rio. Was that Edgar sitting on his shoulder? She hadn't talked to her raven all morning.

"*Valerie.* Why would my pain matter to you?" Griffin caught her chin in his hand, holding it between his thumb and forefinger, and he turned her head, forcing her to look at him.

"I don't know," she whispered. "It just does. And making you feel better would have been such a simple thing. I don't often offer kindnesses, so you should have just accepted my gift."

He studied her far too closely. "You would have hurt."

She was hurting. Because she'd taken some of his pain. It made her heart feel heavy. Made her eyes glisten with tears. But she didn't tell him that. The pain would fade eventually. It always did.

"Why?" he pushed.

She shrugged. "It wasn't a big deal. You were feeling bad. I wanted you better. You stood in front of me when you brother got all handsy, so it seemed like I owed you a payback."

He just stared at her. A furrow appeared between his brows, as if he couldn't quite figure her out.

She tried to distract him. "What's going to happen to your brother?"

"He's not allowed back in the castle."

"Is...um, is he still allowed in shifter land?"

The furrow grew deeper.

"I don't know what in the hell to call this place. I just didn't want your brother getting banished from his home because of me. Doesn't feel right." Actually, it just seemed like another reason for the guy to hate witches.

"He can come and go from this realm as he likes. He's next in line to the throne."

That worried her. "I don't think..." Totally not her place to say but... "I wouldn't exactly turn my back on the guy. You might find claws shoved in your spine." Carmichael *wanted* to rule.

Griffin's fingers slid away from her. "Tell me something I don't know." Sadness there. Bitterness.

How much must it suck to have your own sibling gunning for you?

Her hand flew out. Caught his. Squeezed.

He stilled.

When Valerie realized what she'd done, she stilled, too.

He looked at their hands. "How did I hear the spell? And don't lie."

Okay. Telling the truth wouldn't be as much fun as a lie. It never was. But... "I suspect it's because we're mates." A long exhale. "There's this old, like ancient story, that a witch's true mate can share her power. Her spells are his. His power is hers." There was one tiny part of that story she wasn't going to share. Not yet, anyway. But her brain was spinning. *Hello, possibilities.*

"I don't have any spells."

"Nope. Not a one," she cheerfully told him. "But you do have three beasts. So maybe I'm about to get an all access pass to them."

"You don't want that."

To have a dragon at her command? Uh, yes, please. She did want that.

"And we're not true mates. We're temporary—"

She yanked her hand from his. "How many times must you harp on that point?" She didn't want to hold his hand any longer. She'd rather punch him. Ingrate. Fine. Whatever. Enough chit-chat. "I need to go find my henchman." She brushed past Griffin.

But his hand caught her wrist. His fingers curled over her racing pulse point. "And why the hell are you toying with that boy?"

Her gaze shot to his. "I'm not toying with Rio."

"You don't care about him. You're amusing yourself. Playing a game." Griffin shook his head.

"Don't do that. He matters, understand? His life has been shit, and the last thing he needs is for someone to screw him over again."

Was the pain she felt still from the spell? Or his words? "You're the one planning to kick him out. I'm the one offering him a future." She tugged against his hold. "Let me go."

But he just pulled her closer. His head lowered toward hers. For a moment, Valerie thought he might kiss her. Instead, his mouth went to her ear, and when he whispered to her, she felt the lick of his tongue against her. "Shifters are savage and wild. If he can't transform, he can't protect himself from the others. If he stays, he risks being savaged by them."

Her heart raced faster. "But..."

"So if he can't change by his next birthday, I'll give him a new home in a safe place. A world where he *can* fit in. How is that so wrong?"

Her heart seemed to ache even more.

He lifted his head. Griffin gazed into her eyes. "Maybe I'm not the monster that you think I am."

No. Her shoulders straightened. "I *am* the monster. You should believe all of the stories you've been told about me."

"I don't think so." His thumb slid along her inner wrist.

A shiver moved over her body.

"I think there is a whole lot more to you than meets the eye."

Once more, she tried to jerk her wrist from him. But the shifter was too strong.

"Your magic shouldn't work here. It does. Why." Not a question, a demand.

"Fairies practice dark magic." She would give him this because she'd figured it out for herself. "And unlike most witches..." She rose onto her toes. Licked his lower lip. "So do I," she whispered.

She'd expected him to step back. To evade her. He hadn't exactly been overly eager for her kisses, but—

He pulled her closer. Kissed her. Deep and hard. Wild. Hungry. A kiss that she felt in every single cell of her body. One that made her ache. One that made her want. One that had her pressing close to him. Wishing, wanting so much more.

"Maybe I'm starting to like the dark," he rasped against her mouth. Another slow glide of his thumb over her inner wrist. He had to feel her madly racing pulse.

But then...

He pulled back. Put some nice, considerable distance between them. His broad shoulders straightened. "You keep breaking my rules."

"My magic hasn't hurt *anyone*—"

"No more, Valerie. This is it." His voice was flat. "I've been kind."

Oh, was that what he'd been?

"You break the magic rule again, and you will be punished."

She turned away from him. Gave a roll of her hips as she left him. *Let him see what he's missing.* "Promises, promises..."

***

"You *can't* want him mated to a witch!" Carmichael bellowed, rage nearly choking him.

Warren's expression tensed.

But Elliott just laughed. "I don't care who he mates. Griffin's choice." He pointed at Carmichael. "You won't gain entrance to the castle again. For now, Griffin is allowing you to stay in this realm. Make one wrong move toward *his* mate, though, and you're done."

Carmichael couldn't believe what was happening. His brother was choosing a witch—*a witch*—over him. "She's going to destroy him."

Worry flashed in Warren's eyes.

Carmichael pointed at him. "You know I'm telling the truth. Nothing good will come from a witch being here. Griffin is blinded by lust. Obvious-fucking-ly. He can't protect himself. So it's up to you two..." Now he waved his hand between Elliott and Warren. "You have to step up and do your damn jobs. You're supposed to be his best guards. Guard his ass. Protect him." He heaved out a hard breath. "Get rid of that damn witch!"

But Elliott just gave him a cold smile. "You know mates can't be separated."

Now Carmichael laughed. "He hasn't fucked her yet. You think I would have missed *that?* The mating isn't permanent. When it is, both of their scents will damn well change. The mating won't be permanent, not until he takes her. So you still have time." Not much time, judging by the way his big bastard of a brother had reacted in that throne room. But the mistake could still be corrected.

Because there was no way Griffin got to have a mate. He didn't get a shot at happiness. That ending wasn't in the cards for him.

It's not in the cards for either of us.

"Kill the witch," he spat. "Save my brother some misery now."

Overhead, a raven gave a loud cry.

"For the time being," Elliott took an aggressive step forward, "Valerie Storm is under Griffin's protection. That means *no one* here will hurt—"

Carmichael couldn't control his laughter. "Valerie? That was Valerie Storm?" Yes, he'd heard about her. Who hadn't?

He just hadn't expected the most cursed witch to ever walk the earth to be so sexy. So much for Griffin's happy ending. There was no way he'd find happiness with a woman like Valerie. "The fool is digging his own grave." Perfect. All he had to do was sit back and watch the show.

Soon enough, *he'd* be the one sitting in that throne.

And when he did, Valerie Storm would be long gone.

***

"Kill the witch." The words echoed in Rio's head. He'd followed the others...mostly because he'd never liked Carmichael Bastien. Never trusted the jerk. What most shifters didn't get...even though Rio couldn't shift, he still had all of his shifter strengths. And his sense of hearing was absolutely incredible.

So he easily overheard the conversation. And Carmichael's angry snarl.

Rio's body tensed. He needed to get back to Valerie. To warn her of this threat.

Edgar gave a loud cry. The raven was obviously upset, too. Rio started running back for the castle. He lifted his arm, and the raven flew down, coming straight to him.

He was starting to like that bird.

And he definitely liked Valerie. No one was going to hurt her. Not on his watch.

CHAPTER EIGHT

The sun was particularly bright. The sky was overly blue. She could hear laughter coming from the town. Everyone seemed to be in good spirits.

What an absolutely miserable day.

Valerie hunched her shoulders as she trudged forward. Griffin was attending to some lame ass business with his shifters. Business that she had not been invited to attend. All of the townspeople were avoiding eye contact with her. And she—hell, she was twisted up inside.

Why was she twisted? Because of one arrogant shifter.

Valerie knew his game. He was trying not to fuck her. Because if he fucked her, they'd be mated forever. Edgar had been so helpful to tell her that wonderful bit of information.

She paused her angry walk and glanced up, squinting against the too bright sun. Where was Edgar?

Frustration twisted in her gut. She didn't want to stay in shifter land forever. She didn't want to stay with Griffin, either. The guy was constantly threatening punishments, and she didn't think they'd be the sexy kind. So why, *why* did she keep thinking about him? What in the hell was wrong with her?

And why did she have the stupid thought of...*what if*...?

"Valerie!"

Her head jerked to the left. Rio burst from a line of trees. His face was flushed a dark red as he charged toward her.

Edgar appeared to be clinging to his arm.

She put her hands on her hips. "What are you doing? Slow down." She would *not* admit she was relieved to see her henchman. Maybe she'd been a little lonely. Only because everyone acted as if she were some kind of horrible, demonic person.

Oh, wait. Right.

"Kill you!" Rio shouted. "He wants to *kill* you!"

Now she stiffened. What was Rio raging about? Who'd joined the long line of fools who wrongly believed they could end her very long life?

And then she heard it. Because—contrary to what shifters might think—she also had enhanced hearing. A gift she'd given herself long ago. Enhanced hearing. Enhanced sight. Senses strong enough to rival a shifter's. So she heard the rush of wind that didn't belong. She turned toward the sound, just in time to see an arrow hurtling toward her.

She could hear as well as a shifter. She could see as well as a shifter. But she couldn't move as fast as a shifter. She tried to lunge to the side, but she knew that arrow was going to hit—

Rio slammed into her.

Screams filled the air. Desperate shouts.

All of the air had been driven from Valerie's lungs with the force of Rio's tackle. She pushed against his shoulders, but he didn't move. Rio was heavy against her. She heaved and pushed. "Rio, the danger is past!" He'd saved her, just like the best henchman ever, and he could get up now.

Only...he wasn't.

If anything, he seemed to be a dead weight on top of her.

No. No. No!

"Valerie!" Her name again. A thunderous bellow this time. And then Rio was being pulled off her. Griffin stared down at her, his expression tight with—fear? "Are you hurt?" he demanded.

No, she wasn't.

Griffin tried to grab her, but she shoved his hands away and desperately reached for Rio.

The arrow had gone through his back. It was still in him. So deep. And there was blood. So much blood.

"He's not breathing." That wasn't Valerie's voice. Someone in the crowd had spoken. A crowd had gathered around them. The shifters had *finally* come close to her.

Too late.

"Find the shooter," Griffin snarled. "Find the fucker, *now*."

She looked up and saw Elliott give a grim nod. Elliott was just a step behind Griffin.

Elliott turned away and pushed through the assembled shifters.

"He's not breathing," the same, shaking female voice said. "I-I don't hear his heart beating."

Goldilocks. *No, her name is Lucinda.* Griffin had said she was Warren's niece. The female shifter who'd been the ringmaster of her little crew. Only right then, she'd fallen to her knees beside Rio. She stared at him with wide, desperate eyes. "He's dead."

Valerie shook her head. "No." Her fast denial. She grabbed Rio. Yanked the arrow out of his back.

The crowd gasped in shock and horror.

What else was new?

His blood covered her hands. "Breathe," Valerie snarled at him.

He didn't.

"Stop this!" Now Valerie was shouting at him. "Stop it right now, do you hear me? You *open* your eyes and you breathe."

Murmurs from the crowd. Whispers she could easily catch.

"Is the witch mad?"

"Doesn't she know death when she sees it?"

"Valerie..." Griffin's voice was soft. Sad. "He's gone. I think the arrow went into his back...and punctured his heart."

How did he know that shit? She didn't take her eyes off Rio. "You're wrong. He's not gone. Rio is right here. Don't you see him?"

More shocked murmurs. More talk about her being mad.

Griffin curled his hand on her shoulder. "We need to go. You're not safe out here—"

Now she glared up at him. "I'm not going anywhere."

Goldilocks—Lucinda—was sobbing. So were a few of the other, younger shifters. The pack that had been so cold to Rio before appeared grief-stricken. *Oh, you care now?*

"He saved me," Valerie angrily told Griffin. "Don't you get that? The arrow was coming for *me*. Rio jumped in front of me. He took that arrow. He doesn't die for that."

Griffin's jaw locked. "Baby, there is nothing you can do." Pain was in his eyes. Sorrow.

She smiled at him. "You are so wrong." She pulled in a deep breath. Let it out. And she let loose of the darkness inside of her.

Clouds swept across the sun. Lightning flashed in the sky. Thunder rumbled.

"*Valerie*." A warning edge in Griffin's voice. "What are you doing?"

A tear slid down her cheek because this was going to hurt. So much. "I can't let him die for me." Her words were soft. They were meant for Griffin alone, but those shifters and their damn incredible ears would hear her. "I'm not worth that."

Griffin shook his head. "Valerie—*no!*"

But it was too late. Lightning hit her. Griffin was still touching her when it hit, and the force sent him flying back. She heard him roar his fury, and he charged back toward her.

Too late.

A ring of fire encircled her and Rio. Her hand was on his back, exactly where the arrow had plunged into him. Driving so deep. Hurting so much.

Pain pierced her. Right in her back. Tearing through her spine and she cried out, her whole body jerking.

"Valerie!" Griffin's roar again. "Stop it! Right now!"

There was no stopping, not even if she'd wanted to stop. She didn't.

She could feel hands clawing at her. Death didn't like to give up his prey. So he had his minions clawing at her. Fighting her.

Pain pierced her heart. She knew the tip of the arrow had penetrated Rio's heart. Dammit, Griffin had been right on that point. A burning, twisting agony spread through her blood. *Poison.* The realization burst in her mind. The arrow tip had been laced with poison.

Someone had wanted to make sure she was good and dead.

Someone was going to suffer.

She kept pulling Rio's agony into herself. Kept fighting Death. He was such a greedy bastard. Always demanding a price.

One day, he thought he'd get her.

Not today.

"Enough!" Griffin's shout seemed to shake the very earth itself. But he couldn't stop her. No one could stop her. She was all powerful. She was—

Griffin ran through the fire. His body slammed into hers. He ripped her away from Rio. They rolled, fighting because she had to get back to Rio. She wasn't done.

"You're killing yourself!" Griffin pinned her to the ground. "Not on my watch, do you understand? You will *not* die!"

She glared up at him. She wasn't dying. She was *saving*. Didn't he see that?

"No one can bring back the dead," Griffin told her, voice gruff now, but his hands were still just as fierce and hard as he held her wrists chained to the ground. "Not even you."

Then she heard it...a gasp. A quick pull of air.

And the crowd erupted.

"Rio is moving..."

"What did the witch do?"

"I can hear his heart! He's back!"

"I can do anything." She smiled up at Griffin even as a heavy wave of lethargy swept through her. Valerie knew she wouldn't be conscious much longer. But she needed to bluff this shit out. She could not allow the others to see her weakness.

The circle of flames vanished, leaving only a trail of burned earth in their wake.

Griffin shook his head.

"Wh-what happened?" Rio's voice. Rio's wonderful, cracking voice.

Valerie managed to turn her head toward him. He'd sat up, and he was running his hands over his chest, then straining to find the wound on his back.

Only there was no wound any longer.

"How." Griffin's guttural demand.

Silence reigned all around them.

Valerie figured she had five minutes, maybe ten, before she lost consciousness. And when she went out, it wasn't going to be pretty. Her choices were severely limited. "I broke your rule." *Act like you have this.* She let a big smile stay on her face as she focused on Griffin. "So punish me."

He lifted her up. Hoisted her into his arms and held her against his chest.

Wonderful. She didn't have to stand up. She wasn't sure her legs would have held her. Spoiler...they wouldn't have.

"Put me in the dungeon. Let me stay there until I've learned my lesson." She made sure her voice carried on the wind.

"No." Griffin shook his head. "Something is wrong. Something is—"

"Can't the king keep his word?" Valerie taunted him. "Or should I just break every single rule you have?"

She could feel the stillness and the gazes of everyone around them.

A muscle jerked in Griffin's locked jaw. "Rio," he snapped the name.

Rio jumped to his feet.

Edgar flew to land on his shoulder. She tried to wave at Edgar, but she was already too weak. She *did* have enough strength to send her familiar a mental command. *Look for the shooter, Edgar. Find the bastard. And if you get to him before I do, take his eyes.*

Okay, so *maybe* she was feeling a bit bloodthirsty. Valerie figured she was entitled.

Edgar cawed and took to the sky.

"Are you okay, Rio?" Griffin demanded. He tightened his hold on Valerie.

Dark spots danced before her eyes. She heard the rumble of thunder. Thought she saw the flicker of lightning. Rain drops hit down on her.

"I-I think so." Rio's voice cracked. "*How?*"

Griffin gazed down at Valerie.

She couldn't even muster her fake smile any longer. "I have no idea."

But the whispers had already started. And, once started, they couldn't be stopped.

"Did you see the witch?"

"She brought back the dead."

"No one can do that...impossible."

"Rio was dead. She made him live again."

Then those whispers faded away. There was only stunned silence. She could feel all of the eyes on her. Gazes that had to be filled with fear. Horror. Loathing. Maybe it was a good thing she couldn't see them all.

But they could see her. With her last bit of energy, she lifted her hand. Managed to curl that one finger in a last-ditch salute. She didn't care what they thought of her.

Rio was alive. He was what mattered.

"Take my ass to the dungeon," Valerie muttered as her eyelids sagged shut. "Chain me to the wall. Maybe then you can be safe."

Maybe. It would really just depend...on how bad she got.

***

She was out. Griffin shifted Valerie in his arms, bringing her closer to his body as the rain pelted down on him. She was too pale. Her body too lax. Something was very wrong.

"Valerie?"

She didn't stir.

He tightened his hold on her.

"You can't lock her up."

His head lifted. Rio stood in front of him. The kid's wet hair was already plastered to his head.

"Don't put her in the dungeon." Rio straightened his thin shoulders. "She just—she healed me. I know you didn't want her working magic, but she was helping me."

The kid didn't get it. "She didn't heal you." His voice seemed to boom.

Rio flinched.

"She brought you back from the dead." Something that *shouldn't* have been possible.

For a minute there, he'd feared that Valerie was actually going to trade her life for the boy's. *Not* something a wicked witch would do. But...

She'd been suffering. He'd *felt* her pain. She'd done that, for the boy.

There was far more to Valerie than he'd realized.

"No one can bring back the dead," Rio whispered.

The kid was wrong. Very, very wrong.

Someone could.

The baddest witch in the world just *had*.

CHAPTER NINE

"You have to lock her up." Warren glared at Valerie as she lay cradled in Griffin's arms. "Everyone saw what she did. She *broke* your rules."

She seemed to make a habit of doing that.

"If you don't punish her, they'll all think you're weak. You can't let them believe that. A king can never be weak."

They were almost back to the castle. Valerie hadn't so much as flickered a long eyelash during the desperate trek to his home. Fear twisted inside of Griffin. It was a feeling he *wasn't* used to. He rather hated it.

Guards rushed to open the gates for him. Warren kept pace with him, and the guy also kept up his constant punishment refrain. "She's too powerful to stay loose. If she can bring back the dead, damn, what else can she do?"

What else indeed?

"Why does her magic even work here?" Warren barked. "Witches are supposed—"

"She uses dark magic. Just like the fairies who built this realm. She's not like most witches." Understatement.

He entered the castle. Strode into the great room. Stood with her cradled in front of the fire. The rain had fallen in heavy torrents, soaking him and Valerie. Her hair was wet and drops of water clung to her skin. He should take her upstairs. Get her dried off. Put her in bed.

"Lock her in the dungeon." Warren stood in his way. "She's too *dangerous* to be free."

She didn't look dangerous. She looked weak. Delicate.

Vulnerable.

But Warren wasn't letting up. "Everyone heard, everyone *saw*. If you don't do this, you'll be a weak king."

"Do I look..." Griffin kept his eyes on Valerie. "Do I look as if I give a flying fuck what people think about me?"

Stunned silence.

And then...

Footsteps, rushing to him. His nostrils flared as he caught Elliott's scent. He'd sent Elliott to find the bastard who'd shot Rio, but—

Elliott came in alone.

"He'd better be dead," Griffin barked.

Elliott staggered to a halt. "I...couldn't find anyone."

Impossible. "You picked up a scent—" Elliott was his best hunter.

Elliott glanced at Warren. "I was able to figure out where the archer must have been when he fired the shot based on the angle of the hit. I got to that area. I searched, but I couldn't catch the shooter's scent. He must have masked it."

A task that was possible, under the right circumstances. *And with the right tools.* Magical tools.

"I want the arrow," Elliott added. "That's why I came here. I can check the arrow for the shooter's scent. Maybe pick up on something that can help me."

Rio had the arrow. And the kid was nowhere to be seen. He'd vanished after he'd been told that Valerie had brought him back from the dead. "Find Rio. Bring him *and* the arrow to me."

Elliott nodded. His gaze darted to Valerie. Concern flickered in his eyes. "How is she?"

Out cold. Not fucking good.

"She needs—" Warren began.

A sharp scream came from Valerie. Griffin flinched at the sound. His gaze immediately flew to her face. For an instant, her eyes opened. She stared straight at him. "*Lock me up.*" A rough whisper. "*Before I kill everyone.*"

Then her eyes closed.

For a moment, he wondered if he'd imagined her words.

Her body began to grow warm. Too hot.

Oh, shit. "Get the dungeon ready," he bellowed, "*Now!*"

Guards rushed to follow his command.

"We need to lock up the boy, too," Warren argued. "Who knows what she has made him into now? The dead are monsters. Rio could—"

"Bring Rio back to the castle. Keep him in his room. With a guard." He didn't have time to say more. Valerie's body was almost burning hot. And the fear inside of Griffin was ice cold.

He hurried down the stone stairs that led to the dungeon. Warren trailed behind him.

Valerie was shuddering. He was pretty sure steam was rising from her body. Was his witch about to burn before his eyes? *Don't you dare pull that shit. You will not die on me.*

The cell door on the right was open. He rushed inside. "Lock us in!" Griffin blasted.

"*What?*" Warren's sharp cry.

Griffin lowered her body onto the wooden bed. More of a bench than a bed. She needed better. As soon as he put her body down, smoke came from the wood.

He snatched her right back up into his arms. He whirled to face the door. The still *open* door. "Lock us up! Now!"

Warren's eyes were huge. "You're staying with her?"

He held her even tighter. "She's my mate."

"You don't have to do this. She's just temporary. No one expects—"

"She. Is. Mine." A guttural snarl. Because there was no other choice for him. Maybe there never had been.

Warren slammed the door shut. Griffin heard the heavy lock slide into place.

"Rio?" Valerie's weak cry.

"He's okay. You brought him back." Something Griffin still couldn't believe. "And you're safe, baby. You're—"

Her lashes cracked open. And her eyes—they weren't dark any longer. They were red. Like the fires of hell. "Not s-safe...n-neither are y-you..."

"Valerie?"

"L-leave...*hurry*..."

The hell he'd leave. There was no way—

She screamed. And flames consumed them both.

***

"*OhmyGod.*"

The top of the heavy, cell door was lined with bars. Warren peered into the cell, watching in horror as flames consumed Valerie Storm—and Griffin Bastien.

"No!" Warren yelled.

The flames grew hotter. So hot that—

The cell door blew off, slamming back into him. He flew through the air, and when he landed, the wooden door was on top of him. He shoved it off, screaming for guards. Screaming for help.

The cell was a mass of flames. Smoke billowed everywhere.

"Get water!" Warren yelled. This couldn't be happening. "Get water *now!*"

He knew the witch was dead. She had to be dead. There was no way someone like her could survive the flames. Witches burned, and they died. Everyone knew that.

But Griffin...maybe...maybe the shifter king was still alive. If he'd managed to transform into his beast, if he'd pulled up the dragon before the flames consumed him, then Griffin could still be alive. His dragon could handle the fire.

"*Water!*" Warren shrieked.

They had to put out the fire.

Before it spread to the whole castle and destroyed everyone.

Everything.

***

The pain wouldn't stop. A white-hot agony. The burn was from the inside. Singeing everything. Twisting. Torturing. Then the fire shot outward. Burn. Burn. Burn...

It was—Something cold hit her.

Right in the face.

"*Keep it up!*" A man's shout. Distant. "*More water!*"

And she was doused again. Some of the water went in her mouth, and she spat it out. Cold water. Ice cold.

"*More!*" That same man bellowed.

The water hit her again. Slammed over her body. Poured down her legs.

And she didn't feel quite so hot. The burn had faded. Both on the outside...and in.

More water hit her, drenching her hair. She tried to open her eyes—and got water thrown at her. Valerie lifted her hands. "Stop!"

More water.

"The witch is alive!"

She wouldn't be for long. Not if they kept trying to drown her ass. Water poured over her again, streaming down her body.

Her *naked* body. *Uh, oh.*

Her hand lifted, and she swiped the water out of her eyes. "*Don't soak me again!*"

But they did.

Jaw locking, she jumped to her feet. She ran forward and—tripped over something. Something big. Scaly. Valerie landed with her hands on the still warm stone floor. She turned her head and realized the water that was being blasted into the room—that water wasn't being aimed at her. The men weren't throwing buckets of water at *her* for shits and giggles. They were throwing the water at the fire breathing dragon in the cell with her.

The dragon who'd just turned his very, very scary head toward her. When she'd tripped over his tail, she'd gotten his attention. Now his mouth full of razor sharp teeth was heading for her.

She smiled. "Hi, there." Valerie slapped back her wet hair. "Guessing, um, you had to change when I started shooting fire balls, huh?"

A rumble came from the dragon's throat.

"Okay. Deep breath." She rose to her feet. She was naked. Absolutely stark naked and dripping wet. Her clothes hadn't been fire proof so she figured the material had burned to ash. "I need you to turn back for me. Do me that solid, okay, Griffin?" She held out her hand to him. Just stood before the big, bad dragon...and waited.

Another bucket full of water hit her. "Stop that shit!" Valerie shrieked.

The dragon growled. His emerald eyes gleamed.

She winced. "I get that I have a lot to explain. And I will. But I think you're probably terrifying the water happy shifters, so how about you change back?"

His snout butted against her outstretched hand. A little sigh escaped her, and Valerie shuffled closer to him. "We were in separate cells before. Didn't quite get the full effect of just how *big* you really are." Big, scaly, scary, and dangerous.

His eyes were on her.

She shivered. Because she was dripping wet and cold. And because Valerie realized that she had seriously underestimated the guy. One bite from those giant teeth, and she'd be gone.

She felt like some kind of virgin sacrifice standing before the beast. Dragons and virgins—wasn't that some old story? Well, she sure as hell wasn't a virgin. Not a virgin anything. But she could still try charming the beast. She was his mate, after all, temporary though it may be.

"If you don't change back," she told him, "all of your men are going to keep staring at my naked self. Because they are not letting either of us out while you're still in full beast mode."

The dragon's head turned. He stared at the men with their buckets. Then he let out a wild roar. The whole castle trembled. The beast opened his mouth to blow flames.

Oh, hell! He can't kill his men! This was too much like the nightmare she'd glimpsed. Griffin's worst fear was that his beast would take over, and the dragon would destroy those he valued. Because of her, he'd been forced to pull up his dragon. To shift or die in *her* fire. Valerie couldn't let him hurt his men.

She jumped in front of them, spreading her arms wide. There were gasps from behind her. Valerie glared back at the men—and women—there. "Yes, my ass is amazing. Just settle down."

They blinked. Frowned.

She looked back at her dragon. "Change back."

He didn't. He also didn't unleash a blast of flames at her and the shifters.

The dragon wanted to play hard, did he? Fine. "You all need to get the hell out of here." There was no mad shuffle of feet running away. Seriously? *"Leave,"* Valerie snarled to the fools behind her. "You put out the fire. We aren't going to burn down the castle. But he's too tense with you all here. Too protective. He sees you as a threat, and he's not going to transform back until there are *no* threats to me."

"Maybe he *is* the threat to you."

Who was that? Who'd said that? She slanted a fast glance over her shoulder. Ah, yes, the dick, Warren. They'd tangle soon and not in a good way. "The dragon recognizes his mate. Why do you think he hasn't spewed fire all over me? He wants to hurt you, not me. So get the hell out of here, and I'll calm him down. That's something only I can do. Not you."

Shifters should get that. A mate could always reach past the beast. Even a temporary mate.

Grudgingly, Warren gave a nod. Everyone began to back up. Slowly.

"We won't go far," Warren told her. "If he turns on you, we'll come back to stop the spread of the flames."

Not to save her amazing ass. Right. She got it. They didn't like her. And here she was— protecting them. "You are most welcome!" Valerie called out, voice extra perky. "Happy to risk myself for you all. And, yes, you may name your daughters after me. I will be honored."

"The witch is crazy."

"Insane."

The whispers were normal.

The shifters left. And she was alone with her beast. Her gaze slid over him. "The eyes are the same, you know. You might look terrifying, but when I stare into your eyes, I still see *you.*" She walked closer to him. Lifted her hands. Touched his scales. "They're cold." Seemed odd. "I thought they'd be hot." Her fingers trailed over them. "And they're hard." Almost like armor. Dragons were really badass.

"How about we break the curse? Frogs change into princes when they get a kiss. Let's see what you can become." She pressed a quick kiss to a scale. "Change from a dragon...back into a king. Change for me, okay? Because I'm cold and I'm scared, and if you stay like a dragon, I'm really not sure how long it will be before all your shifter buddies decide to kill me." She shivered again. He wasn't changing. "I need you, Griffin. Change back." She couldn't use magic to help him right then because she was pretty much running on fumes.

His wing lifted. Because he had *wings.* The wing...he wrapped her in it. Pulled her close. Almost like a dragon hug. Kinda sweet. Her eyes closed when she heard thunder. Popping. It was a terrible, terrible sound, one that she could *feel* all around her, and Valerie kept her eyes closed because hearing his pain was bad enough. She didn't want to see it.

But wasn't that being a coward? She'd done this. Forced him to change. So she should have to witness everything.

Her eyes opened. She watched—every moment—as her dragon became a king again.

When the brutal shift was over, a man stood before her. Tall, muscled, his chest heaving, and his eyes still blazing. She should make one of her flippant remarks. Say something outrageous. Tell him that he'd looked great with a tail.

But Valerie didn't say anything.

He put his hands on her shoulders. His fingers were warm. His body was hard and dangerous. And he kissed her. Not some gentle, I-adore-you kiss. They weren't really the adoring type. The kiss was hot. Fierce. Consuming.

It was exactly the kind of kiss that she craved. He dragged her against his body. Her breasts pressed to his chest. His tongue was in her mouth, his scent surrounded her, and his warm, strong flesh was against her.

Desire grew. Again, not some soft, gentle attraction. A greedy, ravenous lust. She went from fear to need. From doubt to craving. Her hands rose. Her nails dug into his back. Their bodies were pushed together, but she wanted more. So much more.

"You were burning." His voice was guttural.

A shiver slid over her. It had nothing do with being cold or scared. That rough voice of his was *sexy*.

"I thought you were going to *die*." He lifted her up and held her as if she weighed nothing.

Her legs wrapped around his hips. She felt the hard length of his cock against her. Valerie rubbed her sex against him. Let out a moan.

"You *never* die. Do you understand?"

She was having trouble breathing, much less understanding everything he was saying.

He carried her across the scorched cell. Her back hit a stone wall, one that still felt warm to the touch. Griffin pinned her there as he glared down at her. "*You never leave.*"

Did it look as if she was about to run away? She leaned forward. Put her mouth on his neck. Licked. Sucked. Bit.

He growled.

Oh, yes. She was definitely into those sexy, rough sounds of his.

His cock was right at the entrance to her body. Thick. Hard. She wanted him *in* her. She didn't want to talk. Didn't want to think. Her heart raced, and her breath heaved. Her breasts were aching, the nipples tight. She wanted his mouth on them. Wanted his cock to thrust deep into her.

She didn't want to stop. Didn't want to think about why they shouldn't be doing this.

She'd never been good with *shouldn't*.

His hands tightened on her waist. He lifted her up, higher, and she let out a cry of frustration because he was moving her away from—

Griffin's mouth closed over her nipple.

Her eyes rolled back into her head when he licked and sucked and lightly bit. The man's mouth. The things he could do...*Yes, please.*

Then he kissed his way to her other breast. Held her up with his easy strength, as if she were his for the taking. Maybe right then, she was. His tongue slid over her nipple. She moaned as he took that nipple deep into his mouth.

Her nails were digging deep into him. *"Griffin!"*

"Gonna take you...*have* to take..."

Did it *look* like she was arguing?

He lowered her again. Her legs were lodged around his hips, her sex open to him. The head of his cock shoved at the entrance to her body, but he didn't sink into her. Not yet. Why in the hell was he making her wait?

She arched against him. *"Now!"*

He laughed. And he gave her *now*. Griffin drove deep into her, so deep and hard that for just a moment, Valerie lost her breath. He'd filled her completely. Her sex clamped greedily around him, holding on tight.

His hand slid between their bodies. Stroked her clit. Had her squirming against him.

Then he withdrew.

Thrust back into her.

Withdrew.

His mouth pressed to her neck, right there in the curve of her shoulder. He licked her skin, and she shuddered. The good kind of shudder. Her legs were locked around his hips, and their bodies arched together as they madly pounded toward climax.

His mouth...

His cock...

She was about to come. Right then. Right there. In a dungeon.

"Forever," Griffin rasped.

He bit her.

Pleasure blasted through her, like a volcano just erupted. The pleasure ignited, and it whipped through her whole body in wave after wave. Not some little pop of release. An explosion that rocked through every cell in her body.

And he was there, too. She felt the hot rush of his release inside of her. Heard the deep bellow of his cry. He held her so tightly. His grip was unbreakable, but she wasn't exactly trying to break free. She was still riding his hard length. Still feeling the pleasure wash over her as she drew it out. Valerie didn't want the moment to end. Not ever. Something that good *shouldn't* end.

He kept thrusting his hips against her. She knew he'd climaxed, but his cock was still hard. And he was still going.

So was she.

They moved hard and fast, staring into each other's eyes. She wouldn't, couldn't look away. The second release hit, a surge that took her breath. He growled. Leaned toward her neck. Licked the mark he'd made before.

And he came again inside of her.

This time, the pleasure slowly ebbed. Her body slumped. She would have fallen, but her big, bad beast still held her up. She was pinned against the wall. Trapped between stone...and—

"*Mate,*" Griffin rumbled.

Between stone and the man she'd just apparently mated, forever.

CHAPTER TEN

He'd just taken his mate in a dungeon. A dungeon.

As the haze of lust surrounding Griffin finally eased, awareness flooded back in an uncomfortable rush. *A dungeon.*

His eyes widened as he stared at Valerie in horror. He was still in her. Already getting hard again, and the woman probably thought he was the biggest bastard in the world. She'd rail at him. Tell him to get the hell away from her. She'd—

Smile?

Her dimples winked. "That was fun." She leaned forward. Pressed a kiss to his lips. "And you picked *our* place. That is so romantic."

A dungeon wasn't romantic. Carefully, he eased out of her before he lowered Valerie to her feet. "I'm sorry."

Her hands went to her hips. The move made her glorious breasts thrust toward him. "You had *better* not apologize for having sex with me."

Never for that. "This wasn't the place. You deserved better. You—" He stopped because Griffin knew he was just a bastard.

She shook her head. "It's *our* place."

Why was she saying that?

Then she gave him her killer smile. "We met in a dungeon. Fate brought us together there. And, of course..." She batted her lashes at him. "A dungeon is where you looked at me—just took that first, incredible look at me—and realized you would love me forever."

His chest ached.

"You did." Valerie winked at him. "You'll realize that truth, one day."

He would never understand her. But...now he had plenty of time to try. Plenty of time—as in, forever. "We're mated."

"We've *been* mated. Darling, did you miss that part?"

Why did he like it so much when she called him darling? Griffin cleared his throat. "Forever now. Once are bodies are joined, there is no going back."

Her gaze slid over him. "There never was any going back."

She was still naked. And when he looked at her body...

Griffin licked his lips.

"Someone looks hungry," Valerie murmured as she arched one delicate brow.

The woman had no idea. But he had to hold his control. *This* time. His people were waiting for him. And there were questions that *had* to be answered. "Could you...summon clothes?"

Her brows climbed. "Are you asking me to do magic?"

"Yes," he hissed.

She wiggled her fingers. Clothes appeared on his body. Pants. A shirt. Boots.

But she was still stark naked.

He was about to grab her. His hands fisted. "*You.*"

"What about me?" She strolled around him, giving him a perfect view of her front and her back. Valerie hadn't just been boasting before. Her ass was world-class.

He might have to kick the shit out of some guards who'd seen too much of her.

"Clothes," Griffin gritted out. "On you."

"Again, you're showing this weirdly prudish tendency for a shifter, but whatever." Her fingers did their little shimmy again, and she was suddenly wearing tennis shoes, jeans, and a black shirt. Her hair had magically dried. "Better?"

Actually, no. She was still sexy as all hell.

"Does this mean that you're suddenly on board with me using my magic?" Valerie wanted to know.

He thought about what she'd done to Rio. The way lightning had traveled through her body and *into* Griffin when he'd tried to pull her away from the boy.

And the way flames had consumed her. "Hell, no."

Disappointment flashed on her face. "Someone is a great lover, but no fun outside of the sexing."

Griffin glowered at her. "You've been lying to me."

She immediately straightened her spine. "I have not."

His fingers curled around her wrist. First things first, they were getting out of the dungeon.

He pulled her with him, moving over the spilled buckets, past the scorched stones, and toward the stairs. "You have lied." They began to climb. "You've tricked and manipulated me from the very first moment we met—"

"And that's why the witch should die."

Griffin's head whipped up. He hadn't sensed anyone else there. Hadn't picked up any odor or heard any sound—until then. Until the moment he heard those dark, angry words.

Carmichael stood at the top of the stairs. A hard glare was on his face. A glare directed at Valerie.

Griffin immediately moved, positioning his body protectively in front of Valerie. "You aren't supposed to be here." He'd given strict orders that Carmichael had to stay *away* from the castle.

"You were dying—or so everyone thought. And if you weren't dead because of the witch, then you were trapped as a beast." Carmichael's shoulders rolled in a shrug. "I'm the next in line of succession so no one tried to get in my way when I came inside."

Probably because everyone had been busy battling a dragon.

"I'm fine," Griffin told his brother, voice curt. "So how about you get the fuck out." He marched up the remaining stairs, bringing Valerie with him. He would cower before no one. And Carmichael sure as hell wasn't going to stare *down* on him and his mate.

Carmichael backed up, moving up the stairs until he was on the first floor. His nostrils flared, and fury flashed on his face. "*Mated.*"

Griffin started to reply—

"Yep, we are," Valerie sang out happily. "And not some temporary link, either. Marked and mated forever now. Boom."

Griffin frowned at her.

She smiled. Blew him a kiss. "Try getting rid of me in a month. See how that works out for you."

A growl came from Carmichael.

Valerie just laughed. "You guys are so growly. It's adorable."

Shock slackened Carmichael's face.

But the shock faded as Valerie stalked toward him. She still had a smile on her face, but her eyes were ice cold. "If I find out you fired that arrow at me..." She lifted her hand. Stabbed her index finger into Carmichael's chest. "I will cut out your heart. Then I will dance on your grave." Her head cocked to the right as she studied him. "That's what I do to my enemies. I love to dance when they're dead."

Carmichael seemed incapable of looking away from her. "You're crazy."

Valerie shrugged.

"You've tied yourself to an insane witch!" Carmichael threw at Griffin. "Why? Because you wanted to screw her? She's hot as hell, but crazy as—"

Griffin had thrown his brother a good ten feet. Carmichael's body thudded into the wall.

Valerie glanced at Griffin, raising one eyebrow. "You moved so fast." Her lips curled down in a pout. "No fair. I was going to throw him. You beat me."

He took her hand in his. Brought it to his lips. Pressed a kiss to her knuckles. "No one calls my mate crazy."

Carmichael slowly rose to his feet.

"*No one* ever disrespects her. She is mine, and I will fight to the death for her."

Valerie's hand gave a little jerk in his. "No need for you to go dying."

His head turned. He smiled at her. And didn't let go of her hand. "I won't be the one dying, baby. Anyone who comes at you will be."

"That is so sweet."

"That's fucking insane!" Carmichael roared.

Warren rushed from the alcove. About damn time. Elliott was right behind him.

Carmichael glared at Valerie. Then at Griffin. "You can't want to be with her forever!"

It was done.

Carmichael focused on Valerie. "And you can't want him! You're playing some kind of game. Using my brother." His gaze cut back to Griffin. "Witches *can't* be trusted. You're the one who told me that, Griffin!"

Because it was a lesson they'd learned long ago. But Griffin wasn't trusting Valerie. He was mating her. There was a difference.

"I won't let you destroy him," Carmichael fumed. "I *will* stop you."

"Promises, promises," Valerie murmured. She didn't look or sound worried.

And she shouldn't be worried. Because Griffin was about to make certain Carmichael never hurt her again. "Take him out of here," Griffin snapped to Warren.

A dark shadow covered Carmichael's face. "Because I'm not supposed to be in the castle. My home. She's taken that over. She's—"

"Out of the realm," Griffin added. "Open the doorway. It's going to be a one-way trip."

Carmichael paled. "What?"

Valerie's eyes widened. "What? You're—you're banishing your brother?"

He fucking was. Griffin's gaze slid to Elliott. "Did you find the arrow?"

Elliott's hands had been behind his back. He gave a grim nod and lifted his right hand—revealing the arrow. "Had to fight to get it from Rio."

Valerie sucked in a sharp breath.

"He is *okay*," Elliott added hastily. "Kid's upstairs. Totally safe."

Griffin stalked forward. Took the blood-stained arrow. Inhaled.

"You can't banish me," Carmichael blasted him. "This is my home! You can't turn me out for a witch!"

Griffin tried to choke down his rage. He turned toward his brother. His blood. "Did you think I wouldn't know?"

Carmichael stiffened.

"I can smell the poison. Your scent isn't there. Right now, the only shifters I can detect on it are Rio and Elliott. But the scent of the poison is very, very distinct." He snapped the arrow in his hand. "A poison designed for one very specific purpose."

Carmichael shook his head. "No. *No!*"

Griffin stalked toward him. Claws burst from his fingertips. "Yes. Only you and I knew about that poison. *Only us.* We were the only ones who knew where it was hidden."

"Griffin?" Valerie's voice was hushed. "What's going on?"

"A poison that can paralyze a witch. It just has to get into her blood, right? But the arrow didn't pierce her skin, so Valerie didn't feel the effects."

Carmichael denied, "I *didn't—*"

"It's the same poison I used on the witch who killed our parents." Because he'd been thirteen when he'd hunted her down, and he'd been no match for her on his own. Getting that poison had been no easy chore. Once he'd had it, though, he'd been able to get vengeance. Finally. And the bit of the poison that had remained stayed locked in Griffin's tower. His secret. His and Carmichael's. Until now. *The secret is out.* "Did you get it when you came to the castle yesterday? You snuck it out, and you tried to use it on my mate?"

"You didn't want her!" Carmichael bellowed. "You hadn't slept with her! Don't act like you're suddenly in love with the witch. It's the mating doing this. You don't give a damn about her."

Griffin stood toe-to-toe with his brother. "You know nothing about me. Or her."

"Griffin—" Valerie began, voice high.

"Banishment." The punishment had been given. "And if you try to fight, Carmichael, if you ever so much as look sideways at her...*death.*"

The tension in the air was palpable.

"Valerie, go upstairs." Griffin didn't look back at her. If his brother fought, he didn't want her watching as he killed his only blood relative.

But she didn't move.

"Valerie..." Griffin glanced back at her.

And he found her staring at him with wide, shocked eyes. "You have a poison...that paralyzes witches?"

Guilt tore through him. *No, no, she can never know the rest. Never.* "We'll talk upstairs." Away from prying eyes and shifter ears.

She shook her head. "Would you have used it on me? Wait—*will* you use it on me? So that I'm too weak to fight back from an attack? So that I can die?"

Did she think he could hurt her? "We're mated now. If you die..." He could lose his sanity. That was how deep the mating went for the shifters in his blood-line. "You won't die."

"That's not an answer. You sonofabitch, *that's not an answer.*" Then Valerie stormed away. He wanted to run after her. To grab her. Hold her tight. But...

Eliminate the threat. His brother couldn't be allowed to stay near Valerie. Her safety had to come first.

From now on, her safety would always be his priority.

***

Valerie flew up the stairs, and she hissed at every guard who so much as glanced at her. Her fingers wiggled in the air—hell, yes, she was doing magic—and she used a locator spell to find her henchman. When she closed in on Rio, she found a tall, dark-haired shifter guarding his door. The fool actually stepped aggressively toward her.

"You do not want to try me right now," Valerie fired at him. "Don't make that mistake."

He backed down. Wise. He was smarter than he'd looked on first glance.

She threw open the door. Rio was on the bed, with Edgar perched on his shoulder. When Rio saw her, he jumped to his feet. Edgar cawed.

Valerie glanced over her shoulder. The shifter guard stood in the doorway. Smiling sweetly, she said, "Back the hell up."

He'd barely cleared the threshold when she slammed the door on him.

Then she was swallowed in a too tight hug. "You saved me!" Rio announced, his voice rising with each word. "I know I was dying. You healed me. You made me stronger. You—"

She shoved his arms away. "What were you thinking?"

"I—" He blinked.

"Who in heaven or hell told you to put your body between me and an arrow?"

Rio pressed his lips together.

Edgar let loose a gurgling croak.

Valerie glared at the raven. "Could you *be* useful? There's witch poison in this place. I just found out that crap a few minutes ago! You're supposed to pick up details like that for me!" She was...scared. Utterly terrified. "Go eavesdrop. Find out what else they've been keeping from me."

The bird flew toward the open window.

"Y-you told me," Rio stammered. "Said it was a henchman's job to always stand between you and—"

Her temples ached. "That is *not* your job any longer."

Was he about to cry? He blinked his eyes a few times. "I'm fired?"

"No. But when danger comes, stand behind me. Got it? Not in front. Behind. You listened wrong before. So everything that happened is your fault. I will *not* forgive you." Her chin jerked into the air. "You pull something like that again, and you will most definitely be fired."

Rio shook his head. "But—"

Valerie tackle hugged him. "Don't ever do that shit again." She'd gotten a stupid soft spot for the kid. "Not ever."

CHAPTER ELEVEN

"I didn't attack your witch!" Carmichael shouted. They were outside of the castle, just beyond the gates. And Griffin was trying to *not* kill his younger brother.

"If I'd attacked her," Carmichael continued, voice grating, "she'd be dead."

Elliott and Warren were on either side of Carmichael. Each man held one of his arms.

Griffin smiled at his brother. "Let him go."

Elliott frowned. "You sure about that?"

"Positive. It's no fun to kick the ass of someone who can't fight back."

Warren and Elliott freed Carmichael.

Carmichael stood there, expression bemused. "What is going on with you?"

Instead of answering, Griffin drove his fist into Carmichael's face. His brother's nose broke with a wonderful crunch. "You won't kill her. You won't touch her."

"Fuck!" Carmichael swiped away the blood. "I told you, I wasn't behind the attack!" He didn't fight back. "And why the hell are you acting so high and mighty?"

A raven flew overhead.

"I know what you were planning! You think I didn't hear? Hell, everyone in this town knew the reason you'd left this realm."

This time, when he hit Carmichael, Griffin would use his claws—

"You were supposed to kill her!" Carmichael spat. "The witch council hired you to take her out because everyone knows Valerie Storm is psychotic. The council didn't think they could handle things on their own, so they hired *you*. You took out the last witch who went bad. You poisoned her so she couldn't use her powers, and then you eliminated her. It's been a century, but who the hell is keeping count?"

Carmichael was, obviously.

The raven suddenly dove low, flying right at Griffin as it released a shrill cry. He batted the fool bird out of his way. It flew up again, cawing.

For some reason, that caw reminded him of Valerie's laugh.

I was supposed to kill her. And if I hadn't been attacked and had to shift into my dragon, I fucking might have done it. Because he never would have gotten to know Valerie. A fact something only those in his inner circle realized...Griffin was a paranormal assassin. He took out the monsters who were too strong for others to handle. That was how he got money for his people. How the shifters kept their power and influence.

And, yes, he'd fucking agreed to kill Valerie Storm.

Before.

Before he'd become trapped as a dragon.

Before a beautiful, wild witch had sat next to him in a dungeon and told him that he had giant claws.

Before she'd saved a young shifter who'd been dead to the world.

Before she'd reached past Griffin's guard. Before his witch had started to make him feel something more than duty and vengeance.

"You were going to kill her, not me." Carmichael laughed at his brother. "I never had those plans for Valerie. I'm not the one who used the poison. So banish me, fine, but you won't be eliminating the threat to your mate. You can't eliminate it." Carmichael closed in on him. "Because you want to know who is the greatest threat to her? Try looking in a mirror to see him." Then, in case Griffin had missed the point, Carmichael thundered, "It's *you,* bastard. You."

***

The raven flew through the window.

Valerie finally stopped hugging Rio. She'd probably hugged him too hard. He seemed to be struggling for breath. She lifted her left hand, and the raven perched on her wrist. "Tell me," Valerie said. "And it had better be good."

Only...it wasn't good.

Her stomach twisted. The room became a little blurry, and that was odd. Why would the room blur? Why did her cheeks feel wet? Why was her chest aching?

"Valerie?" Rio's voice rose with concern.

"He wanted to kill me?" Her heart couldn't be breaking. She didn't have a heart. Ask anyone. Ask everyone.

The raven stared back at her.

Her breath sawed from her lungs. "I can only leave with a shifter." That was how she'd gotten into this cursed realm. Her head turned. She focused on Rio. "You're a shifter."

"But I can't shift—"

"I don't need you to shift." She just needed him to hold her hand. To touch her while they passed through the portal. "We're ditching this world."

"What?"

"I told you before that humans weren't so bad. They're not. They're fabulous. You're going to love them. You'll live a rock star life."

"You're...crying."

"I'm absolutely not." She swiped at her cheek. "My eyes are just leaking. I'm allergic to dragons."

"But—"

"I'm leaving. Are you coming with me?"

"I can't open a doorway." He rocked forward onto the balls of his feet. "Griffin has to do that. I don't possess that kind of power."

Griffin wasn't going to open a door for her. But...

"Banished," Valerie whispered.

"We're not!" Rio instantly denied. "No one told us we were banished from this place!"

They weren't. Carmichael was. That meant Griffin would be opening a doorway for his brother very, very soon. Only Carmichael wouldn't be the only one going through that doorway. She schemed. She plotted. "You don't have to come with me." If she grabbed Carmichael when he went through the door, she'd still technically be with a shifter. "I can go with—"

Rio snapped to attention, standing up straight and tall. "A henchman doesn't leave his witch."

Her eyes were leaking again. "I think I'm also allergic to shifters who can't shift."

He smiled at her.

Her chin lifted as Valerie schemed a little more. "Before we go, let's make sure they remember us, hmm? Give them a show they'll never forget."

Edgar gurgled.

"Exactly, my friend. You read my mind." Her power had returned. The rage and pain she felt fueled her, and she knew just what she would do...

You don't screw with me.

***

Griffin had opened the portal.

"This is a mistake!" Carmichael spat.

"You come back, and I will kill you. Blood or no blood."

"I *didn't* use the poison! It wasn't me!"

No one else had known about the poison. Only his brother. Griffin shoved his brother toward the portal. Before Carmichael could go through that doorway, the ground trembled. A hard, wild shaking. *What in the hell?* Griffin whirled to face the castle. Flames shot from the windows. Smoke billowed into the sky.

"Valerie!" Griffin roared. She was in the castle. Had something happened to her? Were those flames *coming* from her? Without hesitation, he tossed Carmichael through the portal, and then he ran toward the castle. As he ran, he transformed, shedding the body of a man and becoming a beast so that he could get to her faster. Faster.

His heart felt as if it were being ripped from his body. Nothing could happen to his mate.

Nothing.

***

"And *that's* how you make an exit," Valerie murmured. She watched as Griffin became a wolf, charging away from her. Warren and Elliott raced with him.

Elliott became a giant bear. Impressive. A grizzly, if she knew her bears. She did.

While Warren became a big, white wolf.

"Are you sure about this?" Rio voice's held fear.

"Absolutely." She looped her arm through his and then let out a dramatic cry. "Look, a portal! One that some nice person just conveniently left open for us." Edgar landed on her shoulder. Valerie frowned down at him. "You think you're up for the human world?"

Edgar just looked back at her with his black eyes.

"Fine. Whatever. Should be easy enough for you to find worms." As long as the trip through the portal didn't kill him. Valerie pulled in a deep breath. She would *not* glance over her shoulder at the castle. She didn't need to get one last look at Griffin.

At the mate who'd been hired to kill her.

Why, oh, why was she surprised by another betrayal at this point in her life? She should really be used to them by now. The fact that her chest was aching—well, that was the least of what she deserved. She knew better than to let down her guard.

"I...I think it's going to hurt you," Rio whispered.

"It already does." She gave him a big smile. "I'm used to the pain."

"Valerie—"

"The human world is waiting for us." She wouldn't look back. "Let's ditch this hell-hole." They walked through the portal.

She glanced back.

***

The closer he got to the castle, the more the whole thing felt...wrong.

Why wasn't he smelling the fire? The smoke? Griffin could see the flames shooting into the air, but he couldn't smell them. And he didn't feel the heat. He should feel the heat lancing his skin.

He didn't.

It was almost as if—as if he were just watching video of a fire. Scenes of it. An illusion.

Fucking hell.

Valerie's words rolled through his mind, her explanation after she'd scared the ever-loving-hell out of Lucinda. *"I just made it look as if her hair had fallen out. A wee payback spell. She was being rather unkind at the time, and if she was going to worry so much about what people looked like on the outside, I thought it was only fair that I play around with her outside appearance."*

Valerie could work illusion spells like a true master.

There was no smell to go with the smoke. Because illusions didn't contain scents. There was no heat from the flames. Because illusions weren't freaking real.

He stopped. The fire illusion had obviously been created to pull him back to the castle. That meant—

My tricky, beautiful witch. You want me away from something else.

And there was one very dangerous thing out there...something she might want.

He whirled around. Warren and Elliott thundered past him. He didn't care. He lunged across the earth, desperately trying to get back to the portal. Yet even as he ran, Griffin thought...

Surely she isn't trying to escape.

She can't get through the portal without a shifter at her side.

We just mated. She wouldn't leave me.

Why would she leave me?

Then he saw her. She'd just walked into the portal. He opened his mouth, howling his fury. She was with Rio, her arm looped with the younger shifter's arm.

That's how she's leaving! Dammit.

Another howl burst from him. He surged ahead faster and harder.

Valerie glanced over her shoulder. Her gaze met his. He expected to see satisfaction in her dark eyes. Rage. As if she'd been playing with him all along. As if she'd just been jerking around the desperate, obsessed shifter king.

But...

She was crying. Tears were on her cheeks, and pain was in her eyes.

The portal closed.

He howled again, because suddenly, her pain was his.

Oh, the fuck no, baby, you aren't getting away. Not that easily.

***

"Please be okay."

Valerie cracked open one eyelid. She found an upside-down Rio staring at her.

"You're okay!" A wide smile split his upside-down face. And then—then he hauled her upright. So fast and so hard that her head nearly split open, and she *seriously* considered turning the guy into a frog, just for shits and giggles. But he wrapped her in a giant bear hug, and she decided to forgive him.

"You were out for *hours!*" Rio squeezed her harder. "I was afraid you were going to die. I tried to go get help, but any time I walked away from you, Edgar started pecking at me."

She slanted a quick glance at Edgar. He seemed to preen. *Good boy.* If her enemies had found her while she was weak and unprotected, well, that would have been a shit storm. "You can stop hugging me."

Rio pulled back. Flushed.

"I'm fine." Total lie. Who cared? She heard the roar of waves. The pounding of the surf. And beneath her feet—ah, yes, that was sand. Wonderful, wonderful sand. She'd been trying like hell to work her location spell before she'd been knocked unconscious, and if the spell had worked, then the precious sand beneath her bare toes—where were her shoes?—well, the sand meant she was in Key West. *Exactly* where she wanted to be.

Humans didn't know it, but paranormals liked to party in the Florida Keys. The Lord of the Dark, the ruler of all the very baddest things out there—he even had a private island close by. She was counting on Luke Thorne to help her out because Valerie suspected she'd soon have an angry shifter king on her trail.

"What are we going to do?" Rio glanced around, as if he expected an army to appear on the deserted beach and attack them. Hardly going to happen. Hopefully.

She wiggled her fingers. The magic flowed so much better—stronger and cleaner—now that she was away from the shifter realm. She wouldn't have ever told anyone the truth but...her powers *had* been hampered in the other realm. Now, though, she was back to full force.

Watch out, world. I'm back in action. "First, we get clothes. We blend." A finger wiggle in his direction had the guy getting jeans, a black shirt, and a seriously stylish pair of kicks. She also went ahead and gave his hair a new cut. Makeover time. Now he looked more like a young heartthrob and less like the sad shifter who'd died for her.

Then she wiggled her fingers toward her own body. *Hello, sex appeal.* She went for a tight top, one that revealed her belly button. A miniscule pair of shorts. Sandals that showed off what she thought were *precious* toes.

Edgar cawed.

"Yes, go have fun. I'll call you if I need you."

He shot into the sky.

Valerie sucked in a deep breath. A breath of free air.

"What...what's next?"

Ah, now things were going to get fun. "I kill some witches. I take over the council. And I rule the world." She shrugged. "It will be epic."

He didn't look epically thrilled. "What about...Griffin? You're mated. He'll come for you."

Her fingers wiggled. Sparks danced in the air. "Let him come." He'd find she wasn't quite so agreeable to him any longer.

Poison her?

Try to kill *her?*

He'd been working with her enemies all along. What he didn't know...she had her own allies. Always had. And she would not let his attack go unavenged.

"I hear music," Rio mumbled.

Her smile stretched. "Of course, you do, darling. When I arrive, there is always a party."

He blinked.

"Follow me." And she headed for the music. She loved the Florida Keys. The roar of the waves. The scent of the ocean. The sand beneath her feet.

And the bars that always seemed to be open.

She'd picked this place in particular, though, because it was a hangout for her kind. The bad ones. The ones who didn't give a shit about anything or anyone. *Daybreak.* Her favorite dive bar. She could see the ramshackle building with its torchlights glowing. The bar was hardly anything fancy. Why waste time and money on being fancy when the place was right on the beach? No sense competing with that kind of beauty.

She sashayed past the bouncer. Waved her fingers back toward Rio. "He's with me."

Rio straightened. Tried to look tough. Actually succeeded a bit when he hardened his jaw and narrowed his eyes.

Then they were entering the club. Music pounded. Bodies gyrated. Voices rose and fell and then—

Silence.

She *did* know how to capture everyone's attention.

Rio sidled closer. "You sure I shouldn't be standing in front of you?"

The not-so-shifter had definite protective instincts.

She patted his shoulder. "Don't worry. I've got this."

A heavily muscled, heavily tattooed man pulled himself from the crowd. His eyes were pitch black, and his hair was a thick, wild tumble around a face that could only be termed dangerous. "*Valerie.*" His booming voice shook the bar as he closed in on her. With every step he took, his tattoos seemed to swirl and move. Most of his tats were of snakes. They seemed to practically slither. To hiss.

"Oh, shit," Rio whispered. It was the first time she'd ever heard the guy curse.

The man approaching them raked a quick glance over Rio, then focused back on Valerie. "You dare to walk into this place? *My* place?"

Rio tried to slide in front of her. She shoved him back. Smiled at the bar owner. "Of course. Don't I have an open invitation?"

The whispers came, as they always did.

She's the witch. They say she's crazy.

Valerie Storm made a deal with the devil. Lost her soul.

Only works black magic.

She's such a badass.

I would totally fuck her.

"Stefan?" Valerie prompted when the tattooed, muscle man just stared at her and his snakes slithered.

"Are they supposed to do that?" Rio whispered. Only his whisper was, as usual, really, really loud. "Since when do tattoos move?"

"They do that," Stefan replied, his voice sinister, "right before they get ready to strike."

"Oh God." Rio's Adam's apple clicked. "Can they *do* that?"

"Hell, yes, kid. Want to see?" Stefan's rumbling laughter came just before one of the snakes leapt right off his arm and shot toward Rio's terrified face.

Bored now, Valerie's hand flew out. She caught the snake right behind its head. The creature's fangs were open, and its elliptical eyes locked right on her. "We don't bite friends," she chided the snake. Her gaze slid to Stefan. "You should know better."

Stefan smiled at her. A grin that was killer. "Had to make sure it was you."

The snake hissed.

She hissed back.

"There are stories, you see." The crowd was dead silent. "Rumors. You're supposed to be dead."

"Do I look dead?" She let the snake go. It vanished in a blink, then reappeared on Stefan's arm.

His gaze raked her. "Dead sexy."

She would *not* smile at the charmer.

"Stories say you're dead..." Stefan paused. "Or mated to a shifter. Mated *and* trapped in his land. Your power is gone."

Oh, now that was just insulting. "Want to see some power?"

Everyone held their breath.

She wiggled her fingers. Fucking blew the roof off that bar. Stunned silence and then...

Cheers. Laughter. Applause.

"She's back," Stefan called out. Then he was grabbing her, pulling her tightly into his arms, and whispering in her ear, "And just in time, Valerie. Because we've got trouble. Terrible fucking trouble."

She kept her expression haughty. Satisfied. He pulled away from her, and Stefan wore a similar mask. Immediately, his fingers linked with hers. And he began to pull her through the crowd. Drinks were pushed toward her. Hands reached for her.

Stefan's snakes hissed. "She's with me."

Everyone backed away.

Rio had followed. "Um, Valerie—"

They were at the back room. She looked up. The stars were quite lovely overhead. Stefan should thank her for the sky view.

"Put it back," he ordered. *Not* a thank you.

Her fingers wiggled. The roof came back. After all, it had only been an illusion. Just like everything else in her world.

"Valerie," Rio announced again.

"Guard the door," she told him. "I need to get reacquainted with my previous henchman."

Rio's eyes doubled. "He's a *henchman?*"

Stefan swung around and glowered at her. "Him, too? Seriously?"

"It's a very exclusive club. You're both welcome."

Stefan turned back to the crowd. "The kid is part of *my* nest," he bellowed. "If he gets so much as a bruise on him, my snakes will bite every single one of you bastards."

Rio's shoulders straightened.

"*Very* exclusive club." Valerie nodded again.

Stefan dragged her into the back room. Slammed the door shut. Locked it. He immediately put his shoulders against the wooden door and crossed his arms over his powerful chest. "Where the hell have you been?"

No one could overhear the words they said. A helpful witch—*her*—had enchanted the place long ago for him. "In shifter land."

He cursed.

"Mated to the king."

His eyes closed.

"So...I guess that part of the story is true."

His eyes remained closed.

"But I'm back!" *Ta da.*

Stefan didn't appear excited. His eyes opened. For a moment, his eyes looked just like a snake's. Elliptical pupils. Ice cold. Evil. "They're going to kill you. You should have stayed with him."

"He was going to kill me, too." Her voice was low, and for the first time in—hell, she couldn't remember how long—some of her bravado faded. After all, this was Stefan. "He was hired to assassinate me. I thought he was different, but all along, he was just one in a long line."

A long line of people who hated her. Who wanted her wiped from the planet.

Who thought she was nothing but an evil monster.

"I need the others," she said, straightening her spine. "We're going to take down the council. I won't hide what I am any longer."

But Stefan gave a slow, sad shake of his head. "You don't know..." His voice trailed away.

She got a really, really bad feeling in her stomach. "Know what?"

"Fiona is dead."

Fiona...a wonderfully bad witch known as Fiona the Grim. Fiona had earned the moniker because she spread sadness and sorrow everywhere that she went. Not that Fiona could help it. That was just who she was.

Fiona had also been part of Valerie's secret team. A team she'd carefully assembled. One that would take out the council. "How?"

"No one knows who the attacker was, but he took her head."

Valerie sucked in a sharp breath.

"Hurst is gone, too."

Hurst? He'd been one of the oldest witches to ever walk the earth. "No one could catch him off-guard."

"Someone did. He burned in his bedroom. Tied to his bed."

No, that didn't make sense. "He would have just used magic to cut any ropes."

Stefan's eyes flared, the pupils shifting between those of a snake and those of a man. "Not if the ropes themselves were magic. Not if a very powerful witch was the one who imprisoned him."

She sucked in a sharp breath. "Someone is killing my allies."

His face tensed. "It's not safe for you to be in the open. We need to hide you."

Her chin lifted. "I hide from no one."

"They got to Hurst. They took out Fiona. You were counting on their magic to help you, and without them, you're going to be weak."

"I am never weak."

He stepped away from the door. His hands fell to his sides as he closed in on her. She wouldn't stiffen. *Wouldn't.*

His hand lifted. His fingers trailed over her chin. "Tell that to someone who hasn't known you for over a century."

She *wouldn't* cry. She never cried.

He caught the tear on her cheek. "They killed your allies."

They...she had a very good suspicion about who *they* were.

"And they're going to kill you."

Valerie licked her lips. "Not if I kill them first."

Stefan nodded. "I'll have your back."

He always did.

"But what about the shifter king?" His brows rose. "Will he come for you?"

She thought about the way she'd left. The fire. The smoke. The wonderful ground shaking explosions. Valerie shrugged. "I doubt he even notices that I'm gone."

CHAPTER TWELVE

Griffin stood on the beach, his claws out, and his breath heaving. Valerie had *left* him. Fled from him.

His mate.

His.

Oh, the hell, no, she wasn't getting away that easily. They were linked now, joined until death. And he didn't plan on either of them dying soon.

His nostrils flared. It was easy enough to follow her scent. He could follow her—track her—anywhere. There would never be an escape for her again. Didn't she realize that? He began stalking through the sand as the waves battered at the shore. He heard the music up ahead. The laughter. Griffin could smell cheap booze and sex on the breeze.

The bouncer saw him coming. The guy's gaze swept over Griffin, and then his head lowered, a sign of submission. But when Griffin would have bounded inside, the shifter put his hand on Griffin's chest. "You don't want to go in there."

"Something that belongs to *me* is inside."

The bouncer's gaze met his. "Only darkness is inside."

Griffin bared his fangs. "Then she is *my* darkness." Some people liked to paint the world as black and white. Vampires were evil. Angels were good. Shifters...they were mostly on the *bad* side, so why would he be afraid of a little darkness?

He was starting to absolutely crave the dark.

Griffin headed into the club. His gaze raked the place, looking for the one witch who belonged to him. As he stood there, a black raven flew right past him, nearly slamming into Griffin's head.

A familiar bird.

Fuck me. Familiar.

He followed the bird's flight. Saw it land—on Rio. The young shifter stood near a dark door, his hands crossed over his chest, his chin out in a tough-guy pose. A waitress had sidled near Rio, one clad in a very short skirt and a barely-there top. She pushed a drink toward Rio.

"He's not legal," Griffin barked as he closed in on them.

The waitress laughed. "Like anything in this place is legal?"

He growled at her.

She laughed again. "Oh, man, you're not even the worst thing I've seen in the last five minutes." She winked at Rio. "You want some fun, you come find me."

Rio's eyes were the size of saucers as he watched her walk away. "This place is...awesome."

"No, it's the pit of hell." Griffin snapped his fingers in front of Rio's face, trying to draw the kid's attention away from the waitress's ample ass. "Where's my witch?"

Rio shook his head. Seemed to finally focus on Griffin. "What are you doing here?"

Griffin almost rolled his eyes. *I've been around my witch too long.* "I'm here to claim what's mine." A hard edge punctuated each word. "Where is she?"

Rio gave a telling glance back at the door.

Griffin frowned. Valerie's scent had stopped right there—right at Rio. No scents and no sounds were coming from inside whatever room that was. *Probably because the place is enchanted.* "Move aside."

"She's...not alone."

Griffin kicked in the door. It went flying back with a heavy crash and standing there—his witch. His beautiful, sexy as sin witch. And she was *not* alone. A big bastard with too many tats stood *touching* her. Touching her? He damn well dared?

Griffin's claws lengthened as a red haze seemed to cloud his vision. "You're going to lose that hand."

The guy laughed. "Good thing I can regrow another." And his hand *lingered* on her cheek. The tats on the guy's arms seemed to slither.

"I sure as hell hope that's the case," Griffin muttered. He'd warned the bastard. Griffin lunged across the room, his claws flying.

And a fucking *snake* shot out at him.

His claws cut right through the snake's head.

It vanished before it hit the floor.

The guy barreled at Griffin, but he just drove his fist into the fellow's jaw. The man was big, but Griffin was fucking pissed. His blow drove the

SOB across the room. The guy slammed into a wall. The whole building shook.

"Oh, I'm going to like kicking your ass." The guy's eyes had changed. Gone absolutely serpentine. Hisses seemed to surround him. He surged forward.

"Stop." Valerie stood between them. One hand was on Griffin's chest. The other was on the soon-to-be-dead asshole's chest.

Griffin felt her touch resonate all the way through his body. Her touch seemed to burn. To mark him. And some of the desperate tension he'd felt since she left him finally faded. *I've got her back. I won't lose her again.*

But Valerie slowly turned her head. Her eyes seemed ice cold. "You're not wanted here, shifter."

His body stiffened.

"So why don't you just drag yourself back to shifter land?"

Hell, no. "Not going anywhere, not without you."

She lifted one brow. "You sure about that?"

"Abso-fucking-lutely."

Valerie's smile was almost angelic. She turned away from the SOB to focus totally on Griffin. At her move, it sounded as if the SOB snickered. Both of Valerie's hands rose to press to Griffin's chest. "I never finished going over all of my rules with you."

Her scent was all around him. Driving him insane. He wanted to grab her and pull her close. To take her as far away from this place as possible. To take her *home*.

"I have one very, very big rule. Should have covered that, but, honestly..." She exhaled. "I thought it was a given."

"Valerie—"

"Never betray me."

A cold chill slid up his spine. No, no, there was no way—

"*Never* try to kill me." She rose onto her tiptoes. Her lips slid over his. A light, tempting caress that had him yearning for so much more. "Because if you do, I'll never forgive you."

"Eye for an eye," the dumbass behind her called out.

She kissed Griffin again. "Yes."

Griffin breathed out slowly. "I haven't tried to kill you."

Her smile lingered. A smile that never reached her eyes. "Intent is a very dangerous thing."

Oh, fuck me. Somehow, she knew. "Valerie—"

"I don't forget. I don't forgive." Now her smile faded. "And, you, shifter, are now my enemy." She started to back away.

His hands flew up and clamped around her shoulders. "I'm your *mate.*"

Valerie stiffened. "That, too. Enemy, mate. But you know the thing about *mates?* That bond only gets beneath your skin, it only drives you *mad,* if you're a shifter. And in case you haven't noticed..." A little shrug. "I'm not."

He wouldn't let her go. He would explain. He would tell her—

"Now, *bippity, boppity, fuck you.*" She wiggled her fingers.

He *flew* through the wall of the club. Flew back, back...until his body slammed down into the ocean. He burst up, spitting out salt water, and shaking. He swam back to shore, then stomped up the beach.

Valerie was there. His beautiful witch. Her hands were clenched at her sides. Rio stood a few feet behind her. The tattooed bastard was there, too. Watching. Grinning.

"Uh, oh," Valerie murmured. "Someone looks like a wet dog."

Griffin ran his hand over his head, sending drops of water flying.

"I could have drowned you." She shrugged one shoulder. "Wiggled my fingers and the waves would have kept you prisoner forever. So easy to do."

He stalked toward her. Only stopped when he was right in front of her. When he towered over her. Griffin wanted his hands on Valerie. All over her. But he kept them at his sides. For the moment. "Why the hell didn't you?"

Her gaze jerked away from him. "I gave you a warning."

Bullshit. "Since when does the queen of all evil give warnings?"

Her lower lip trembled. "You will stay away from me."

"The hell I will. Listen, dammit, I don't know what you heard or how—"

A raven torpedoed him. Shit. *Shit*. Griffin slapped at it, and the bird dodged easily. Then...the raven perched on her shoulder. "Fucking familiar," Griffin muttered.

Valerie's dark eyes glittered. "You were going to poison me. Kill me." The wind seemed to pick up with each word she spoke. "You didn't even know me, yet you took the job as my assassin."

Okay, so now he was understanding. Too much. His chest ached. Burned. "I was told of your crimes." A very, very long list of crimes.

Her gaze cut away from him, as if she couldn't stand to peer into his eyes right then. She stared at the waves. "So you decided to be my executioner?"

"Don't play innocent!" No, dammit, he hadn't meant to say that. He grabbed onto his control, a hard feat when desperation gnawed at him. "You...you killed, Valerie. You were out of control. You took out your own kind. You took out demons. Vampires. You had to be stopped."

"And you were the man to stop me?" Still, she wasn't looking at him.

He wanted her to look at him. He needed her to look at him. "Things are different now. You're my *mate*."

"You never would have chosen me on your own." Was that sadness? No, she could *not* be sad. "If you hadn't been trapped as a dragon, if you had met me in the form of a man..." Now her gaze turned to him. "Would I be dead right now?"

Kill her? Could he have done it? Stared into her dark, deep eyes and taken her life? He remembered all of the stories about her, the proof he'd been promised by the council... "I can help you," Griffin heard himself say. "You can change. You can be—"

The wind whipped harder against him. "You want to change me?" Valerie demanded. "Because I'm not good enough for you just the way I am?"

He hadn't meant—

"You didn't answer my first question, shifter. If you hadn't been trapped as a dragon, if you hadn't needed my magic, would I be dead right now?"

He'd taken some of the poison with him to the meeting with the council. He'd intended to use it on Valerie. To paralyze her so she couldn't work her magic against him. But then everything had gone to hell when he'd been attacked. An attack he'd never even seen coming. He'd taken the poison and—"Fucking hell."

"Is that a yes?" Valerie asked in her sugary sweet voice. "Or a no?"

"I lost the poison." Something he'd just freaking realized because he'd been more than a bit distracted.

She stiffened.

"I was going for a meeting with the council. They were going to show me proof of your crimes before I handed down your sentence. But I was attacked. Panthers attacked me—"

"Panthers? Shifter panthers? I'm supposed to believe they attacked their own king?"

"Not all shifters swear allegiance to me." If only. Life would be much easier. "I transformed into the dragon because there were so many of them. When I transformed, I ripped through my clothes. I had a pack with me. The poison was *in* the pack. I don't—hell, I have no idea where it is."

She sucked in a quick breath. "Someone has your witch poison out there?" Her gaze was frantic. "Tell me, *exactly* what it does."

She wasn't going to like this. His gaze darted over her shoulder. Rio and the other bastard were watching. Listening. And if shifters were inside that club, they could hear, too.

"I can't tell you, not while we're in the open." He offered his hand to her. "Let's get out of here. I'll reveal everything, I swear I will."

She peered down at his hand. "I don't think..." Now her gaze rose. "I don't think that I can trust you."

"Valerie—"

"Fool me once," she whispered.

Griffin shook his head. "You are my mate. My duty is to keep you safe now. Despite what you've done—"

Fury flashed on her face. Her hands came up, little electric sparks flying over her fingertips, and she shoved against his chest. *Hard.* "What I've done? *Me?* You're the one who lied. You're the one who betrayed. You're the one who *hurt* me."

He didn't want to hurt her. He didn't want—

"Now." She released a long breath. "You're the one who is dead to me."

The wind whipped against his body. He was lifted up. High, higher. "Valerie!" Griffin roared her name.

Then he slammed down into the ocean. He was pulled down, down, down...and the angry waves held him tight.

***

Valerie stared at the swirling water. Her whole body ached. But the pain wasn't coming from the outside, not from some powerful blows that she'd been given. The pain came from inside. From a heart most of the world would swear she didn't have. "Henchmen!" Valerie called out as she turned her back on the churning ocean.

Immediately, both Rio and Stefan stepped forward.

Rio stared at her with worry.

Stefan...he just waited.

"I have to go on a little mission."

Stefan's gaze darted over her shoulder. His shoulders tensed. "He's swimming toward shore."

Of course, Griffin was. Because she couldn't kill him. So much for being the queen of all evil. She had a soft spot. A weakness.

Her assassin was her weakness.

"Stefan, keep Rio at your side until I return."

Rio immediately shook his head. "No! I go where you—"

"This time, it's too dangerous." The man she was seeking out was too dangerous. "You stay here, okay? Try to figure out how Stefan got those tats."

She could feel Griffin's gaze on her. Boring into her back.

Valerie lifted her hands. Sparks were dancing near her fingers.

"I can kill him for you," Stefan offered in his booming voice. "If it's too...hard...to do the deed yourself."

Only shifters were supposed to feel that soul deep bond that came from a mating. Only shifters were supposed to feel like they'd found the other part of themselves.

She wasn't even supposed to have a soul. Ask anyone.

For a witch to actually form a true bond with someone else—that was so rare as to be nearly mythical. A bond like that, one pure and true and deep...a bond like that was supposed to be stronger than death itself.

She did *not* have a bond like that.

"Do you want me to kill him?" Stefan pushed.

"Don't," the one word bit from her. "I need him alive."

"Why?" Stefan seemed genuinely confused.

So was she. But... "Because I like the world better when he's in it." Even though he was a deceptive bastard, and she would *never* ever trust him again.

The wind whipped around her, and Valerie vanished.

***

Griffin roared his rage when Valerie vanished. One moment, she was standing on the beach, her hair blowing in the wind, and in the next instant, she was gone.

Gone.

No, oh, hell, *no.*

"Oh, look, a wet dog."

She was gone, but that bastard with the tats was still there. And he had his arm slung over Rio's shoulders. "Let him go, *now,*" Griffin ordered.

The guy lifted his brows. "I'm not going to hurt him. He's part of my nest."

What was that supposed to mean? "Rio, we're going home."

Rio stepped toward him.

The SOB jerked him back. "*Rio,* you are home."

Rio swallowed.

Griffin sized up his enemy. "How many freaking snakes do you have on your body?"

"More than you can guess." Laughter. "I'm Stefan Medusa."

No way. *No way.*

Griffin's expression must have shown his shock because Stefan preened. "Oh, you've heard of me? That's good. Because I've certainly heard of you, Griffin Bastien."

"Rio, move away from him, *now.*"

"I wouldn't hurt the boy. He's under Valerie's protection, so that means he's under my protection, too. But I do believe in free will so..." He let Rio go.

Rio took a few steps toward Griffin. Stopped. Frowned. "Valerie is mad at you."

"A misunderstanding. I'll find her and fix things."

More laughter from Stefan. "You can't fix what's been broken." He pointed at Griffin. "*You* did that." A disappointed sigh. "You're so lucky she wants you to keep living. My snakes could have a feast with you."

Griffin marched toward him. Stefan kept his taunting grin in place. "Listen well, *Medusa.*"

Stefan lost his grin.

"Valerie is *my* mate. Bound to me body and soul. I will not be separated from her. No one will take her from me. And if someone tries...if you try...I will end you."

"I'm not the one you need to worry about." Stefan was suddenly dead serious. "I'd die for her a million times over, and never hesitate."

Fuck. He loves her. Griffin's dragon began to stir, his body heated, he—

"She's gone to another. Someone even stronger than I am. And if she finds him, well, the guy does owe her plenty of favors. If anyone can break the bond between you, the Lord of the Dark will be the one to do it."

Lord of the Dark.

Griffin shook his head. He'd *better* have misheard.

"Why else would she come down to the Florida Keys? She wants out of this mating with you, and her ex is just the guy to do the job."

The thundering drumming of his heart filled Griffin's ears. He was pretty sure he could taste smoke on his tongue. "Her *ex*?"

"Um, yes...I mean, you're the king of shifters. Wow. Badass." Stefan didn't seem even mildly impressed. "But she likes to dirty dance on the dark side. Her *ex* is none other than Luke Thorne, the ruler of every bad thing on the planet. If anyone can get her out of her current predicament, then it will be him."

Wings burst from Griffin's back. His beast couldn't be contained. His fury was too great. Someone was going to try and take Valerie from him? Someone was going to sever *his* bond with her? *No, never.*

"Well, that is something new."

Scales sprang over Griffin's body. His bones snapped and elongated. And when he took to the sky—

He was a mother fucking dragon.

CHAPTER THIRTEEN

Valerie appeared in the middle of a lush living room. Huge chandeliers hung overhead. Ming vases were strategically positioned around the room. The rug beneath her was so thick and deep her feet sank into it. And right there, sitting on the couch and staring at her as if she had two heads—

"Luke!" His name emerged from her as a sigh of relief. Valerie surged forward and hugged him. "I am so happy to see your bad self right now."

But...

He didn't hug her back. In fact, he stiffened. His hands flew up, and he pushed her away. Then he stared at her as if he'd never seen her in his very long life.

Oh, damn. Her luck could not be this bad. No way. No way on... "You're not Luke."

Luke Thorne. The Lord of the Dark. All around badass and the guy who happened to owe her a long list of favors.

The man on the couch shook his head. He *looked* like Luke. Same dark hair. Same incredible sex appeal. Same intense, golden eyes. Same drop-dead gorgeous features.

But...

"Dammit, you're the other one." Valerie bounded across the room because she wanted to put some serious space between them. "What are you doing here? Luke will *kill* you when he finds out that you're in his house."

"Right...about that..." The guy slowly stood as he rubbed the bridge of his nose. "Guessing you've been out of touch for a while? Not exactly communicating frequently with my brother?"

Brother. Another nail in her coffin. But she'd already worked this part out. "You're Leo." And she was in trouble. Luke Thorne was the all-powerful being who ruled over the so-called "bad" paranormals, but his twin brother—the guy who was standing right in front of her—Leo was the Lord of the Light. Ruler of all the goody-two-shoes and annoyingly perky paranormals.

"Guilty," he confessed.

"What are you doing here?" All of her fine plans were going up into smoke. "I need Luke. He owes me."

Leo's brows lifted. "Does he? Good luck getting him to pay up."

"Where. Is. Luke?"

Leo pointed up.

"He's upstairs?" Relief crashed through her. "Why didn't you just say that crap to begin with? No need for stupid games." She whirled and hurried for the stairs.

"He's way, way up."

Leo's words stopped her.

"We switched places."

She spun back to face him. "This is not some Disney movie. You do *not* trade places."

His lips twitched. "We did. Sorry."

No, no, *no*.

"Guessing you're...um, bad, right?"

She seethed.

Then a woman came strolling in. An absolutely beautiful woman who seemed to crackle with power. She took one look at Valerie and stopped cold, her blue eyes widening. "Oh, shit."

"Mora." Valerie said the woman's name like the curse that it was. Only Mora wasn't the woman's *real* name. Her real name—that would be Fate. As in...the Fate. The all-knowing, ever-powerful, ancient Fate. "What are you doing with him? That's not Luke!"

Leo caught Mora's hand. Brought it to his lips. Kissed her wrist.

And nearly made Valerie gag.

"I know." Mora's cheeks flushed. "Leo and I are, um—"

"We're a thing," Leo announced.

Valerie shook her head. There was only one response to give in this particular situation. "I'm so sorry," she told the other woman.

Leo stiffened.

Mora's lips curled. "I've almost missed you, witch." Her dark hair slid over her shoulders.

"Yes, everyone misses me. I am unforgettable and amazing and your worst nightmare all in one." She rushed to Mora and ignored Leo. She had no use for him. "Where is Luke? I need him, like, pronto."

Mora lifted her eyes to the ceiling.

"Do *not* say up," Valerie snapped.

But then...then she heard something. A rumble? Thunder? And the doors of the house—gloriously elaborate French doors—suddenly flew back. Curtains swirled in the air. The wind shoved through the house, making her stagger.

"Are *you* doing that?" Mora asked her.

If only.

They all rushed toward the now open French doors. The wind was stronger. Wind that was coming from the force of two giant dragon wings.

"I'll be damned," Leo whispered. "You don't see that every day."

The dragon landed. Smoke billowed around him.

"*This* is why I needed Luke," Valerie muttered. Time for her to disappear. She lifted her hands, but—

Griffin appeared. He'd just done the fastest transformation she'd ever seen in her life. *Someone* had gotten great control of his beast. He should thank her for that. The guy walked—naked as the day he'd been born—out of the billowing smoke. His jaw was locked tight, tension coated his hard muscles, and his glittering gaze pinned Valerie in place.

"Mated," Mora pronounced with an air of satisfaction. "The beast and his wicked queen."

Valerie shot the woman a death glare. "Tell me that isn't some forever vision you just had. Because I came here in order for the Lord of the Dark to *break* the mating."

"*No!*" Griffin's snarl.

"Even death can't break the mating." Mora's voice had turned distant. Her eyes flared with power. "He's with you until your last breath and beyond."

Hardly reassuring.

"Even when you die," Mora continued, the words coming faster, "even—"

Griffin grabbed Valerie's hand and yanked her toward him. "She's not dying!"

"So says the man who was hired to *kill* me!" Valerie glared at him.

He glared back harder. "You will not die."

"Shifter, you are getting on my nerves."

Mora cleared her throat. "Is that because he's also getting into your heart?"

Valerie gasped. She spun toward the other woman. "You *know* I don't have a heart!"

But Mora just smiled. "Everyone has a heart. Some of those hearts are just a wee bit...small. You know, like the Grinch."

She did not know. "Change my fate."

Now Leo stepped in front of Mora. "I don't like the tone you're using with her."

"And I don't like the fact that you're here, talking to me, when Luke is the one I want!"

Griffin growled.

She would not find his growls sexy. Not anymore. Her fingers wiggled toward him. Sparks flew. Clothes covered his hot nakedness. "Stop growling at me."

"You will *not* want another man. We are mates, we are—"

Valerie narrowed her eyes at him. "Stop being crazy. Luke is the Lord of the Dark. The guy who should have been able to sever this stupid bond."

Leo coughed. "Um, he *was* the Lord of the Dark. I'm sort of...in charge of the bad things now."

For a moment, Valerie couldn't breathe. Not at all. Then she sucked in a deep, desperate gulp of air. "We are so screwed." No, she was screwed.

"Maybe." Leo coughed again. "I'm still trying to figure this shit out, but if you told me your problem...uh, you are *obviously* something bad...then I think I might can...help?" He sounded so uncertain with all of his little pauses.

She gave Griffin another glower. Then she faced off with Leo. "Obviously," she drew out the word, "I am bad. The baddest. I'm Valerie Storm."

Leo's eyes flared in recognition.

"And my problem? It's him." Valerie jerked her thumb toward Griffin. "My *mate* is also the assassin who was hired to kill me."

Leo's jaw dropped as he cut his eyes toward Griffin. "You want to kill your mate? But you're a shifter. I can tell. I can smell the beasts on you and—"

"I *don't* want to kill her," Griffin rasped.

"So says the man who keeps witch poison at his home. Who does that?" She nodded. "There was an attempt on my life. Right under his nose. I'm supposed to buy he didn't have anything to do with that? I'm supposed to *trust* this liar?"

Griffin's hand closed around her shoulder. "I had nothing to do with the attempt on your life." His voice was gruff. "When I saw you on the ground...Rio was covering you. I couldn't tell if you were hurt or not."

She slanted a glance back at him.

"I couldn't tell if you lived." He swallowed. "The world...it got very dark for me."

"Big deal. The world is always dark for me." *Welcome to my paradise.*

"I feared." He pulled her closer. "I don't fear anything."

"You *should* fear me," Leo pointed out. "I'm the ruler of the bad things, and—"

Griffin looked at the other man. Just looked.

Mora tapped Leo's shoulder. "He doesn't fall under your domain."

Leo was staring at Griffin in confusion. "Why the hell not?"

"Because *parts* of him are good, and parts of him are bad. He carries three beasts inside." Her eyes were glowing again. "And those beasts may one day rip him apart. They may make him choose a side—good or bad. Bad or good. But for now...now they just want..." She blinked. Focused on Valerie. "*Her.* He wants her."

Her day was getting better and better. "I don't have time for this. I have too many enemies and a world to take over. It doesn't just rule itself, you know?" She jerked away from Griffin. Wiggled her fingers. "I'm out of—"

"No."

Her brows rose. "Excuse me?"

His hand locked around her wrist. "You don't leave me."

She laughed. "I do anything I want."

"I'm your mate. Where you go, I go."

Precious. She leaned in close to him, and, her voice a lethal whisper, Valerie told him, "You could've had something. Something absolutely spectacular. Something others would have killed to possess." Her gaze cut into him. "You could've had me. But you lied to me. You tricked me. I won't make the same mistake with you again."

His hold tightened on her. "Like you didn't lie? Didn't trick me?"

"That's the thing. I didn't." Her smile hurt. "I should have learned from my previous mistakes. You won't be hurting me again."

His face went slack with surprise and his grip loosened. "I hurt—"

Her fingers wiggled. She left him. Left before the bastard could see that he'd made her cry. Pain was good, though. Pain would give her more strength.

And she'd need that strength for the battles ahead.

Someone was taking out her allies. The team she'd carefully assembled. Two were dead. That left...

Only one more witch on my side. A somewhat reckless witch named Calliope Briggs. Valerie had to find her, fast. Before someone took Calliope out of the equation.

***

Valerie had left him, again. And before she'd left...had those been tears in her eyes?

Griffin rolled back his shoulders, pulling up his beast, ready to hunt and—

"Uh, yeah..." Leo cleared his throat. "I don't think she wants to be with you, buddy. Probably want to give her a little bit of space."

Griffin turned his head so that he was staring at the Lord of the Dark. Yes, he knew who the bastard was. He kept tabs on both Leo and Luke. The two brothers—identical twins—had recently switched places, courtesy, he suspected of Fate.

Fate gave him a weak smile. "Valerie seemed really pissed."

"No." Griffin shook his head. "She was hurt. There's a difference."

"Not for her," Fate argued. But, wait, she went by the less glamorous name of Mora now. He'd have to remember that.

Griffin rubbed his chest. His heart seemed to ache again. "It was just a job that I took. She was a menace."

"Was?" Leo latched onto that word. "Past tense? Has the evil witch suddenly changed her ways?"

No, he didn't think she had.

"Or maybe..." Leo continued carefully. "You've just realized that things aren't always black and white."

His chest ached more.

"If that's the case, then join the club." Leo lifted his hands. "How the hell do you think I wound up here?"

Mora stroked her lover's arm. "Valerie has a lot of enemies in the world. They are closing in on her." Her stare didn't leave Griffin's. "Will you let her face them alone?"

They should be clear on this. "Anyone who wants to hurt *my* mate will have to go through me first." And she would only be hurt over his dead body.

Mora's smile became absolutely brilliant. "That's what I thought. But I worried because, you know, you're still *here*. And Valerie is—um, wherever the hell she wants to be."

Every instinct he had screamed for Griffin to give chase. Instead, he squared his shoulders and held the gaze of the new Lord of the Dark. "Who are the ones after Valerie?"

"The witch council, of course." It was Mora who answered. "You were there when they tried to burn her. You were there when they banished her. What do you think they'll do when they learn she's back? *Against* their orders? The only punishment can possibly be death."

"She's my mate. They wouldn't dare." He had an alliance with them. Didn't he?

"Why don't you go find out why Valerie hates them all so much? Learn the story of her pain. Because Valerie's pain..." Mora winced. "She is so not going to like me telling you this. But we *do* go back forever, so I know her secrets."

He took a step toward Mora.

Leo stiffened.

"Pain fuels Valerie." Mora's voice was sad. "She was supposed to be the most powerful witch to walk the earth. The ruler of them all. That's what I saw when I first met her. *That* is the fate that should have waited for Valerie."

"Instead she became the one they all want dead?"

Leo cleared his throat. "She does have a long history of death and dismemberment. I'm still getting caught up on all the back stories for my new...paranormals, but Valerie, let's just say she's at the top of my danger list. From what I can tell, though, Luke was protecting her for some reason. Letting her get away with crimes that he would have killed others for committing."

Griffin's brow furrowed.

"Oh, that's just because they used to be lovers." Mora waved that bit away. "Luke probably had a soft spot for her—"

Rage. Jealousy. Raw fury. *"She ran to her ex-lover?"* Valerie had dropped him in the ocean and then taken off to find her ex? And if the two brothers hadn't switched places, fuck, she *would* have found Luke Thorne. Would the bastard have severed her mating bond with Griffin?

"She had him wrapped around her little wiggling finger," Mora added, eyes gleaming.

Griffin roared. He shot into the sky as his dragon's wings ripped from his back.

***

Leo watched as the king of shifters flew away. "I'm not sure you should have mentioned Valerie's past with my brother." The shifter's wings were covered in scales. And the fellow had been *pissed*. "I think you might have pushed him over the edge."

Mora just laughed. "Griffin needed to be pushed."

Leo wasn't so sure. "Did you see his face? Killing fury is the way I'd describe his emotional state."

Her fingers slid down his arm. "If he's going to fight with Valerie, if he's going to be strong enough to handle her, then he needs some fury. He needs to understand exactly what he's fighting to protect."

Leo glanced down at her. His Fate. If anyone tried to take her from him, he'd fight like hell. There was nothing he wouldn't do. No line he wouldn't cross.

He'd trade his very soul to keep her safe.

"I just hope he understands before it's too late." Sadness flashed in her eyes. "Because time is running out. Death is tired of waiting."

CHAPTER FOURTEEN

He landed on the beach. The moonlight gleamed overhead, and the waves pounded on the shore. Valerie's scent lingered in the air. Griffin's nostrils flared as he drank in that delectable scent. Did she truly think she could hide from him? There was no place she could go that he wouldn't follow.

"You didn't keep your end of the deal." The low, masculine voice came from the darkness.

Griffin stiffened. He hadn't sensed anyone else nearby, and his senses were damn sharp. Since he hadn't realized the guy was there... "Using magic to cloak yourself, Devon?" he asked as he slowly turned around to face the threat.

The witch materialized from the shadows. "I didn't exactly want to announce my presence to every beast in the Keys." His stare raked Griffin. "You want some clothes?"

He'd ripped them to shreds during his shift.

"Before I go blind...here." Devon snapped his fingers. Clothes covered Griffin. "Don't say I never did anything for you."

Griffin didn't move.

Devon began to pace. "You said you'd keep Valerie in your realm. You promised."

"How do you know she's here?" Who'd told the bastard?

Devon stilled. "I *felt* her. Valerie's magic is so strong, every witch felt it when she left. Trust me, there was great rejoicing." His shoulders rolled back. "Then when she returned, well, let's just say a whole lot of people went into hiding, very fast."

Griffin realized Devon had been cloaking himself for a very specific reason. "You were hiding from her. You're *scared* of her."

The witch didn't deny it. Instead, he slowly marched toward Griffin. "If she has the chance, Valerie will kill me."

"Only fair, considering you tried to burn her at the stake." And, yeah, his claws were coming out at that memory.

But Devon shook his head. "That's not why she wants me dead. She wants me dead because of Tomas."

"Who the fuck is Tomas?"

Devon laughed. The sound really got on Griffin's nerves.

"What?" Devon drawled. "Your *mate* never mentioned the human that she loved? I think he's the only person she ever did love. And the only one she ever will love. She lost her heart because of him."

Another fucking lover. Griffin's back teeth clenched. "Where is Tomas?" The man would *never* see Valerie—

"Dead, of course. Why else would Valerie want to kill me? She blames me. Like I could have stopped what happened." His face twisted in disgust. "She changed after him. Went mad. She doesn't understand right and wrong, doesn't care who she hurts, all because of a man long dead. A human."

A human she'd...loved?

"You mated her. You poor bastard."

Griffin attacked. In a lightning fast move, he grabbed the witch, his claws going to the fool's throat. "I can take your head right now. Let it drop to the sand. I could cleave it before you even draw the breath to scream." He could smell Devon's fear.

"S-stop!" Devon gasped. "I-I have...s-something...help..."

Griffin eased his hold. If the jerk tried to work magic, he was a dead man.

But Devon just pulled out a pair of gold bracelets from his pocket. Gold bracelets, wrapped with lines of diamonds. "These can help you."

How the hell were those trinkets supposed to help him?

"They're bewitched. They can control Valerie's magic. You put these on her, and she won't be able to work *any* spells. She can't disappear. She can't kill. You can take her back to your realm—*like you promised*. Take her back, live forever with that psycho if that's what you want to do. She won't be my problem any longer."

Griffin punched Devon. Hard enough to send the guy flying back and landing in the sand. "Don't ever talk that way about my mate again." He bent and picked up the bracelets that had fallen. He shook the sand off them. "If you had these before, why didn't you put them on her? Why not use them sooner?"

Devon dusted himself off. "Because I *didn't* have them before. It takes a very special magic to forge them, and I just got strong enough to make them. Made them just in time, the way I see it. Because if you don't use them, if you don't get Valerie out of here..." He blew out a hard breath. "Genevieve will not stop until your mate is dead. She knows Valerie wants to take over the council, and the only way Valerie can do that—it's if Genevieve is gone. They are the two strongest witches. They will battle to the death and in the end..." His words trailed away.

But Griffin knew what the man had been going to say. "In the end, you think that Valerie will defeat Genevieve."

A nod. "And I think the whole world will suffer for it. Genevieve's defeat *can't* happen. That's why multiple assassins have been hired. Why *you* were hired."

Oh, the hell, no, the guy hadn't just thrown that back at—

"Valerie has to be stopped. She's sexy as fuck, I get that, but she's dangerous. If you want her, fine, keep her—in your realm. Keep her, screw her, and go mad with her. Whatever. I've just given you the tools to do that. But if you can't take her back, if you can't control her, then she will die here. There is no other option."

The waves crashed against the beach.

"Do we have a deal?" Devon pushed.

"No." He pocketed the bracelets. "We don't. And if you—or any of these other *assassins*—so much as bruise her skin, I will rip you apart. Tear you into pieces. Then I'll let my dragon burn you to ash." Griffin smiled. "Understand?"

Devon's face flushed a furious red even as lightning crackled across the sky. "You are making a mistake!"

"No, you are. You're standing in front of me, threatening *my* mate. You must be fucking insane." And his claws slashed out, cutting into the bastard's cheek. "No one threatens what is mine. You think I'm going to make some kind of deal with you? Screw that shit. She's mine, and I'm keeping her. Anyone tries to take Valerie from me—it's gonna be the last mistake that person will ever make. Period."

Blood dripped down Devon's cheek. "You want a war with the witches? Because of her? You'd risk all of your kind for *her?* She doesn't love you, probably doesn't even like you. She's running from you now."

"A temporary issue, one you don't need to worry about."

"You're as crazy as she is!"

Griffin shrugged. "Maybe."

"Has she put you under a spell?" Devon's eyes widened. "She has! She's bewitched you! That's why you have to use the bracelets. Use them, and then you'll see reason again. She's clouded your mind. It's not the first time she's used a lust spell to get what she wants. That's an old witch trick. *Use* the bracelets. Then we'll talk again. I will break the mating bond she has with you. You can be free of her."

The bastard vanished.

It's not the first time she's used a lust spell to get what she wants.

Griffin marched up the beach, heading for the club. The same damn club he'd found his witch in not so long ago. Only this time, no music drifted from the place. No voices. No laughter. When he got there, the place was pitch black.

But it wasn't deserted, not yet. He could hear the faint footsteps inside. So Griffin kicked in the door. Seemed like an easy enough way to make his entrance. He strode inside, and the man who'd introduced himself as Stefan Medusa was waiting for him.

Stefan had a beer in one hand. He saluted Griffin with the beer, then took a long swig.

Griffin braced his legs apart and glared at the bastard. "Are you one of her lovers?"

Stefan laughed as he sat down the beer, slamming it against the bar's counter. "I wish."

Griffin glowered.

"Ah...wishing *you* were her lover, too, right? I do know that look."

He *was* her lover. He'd had her, once. *And I want her again. And again. Fucking again.* Because of a spell? Or because of something more?

"Where is Rio?" Griffin demanded.

Stefan's fingers tapped against the bar top. "He's still in training, so she took him with her. She's in her hyper-protective mode. I figure something must have happened to the kid recently because Valerie only gets all motherly like that when she's worried."

Motherly? Valerie?

A rumble of laughter came from Stefan. His tattoos twisted. "You have no idea who Valerie is, do you?"

Griffin advanced. "You seem to know her very well."

"Yeah, I do, but shove that jealousy back down, shifter." His laughter was gone. "I know Valerie well enough to say I'd lay down my life for her in an instant."

"Why?"

A shrug. "Because she gave me life."

What the fuck?

"No, shit, stop looking at me like that. She's not my mother." Stefan rolled his eyes—a move totally reminiscent of Valerie. "I'm a Medusa. You know what that means?"

He did. "You turn people to stone."

"Sometimes." Stefan's grin came and went. Then his face tensed. "It's also common knowledge in certain paranormal circles that if you take my head, you get a surge of powerful magic. *My* magic. When I was younger and didn't quite understand that people couldn't be trusted, I was jumped. My attackers knew how to kill me. Every single snake was stabbed, and their venom was drained." He looked down at his arms.

Hisses filled the air.

"After the snakes were gone, they came for my head. The knife sliced right through my throat. They were *draining* me. Taking all my blood. Biting me. No one was coming to my aid. No one was helping me. I couldn't even scream." He swallowed. The snakes were sliding up and down his arms. "I was dead. I felt myself die."

Griffin didn't speak because he knew there was going to be more to this story.

Rio was dead, too. Then Valerie touched him.

"She pulled me back. I know I was gone, but Valerie pulled me back to this world. And she was screaming and hurting. I saw the pain. She'd taken *my* pain. I didn't know anyone could work that kind of magic. Nothing should reverse death, but she did. Then the fire came, burning over her, and I thought she was dying. I heard her agony, and I couldn't do anything but lie on the ground." His eyes flashed serpentine. "But the flames didn't kill her. Instead, the fire killed the bastards who'd come after me. A group of vamps. The fire lit them up, and when the smoke cleared, I was alive. Valerie was alive. And I knew I'd always do *anything* that witch wanted."

"Because she saved you. You owed her."

"Because she was the only one who fought for me. Valerie didn't even know me. She stumbled onto me in that alley. I was a stranger. A dead Medusa. But she...fought. Even gave me back my snakes. She told me I was her henchman after that, and I was under her protection. She kept me at her side until I learned to fight for myself. Until I realized who I could trust and who I couldn't." He lifted the beer. Drained the bottle. "Want to know what I figured out? I could trust *her*. Always. Maybe you should try learning that same lesson before it's too late."

Trust. "Valerie isn't crazy."

But Stefan said, "We're all crazy. That's what makes life fun."

He *had* been around Valerie too much.

"She's no saint. Never will be. Goodness gets on her nerves. But she's not the all-consuming evil that some say. She's something so much more than that. If you're smart, you'll find her and you'll put the world at her feet." Stefan flashed a cold smile. "And if you're not smart, you'll keep hurting her...and then I'll have to kill you."

Griffin raised his brows. "You really think I'm scared of a few snakes?"

Stefan strode toward him. "All it takes is one bite. You'd be surprised what my venom can do."

"You're playing out of your league." The only warning he'd give. "And as far as Valerie is concerned, I'll protect what's mine."

"Good. You'd better." He glanced over Griffin's shoulder. "More shifters? Guess they didn't get the memo that the party is over."

He didn't look behind him. He'd already caught the familiar scents in the air. Warren and Elliott had followed him from the realm of shifters.

"Just a parade of you guys tonight," Stefan murmured. "First the one who looked a little like you, rushing through my place as fast as he could, and now—well, just a regular reunion, isn't it?"

Tension swept through Griffin. "The one who looked like me?"

"Um. Guy came in after Valerie had already left. Sniffed the air—rather dog-like, don't you think?—and then he took off. Since your scent was all over him, I figured you'd sent him to hunt her."

"*I'm* hunting her." And shit, it sounded like Carmichael was, too. Not a good sign. "If you see him again, I need to know."

Warren and Elliott closed in.

"Where's the witch?" Warren called out.

Stefan's snakes hissed. "They don't like him," he noted.

Warren took up a position on Griffin's left. Elliott waited at his right.

Stefan took their measure and didn't look impressed. "I'll give you guys two minutes to get out of my bar. Two minutes, and the snakes come out." He turned his back on them—as if they weren't a threat—and headed behind the counter. Stefan grabbed another beer.

"Are his tats *moving?*" Warren asked, too loudly.

"It's fine as long as they don't strike," Griffin dismissed. His head was cocked as he studied Stefan's back. The guy was a friend to Valerie. That meant... "Stefan Medusa is under pack protection. Make sure word spreads."

Stefan whirled toward him. "I don't need protection."

"Where is Valerie?"

"You're her *mate*. Find her."

"Devon was on the beach. He's tracking her, and he can move faster than I can." Tension had crept into his words. "Where is she?"

Stefan glanced out at the darkness beyond the club. "She was looking for a witch she trusts. Calliope. Word I have...Calliope is close by. She's been screwing a vamp, so she's under *his* protection." His lips twisted. "Guess that shit is going around."

Griffin waited.

"The vamps were having a blood party. They'll be partying until dawn. If you take to the air, I'm sure your shifter nose will lock on to the scent of blood fast enough. Especially if that blood comes from a witch."

They'd better not drink from my witch.

"Vamps love magic blood. You offer them the right prize, and they'll work any deal." Bitterness hardened his gaze. Griffin was betting that, once upon a time, Stefan Medusa's magic had been the prize that vamps sought. Stefan continued, "Valerie wouldn't let me go with her. She knows vamps and I...well, I fucking believe the bloodsuckers should die. I don't think she was in the mood for a bloodbath, though, not yet."

"Where is Rio?" Warren muttered. "My niece is freaking the hell out. She was crying about him when I left. If some vamp is draining him dry, if your witch is offering him up in some deal..."

Stefan's head turned toward Warren. "She's not. And I really don't like you." He rolled back his shoulders. "I did my part." He focused on Griffin once more. "Now do yours." He smiled at them all. "Get the hell out of my bar. *Now.*"

***

The long, black dress slid over her skin, silken and soft. Her hair trailed down her back, and the high heels she wore screamed sex. Valerie knew that because she'd picked the spiky heels deliberately.

When you crashed a blood party, you'd damn well better be bringing your *A Game*.

Valerie was bringing it.

The penthouse smelled of blood. And of money. Women were in corners, their throats bared, as vamps drank from them. Men were up against the walls, while female vamps sank their fangs into flesh.

Humans were prey. So were paranormals.

A woman in a white dress played a harp. Blood dripped from her neck.

Power was everywhere, in every single place she looked, but Valerie didn't see the one person she'd sought. Calliope.

Fingers trailed over her spine. Icy fingers. "Valerie, darling..." A male voice purred. "Didn't realize you were still in the land of the living."

Her head turned, and she met the midnight black stare of the vamp. Not just any vamp. The leader of this den. Enzo Romano. Dark hair, dark eyes, golden skin. And really, really sharp fangs. With her voice flat, Valerie announced, "I'm here for Calliope."

He frowned, then stroked his slightly pointed chin. "Don't think I know her."

Seriously? "And I don't think I'm in the mood for your brand of stupid."

His eyes narrowed.

"You're hiding Calliope. She knows Hurst and Fiona are dead so she's running scared. Only she doesn't need to run anymore. I'm here."

One roll of his right shoulder. "Hurray. The world is safe."

She shifted her body and put her hand on his chest. "No, the world is about to be plunged into madness. You should approve."

He licked his lower lip.

"Calliope," she repeated. "I want her. Now."

His fangs were poking out. "Witch blood tastes good. Feels good, too. If I were a human, I'd say it's like getting a shot of heroine."

She didn't look away from him.

"You want Calliope, then you're gonna have to bleed for me." His hand rose, and his fingers slid over her pulse. "Bet you're even better than heroine."

"I am." He had no idea. Her gaze slid around the room. "Not here. Alone."

He was almost salivating.

"I let you drink. You take me to Calliope."

"Absolutely."

He gave in too fast. She had, too, but then, she'd been lying to him. She lied to everyone but— well, Griffin.

Don't go there, not now.

She had no intention of letting Enzo put his fangs anywhere near her. She *did* intend to torture him and get Calliope's location. The torturing would just be accomplished easier when they were away from prying eyes.

"Follow me." He gave her what he probably thought was a sultry, seductive glance. Vamps and their sex appeal. Highly overrated. She'd rather have a wild, fierce beast any day of the week.

What in the hell? Had she seriously just thought that?

She didn't want a beast. Did *not*.

Or maybe she did. Dammit.

But she still followed Enzo into what turned out to be a bedroom. He shut the door behind her.

Then he strolled across the room and lowered himself onto a big, black leather chair. His fangs flashed as he smiled at her. "I'm waiting."

He'd continue to wait. "Calliope isn't at the party."

His brows furrowed. "Do I look like the sharing sort?"

What in the world did Calliope see in this douche? "Tell me where she is."

"Bleed for me first." His gaze dropped to her throat. "As strong as you are, your blood has to be amazing."

"Better than heroine," Valerie reminded him as she strolled forward. Nice and slow. She knew how to do a sexy walk. Her heels really helped. "But I'm not giving up my blood, not until you tell me where my friend is."

He laughed. "She's *not* your friend."

That might be true.

Valerie wiggled her fingers, sending out the spell that would immobilize him. "I still want to know where she is."

But instead of being frozen in place, Enzo lunged out of his chair. He grabbed her and held her wrists tightly in his hands. "Guess what I learned?" His breath blew over her face. "You take enough blood from a witch, and suddenly, their spells don't work so well on you. You drain a witch dry, and you get to keep some of her magic after she's gone."

After she's gone.

No, no. Calliope couldn't be dead.

"Better than heroine," he repeated. She couldn't break free of his hold. He was too strong.

"At least, you'd better be." His fangs shot toward her throat even as her knee shoved into his groin.

He grunted and—

The window crashed in. Shards of glass flew across the room. One sliced over her arm, making blood spill onto her skin. Enzo let out a ragged groan, and he yanked her arm upward. His mouth closed over the wound, and he sucked—

"Get your fucking mouth off my mate."

But Griffin didn't wait to see if Enzo followed his order. He ripped the vamp away from her, and Enzo's fangs scraped over Valerie's skin. She gave a little cry, mostly in anger, and Griffin immediately pulled her into his arms.

"He hurt you." Rage was there, glittering in Griffin's eyes. "He's dead."

Griffin whirled away from her before she could tell him that technically, Enzo was *undead*.

The vamp stood near the bed, fangs bared, face twisted in fury. "I was having a *meal*!" Enzo yelled. "You don't interrupt a—a—" His knees gave way. Enzo fell and slammed face first into the floor before Griffin could so much as touch him.

Valerie glanced toward the closed door. No vamps had come swarming in. Maybe they were too distracted by the blood party to notice all of the noise. Or maybe Enzo had given orders that he wasn't to be disturbed during his "meal" time, no matter what sounds might come from the bedroom. Valerie was sure plenty of screams had echoed off those walls before.

"What's wrong with him?" Griffin kicked the vampire onto his back. "Why does he look like that?"

Enzo's face had frozen into lines of agony. Blisters lined his mouth. His hands were raised and stuck in curled claws.

"He took a hit of heroine. Or something like that." Valerie took her time advancing toward the vampire. It wasn't like he could go anywhere. She frowned at Griffin. "I had the scene covered, by the way. Didn't need you rushing in." Glass crunched beneath her high heels. "So you're just...what...flying all the time now? Not even worrying that any pesky humans might glance up and see you?" At least he'd only partially shifted—just sprouted dragon wings. She reached for his shoulders. Big, powerful, broad shoulders. She spun him around and saw that his wings had cut right through the back of his clothes. The wings were gone now, though. "It's a good thing I can work magic for you. I swear, you destroy too much clothing." She wiggled her fingers. And because she was the one dressing him...she went for something different. Something very new for her edgy beast. Not a t-shirt and jeans. Not this time.

A black tux. Rich elegance. Sex appeal in a bottle.

"Much better. You'll fit in with the party group now."

He glanced down at his body. "I don't give a fuck about fitting in."

Obviously. And he didn't fit, not exactly. He stood out. Lickably gorgeous.

His head cocked. "You're not...angry at me any longer."

"Of course, I'm still furious. Totally enraged." But...hadn't she been just the tiniest bit glad to see him when he burst through the window and told the vamp to get his fangs off her? That had been hot. She wouldn't lie to herself. "And this changes *nothing* between us."

He stared at her. His emerald eyes were positively killer.

The vamp twitched.

"I should kill him," Griffin said. "He put his mouth on you."

The vamp's eyes rolled toward him. Then her.

"We *will* kill him, but I need information first." She knelt next to the vampire. "Someone can't handle his heroine."

Another twitch.

"Drugs are bad for you." Valerie smiled. "My blood is a very, very bad drug for vampires. First, it freezes you. Shuts you down so that you can't move at all. Then it burns. Has the burning started yet?" Valerie peered at him closely. "I don't think it has."

A keening cry came from him.

"Is that a yes? Or a no?"

Griffin's fingers slid over her shoulder. "You're still bleeding."

Her arm was bleeding. Not too badly. It would stop, eventually. "A long time ago, a group of vampires tried to drain a friend of mine. First, they made him weak. Took out his protection. Then they sliced open his throat. When his blood flowed, they fed and fed on him. They wanted his power. They pissed me off." She gave a quick smile to Enzo. "So I killed them all. And then I thought...if vampires like the taste of power, of magic blood, they are going to want me. Because, as we all know, I'm awesome."

A gurgle was his response.

"So I made sure that any vamp who took my blood—that vamp wouldn't ever forget me." Her fingers tapped against his forehead. "You won't forget, will you?"

Sweat covered his body.

"Is Calliope dead?" The question came from her, quiet and calm. She'd locked down her emotions.

Enzo keened.

"I don't think he can talk," Griffin muttered.

Right. Her bad. "Enzo, blink once if she's still alive. Twice if she's dead."

And...one blink.

So he'd lied to her before. *Or he's lying now.* "You tricked her, didn't you? Promised her protection, but you just wanted her blood."

One blink. She took that as a yes. "You've got her hidden, don't you? Where?"

No blinks.

Valerie sighed. "I can stop the pain. I can make it all go away. And you can go about your business biting humans and scaring the world. But I need to know where Calliope is. *Right now.*"

He hadn't taken enough of her blood to kill him. Unfortunately. And as she watched, some of the tension left his body. His hands uncurled. His mouth parted. Enzo turned his head toward her. "You bitch."

Griffin pounded a powerful fist into the vamp's face. "Don't talk to my mate that way."

Warmth spread through Valerie. Ridiculous, of course. She was furious with Griffin. He'd betrayed her. But it was nice to have someone at her side. To have someone defending her.

He also looked super sexy.

Focus. The mating had to be messing with her head. She was *not* the forgiving type. Valerie cleared her throat. "Tell me where Calliope is, or the shifter will rip you apart."

Enzo looked at her, then Griffin. Then her. "Your blood is poison."

"Don't ever forget that. Spread the word to all of your vamp friends."

"Calliope tasted better." Enzo smiled at her. "Just a little blood left in her. Almost finished her off—"

Griffin punched him again. The vamp's nose broke. *His* blood trickled down his face.

"Calliope," Valerie spat. "Now. I won't ask again."

Enzo's tongue licked away the blood that had dripped onto his upper lip. "She wanted to hide from the witches. If I tell you where she is, then Calliope isn't exactly hiding, is she?"

The sonofabitch. Valerie could only shake her head. "You've been lying to me."

Griffin's claws were out. He went for the vamp's throat.

"Don't!" Valerie grabbed his arm, stopping him. "He hasn't hurt Calliope." The guy had kept her location secret, even when he knew death would be coming. "I think the dumbass might have even fallen for her."

"I have *not!*" Enzo instantly denied.

"Whatever." She let go of Griffin's arm. "This is how it will work. Tell Calliope I'm back. She's in serious danger, and she needs my help. Get her to meet me at Stefan's club, Daybreak, at sun—"

"She will *not* meet you at sunrise," Enzo cut in. "And she won't be meeting you alone. I'll be at her side." His eyes turned to slits. "Sunset."

"Fine." She'd accomplished her mission. "But you keep her alive until then, got me? If something happens to her..."

Enzo glared at Griffin. "You'll sic your dog on me?"

"He's not a dog." Sparks danced above Valerie's fingers. "He's a freaking dragon. And you won't have time to scream before he burns you to ash."

Enzo's Adam's apple bobbed.

"See you at sunset, vamp." She reached for Griffin's arm. "Let's go."

Griffin stiffened. "You're...not trying to leave me?"

She wasn't having this conversation with a vamp watching her. "I'm still bleeding, and my blood is going to smell like heaven to every vamp out there. So keep me close, would you?"

He pulled her closer.

She could have used some magic to bounce herself out of there except...

Except the bite from the vamp had drained her. She was totally bluffing right then. She was weak and her stomach was twisting, and she seriously needed her shifter to protect her ass.

Her blood was a paralytic drug to vamps, but when she got bit—her power was drained. That was the way magic worked. You never got something for free. She had to pay a price for what she could do to the vamps.

She'd be okay again, just not in the next few moments.

Griffin opened the bedroom door. Sure enough, as soon as they started strolling through the penthouse, all of the vamps jerked to hard attention. Some took frantic steps toward her.

"Don't even think about it." Griffin flashed fang at them. Wonderful, sharp, shifter fang.

The vamps backed down. Watched her with hungry eyes. Licked their lips.

She pressed even closer to Griffin. Walking in her heels was an effort. Staying upright was an effort. Enzo had only taken a few drops of her blood, but she felt the pull of weakness so strongly.

This one particular spell cost her too much.

Griffin had his arm around her shoulders. His body was hot and strong against her. She wanted to press closer to him, but doing so might reveal her weakness. She couldn't let him know her secrets. No one could know them.

One vamp tried to touch her. Griffin caught his hand before the guy could make contact. Snapped the fellow's wrist and threw the foolish vamp through the air. A piano broke his fall. The vamp didn't get up.

And Griffin still had one arm around her.

Once they were in the hallway, she pulled in a deep breath. The vamps might follow her, though, so they needed to get out of the building. "I'm hoping you have a car waiting." If not, then she would be flying dragon skies.

"Elliott is downstairs."

Great. The whole crew. She would've made a flippant remark but...

It's been one hell of a night.

"What's wrong?" Griffin asked, voice gruff.

They were in the elevator. Heading straight down. Her lashes had fallen, but she forced them open. His bright stare was on her. "Are you all right?"

"Of course." She swallowed. "Nothing I can't handle."

"Valerie..." He caged her against the elevator wall. "What the hell is going on? The last time I saw you, you were ready to rip my eyes out. And that was *very* recently."

She could give him this truth. "I'm tired." A sigh slipped from her as her hands rose and pressed to his chest. His very big, very powerful chest. "And I could use some strength." Having a dragon at her back in the coming battle would only be a good thing. If she could trust him.

If.

"You'll need to grovel." She let her eyes close. "Prepare for that. I deserve a million apologies. I will get them."

Silence. Then he moved away from her. Her hands fell back to her sides. She could totally just fall into a puddle right there. Not an option, of course. But...

"Valerie." Griffin said her name differently this time. Harder. Rougher.

She forced her eyes to open. She looked straight ahead, then down.

Because he was on his knees before her. The king of shifters? Kneeling for her? Oh, shit, she must have passed out. She was having a dream. Wonderful. In reality, she was probably sprawled in front of him in an unconscious heap on the floor.

Gazing up at her, he said, "I swear allegiance to *you*."

His voice seemed to drift straight through her. Her right hand rose. Lingered in the air above his shoulder.

"I will not turn on you. I will not betray you."

She couldn't look away from his eyes. If this was a dream, it was the best one she'd had in ages.

"I will stand between you and danger. I will *never* use poison on you. I will *never* hurt you."

Her heart was beating too fast. Her fingers latched onto his shoulder. Pinched.

His lips curled even as the elevator dinged. "What's the pinch for?"

"To see if I'm dreaming."

"Shouldn't you have pinched yourself?"

Why? She wasn't into self-pain. "You're on your knees."

The doors slid open.

He stayed there. "I'm sorry. I didn't understand...who you were."

Her tongue swiped over her lower lip. "You still don't."

Now he rose, towering over her. "Don't be so sure of that."

But she was sure. How could he know her? She didn't even know herself. He twined his fingers with hers and led her out of the elevator. They strolled through the gleaming lobby and headed right past the vamp guards who watched them far too closely.

Then they were outside, walking into the moonlit night. An SUV waited near the curb. Curious, she asked, "Where'd you get a ride so fast?"

"Sweetheart, there's something I should tell you."

Her head turned toward him.

"I'm fucking rich as hell. I own an island close by. One that's even bigger than the Lord of the Dark's."

She schooled her expression. "Size doesn't matter."

He crowded closer. His mouth was just inches from hers. "Liar," he whispered to her.

She laughed. She shouldn't laugh. Things were screwed to hell and back. Vamps were watching her. Her allies were dead—or missing. She was being hunted.

But she still laughed.

And maybe that was okay. After all, everyone said she was crazy, anyway. Maybe they were all right.

Griffin's hand lifted, and his fingers curled under her chin. "I love your laugh."

Okay, maybe *he* was crazy. She knew what her laugh sounded like. No one loved it.

No one loves me.

She shook her head, slamming the door shut on that particular thought. Absolutely not. She was amazing. She didn't need others to love her. She loved herself. "Take me to your island. Let me judge for myself if it's big enough." She yanked open the SUV's back passenger door and slid inside. Valerie wasn't at all surprised to find Elliott in the driver's seat.

He'd turned his head to watch her. When her dress slid up and the slit in the side gave him a glorious view of her legs, Elliott let out a low whistle. "You cleaned up nice."

"I always do."

Griffin jumped in beside her. Her shifter king made the big back seat suddenly seem small as he crowded close to her. "Get us out of here," he barked.

Griffin hadn't complimented her. Hadn't said her legs looked killer. Hadn't told her that the dress made her look like sweet sin. All compliments plenty of other men had given her in the past. He hadn't even said she looked beautiful.

But...

"*I swear allegiance to you.*" He had said that. And..."*I will not turn on you. I will not betray you.*" And even her eternal favorite... "*I will stand between you and danger.*"

"Don't fucking ever look at her legs again," Griffin ordered, voice sharp. "Keep your eyes on the road, asshole." He turned toward her and immediately yanked her dress down to cover Valerie's legs.

Her hand caught his. "How do I look to you?"

"Like you need more clothes."

Griffin was truly the most prudish shifter she'd ever met.

But his gaze narrowed. She could see him perfectly in the dark. Thanks to her spells. Why have magic if you weren't going to use it to its full potential? A question she'd always asked the others. The ones without imagination.

"What do you want to hear?" He pressed even closer. "That you're beautiful? The most gorgeous thing I've ever seen? That I want to rip the dress off and fuck you right here?" Anger hummed in his voice. "I'm sure you've heard those words from plenty of men."

"Yes." Plenty.

He gave an animalistic rumble.

Why did she like that sound? What was up with her and her new attraction to rough beasts?

"You are beautiful." His hand slid to her cheek. "You are gorgeous. I want to fuck you every minute."

Okay, now she was getting turned on. *Liar.* She'd been turned on from the minute he'd burst through the window. Other than her henchmen, she didn't often get heroes rushing in to save her day. And certainly not heroes like the shifter king. "Fuck me...and not kill me?"

"You aren't going to let that go, are you?"

Probably not. But maybe.

"You're getting color back in your cheeks." And his fingers lightly caressed her skin. "You gonna tell me what the hell happened back there?"

"I'm supposed to tell you all of my secrets?" Had he missed the part where she'd repeatedly run from him?

"That's kind of the deal with mates."

Ah, that word. "Are you going to keep questioning me or are you going to kiss me?"

Silence. She didn't think her question had been that hard.

Then his answer came. Deep. Gravel-rough. "If I kiss you, I won't stop. I'll fuck you in this SUV."

Goosebumps rose on her skin. The good kind.

"And I don't particularly want to give Elliott a show, so I'm keeping my mouth off you." A pause. "For now." He leaned closer to her, and his breath teased her ear as he promised, "But when I get you to *my* island, you're mine."

Her heart was beating a little too fast. "I thought I already was yours." Wasn't that why he'd run after her? The mating bond? Because he didn't have a choice.

For some reason, the thought made her sad. She wasn't the sad sort.

"You'll always be mine. Don't forget that."

He eased back.

She felt colder.

"Where's Rio?" Griffin demanded. "We need to pick him up and take him to the island with us."

"Not happening." She smiled. A dazzling display, she was sure. "As of very recently, Rio has been removed from the equation."

Silence. The scary kind. Her kind.

"You *killed* him?" Elliott demanded from the front as the SUV swerved.

"Seriously?" Now she was insulted. "In case you missed it—and, honestly, I can't remember if you were there for the fabulous show or not—but I brought Rio's ass back from the dead because I am amazing." How many times did she have to tell the world that truth? "Why would I go to all the trouble of saving him, only to then kill him? Makes no sense." She was huffing a bit because he'd made her mad. "You don't kill your own henchman. That's like villain 101. Pick up a book."

Griffin caught her hand in his. His fingers stroked along her inner wrist. "You hid him, didn't you?"

"He's *my* henchman. Right now, that can be a bad thing. Someone wanting to hurt me may decide to go after him." She was just handing out truths left and right. She almost felt virtuous. Almost. "He's not strong enough to face my enemies. One day, he will be." He'd never be pushed around again. "But until that day, I'm going to make certain he doesn't get pulled into my war."

"Are you sure he's safe?"

"Absolutely." She'd certainly used enough magic on that particular spell. Rio was far away, currently enjoying the sweet life in Colorado and being guarded by beings she trusted completely.

Trolls.

Another story. For another day.

Griffin's fingers slid over her wrist in a slow caress. "What about the raven?"

The vehicle braked. They'd sure made a fast trip to the pier. They got out, their little group sticking close together, and she didn't answer him. While Elliott prepared the boat, she made sure to get herself a life vest—witches didn't always *love* water. That went back to their Salem days and the stupid idea of testing to see if a person was a witch by tossing her ass into water. Since she'd actually been alive during the Salem trials, she had personal experience with the old "swimming" test.

She'd failed the test, by the way.

Those bastards had tried to drown her as punishment.

She *might* have killed them.

The boat's motor kicked to life. In moments, they were shooting away from the pier. The wind and ocean spray hit her face.

"Valerie."

Griffin was in front of her. Elliott steered their boat. A nice boat. Or, rather, yacht. At least a thirty-footer.

"What about your raven?" Griffin pressed.

"I don't have a raven," she replied, raising her voice to be heard over the roar of the waves and the boat's engine.

Then...

Edgar flew down. He landed on her shoulder.

Griffin kept gazing at her. One dark brow rose.

"I don't have a raven," she said, telling the truth. "The raven has me." That was the way of it. "Familiars pick their witches. We don't pick them." Her hand lifted, and she stroked the raven's glorious feathers. Such a beautiful black. "Edgar chose me. He's brilliant that way."

Edgar cawed.

"Yes, thank you." She smiled at him. "We match like that."

"Are you *talking* to the bird?" Griffin demanded. It sounded as if her shifter was choking on something.

"Of course, I'm talking to him. I can talk to *all* animals."

He took a step back, as if she'd truly surprised him. "That's...that's how you knew about me working with the witch council. You've been using your bird to spy, haven't you?"

"Better fly high, Edgar," she murmured to her friend. "We'll chat later." He took to the sky. Valerie considered Griffin's question. "Spy is a strong word. I prefer eavesdrop."

Elliott laughed.

She rose and let her body brush against Griffin's. He wasn't laughing. Neither was she. "You were going to get rid of me after a month." More anger there, burning inside of her, and if she looked deep enough...hurt. "If you didn't have sex with me, the bond wouldn't hold. You could get rid of me. Even kill me."

His lips parted. "You were trying to seduce me."

"I didn't have to try very hard."

Griffin shook his head. "You didn't want me? It was...an act?"

"I wanted you. I still want you." When would he get that she wasn't lying to him? Not him. "And I didn't understand why you didn't feel the same attraction I did." Her hand rose and pressed over his heart. "I haven't ever wanted anyone the way I seem to crave you."

There. She'd told him. She waited, wondering how he'd respond since she'd absolutely just bared her tattered soul to him. He would—

"Didn't you crave Tomas?"

For an instant, the wind seemed to stop blowing. The waves stopped battering the boat. She felt all of the blood drain from her head. Felt ice sweep over her body.

Then the storm hit.

CHAPTER FIFTEEN

"He's going to die!" Tears poured down Valerie's cheeks. "Every single day, he grows weaker and weaker." It shouldn't happen. A body shouldn't be so frail. So weak.

Death shouldn't take the young.

Genevieve gave a long sigh as she looked up from her book of spells. "Of course, he's going to die, Val. He's human." She shrugged one elegant shoulder. Genevieve was always elegant. Always dressing as if she was the queen of the world and not the illegitimate daughter of a council witch. "Humans die. That's their thing."

"Death isn't for Tomas. He's only twenty-five. He's young. He's strong."

"He is sick. One of those terrible human conditions that eats away at the body. I could see his weakness the first time you introduced him to me." Genevieve closed her book. "I wondered why you were wasting yourself with him. He's hardly your type."

"He makes me laugh." He had such a quick smile. And he loved *her*. "He can't die. We can fix him." She ran forward and grabbed her best friend's hand. "I'm not strong enough to do it on my own. But together, we can. We can do anything."

Genevieve's eyes flew wide. "We can't heal a human!"

"Of course, we can! We're the best witches on earth."

"He's a *human*. That's forbidden! We can't show magic to him."

Valerie glanced away from her friend. Guilt flushed her cheeks.

"You've already shown him magic." Genevieve's voice was hushed.

He'd been so sick. He hadn't been able to get out of bed. She'd wanted to make him smile. Tomas had such a great smile. So she'd made it snow in his room. He'd laughed and laughed.

Then he'd started coughing and hadn't been able to stop.

"You're going to get in trouble." Now Genevieve was holding her hand, gripping it too tightly. "You'd better hope he dies before he can tell anyone!"

What? Valerie snatched her hand back. "He's not going to die. We're going to heal him!" She had plans. "And then we're going to make him immortal. He'll be able to stay with me forever."

Genevieve shook her head. "You can't do that."

Why not? "I can't let him die. That's what I can't do. I love him."

"You don't. You can't love anyone, Val. We all know that's your curse. The strongest magic, the coldest heart. That's what everyone said when you were born. You think you love him, but you don't.

You pity him. And you're just getting your emotions all confused. He's going to die, and you'll see. You'll go right on living. You'll probably be even more powerful. A witch's magic grows with pain, and you—"

"I want you to help me!"

Genevieve drew herself up. Stood tall. "I am."

No, she wasn't. "Heal him. If we put our power together—"

"I won't use magic on your mortal. He's going to die."

Frustration poured through her. "I won't lose him!" She whirled for the door.

Only to find her path blocked by Devon. Valerie blinked. She hadn't even heard him arrive. He must have used magic to slip into the room. Devon was strong, almost as strong as Genevieve. "You can help me." She gave him a dazzling smile. He usually fell for her smiles. "We can put our magic together, and you can help me—"

"I am helping."

His words were too similar to Genevieve's. A chill swept over Valerie.

"He's dying right now," Devon said. No emotion was in his voice. Just a flat calmness. "It's good to let him go."

No. "*No!*" She lifted up her hands, she just needed to pull some magic—

Devon broke her fingers. Both hands. He grabbed them. Twisted. Had pain spiraling through her because she'd never expected the attack. She cried out even as—

As they surrounded her. Genevieve moved in close behind her. Devon was before her.

Genevieve and Devon locked hands, trapping her between them, and then they began to chant.

"No!" Another scream burst from her. They were binding her. Trapping her right there. Holding her between them. Her fingers throbbed. Her skin seemed to *burn*.

"The human dies," Devon gritted out. "We won't lose everything for your latest pet."

"We're taking over the council." Genevieve's voice showed the strain of the magic. "You're our third. We need you for our plan to work. They won't look at us as if we're garbage any longer. We'll light the way. We'll be the power."

"But not if you destroy everything!" Devon raged. Sweat slid down his cheek.

Her magic pushed at him. *Pushed*.

But he and Genevieve held her back.

They held her trapped, even though she was stronger than them both because...

She'd linked herself to Tomas. Already used magic to buy him time. Part of her essence was within him. So as he fought, as he lay dying, as he struggled to take his last breaths...

So did she.

Her lungs closed up. Coughs choked her. Her body shuddered as she fell to the floor.

But Genevieve and Devon didn't ease their magical locks. They kept her trapped.

Tears slid from her eyes. Pain cut into her. Her heart raced too fast, then the beats became too slow.

Thud.

Silence.

Thud.

She could barely breathe. Couldn't take the air inside her lungs. Couldn't move at all.

But she could feel—she felt Tomas. Felt him reaching for her. Felt him—

Dying.

Just as she died.

***

Griffin knew he'd said the wrong fucking thing to Valerie. Jealousy had been driving him, a ferocious monster tearing him apart from the inside, and he'd blurted out the other man's name.

He'd never wanted to take back words more than he did in that moment.

"I didn't mean...I'm sorry, Valerie." His hands curled around her shoulders.

She seemed to stare right through him. Her dark eyes were so deep and fathomless.

"Valerie?"

Elliott killed the yacht's engine. "Something is very wrong out here."

Something was very wrong right in front of him. Valerie was statue-still, and she barely seemed to breathe. "Baby?" His hold tightened on her.

"Is it me..." Elliott muttered. "Or have the waves stopped moving? And what the hell is up with the wind? Shouldn't it...you know...blow?"

Griffin gave Valerie a little shake. He had the weird feeling that she'd just left him. Gone somewhere far away. "Valerie?"

Nothing.

This wasn't right.

He pulled her closer. Locked his arms around her. "You come back to me. Right the hell now."

She trembled in his arms.

"Fucking hell!" Elliott's alarmed cry. "Do you see that wave?"

Valerie jerked against him. "Griffin?"

He looked into the distance. Saw that the ocean was definitely moving again. The biggest wave he'd ever seen in his life was charging right for them.

Valerie tried to pull free, but he just held her tighter. Elliott ran back for the wheel, and the monster wave slammed into them. Salt water poured onto them, battered the vessel, and the yacht listed to the side as Elliott fought to hold the wheel.

The water fell like an avalanche, and Valerie was torn from his arms. She flew over the port side, a scream breaking from her lips.

"No!" Griffin roared as he rushed after her. Not hesitating, he dove right over the side of the vessel. He hit the water, desperation plaguing him because everyone knew witches and water didn't mix.

Valerie bobbed up beside him. Her bright life vest was still bound tightly around her. She shoved a wet mess of hair out of her eyes.

He grabbed her and hauled her into his arms.

"You jumped in after me." Valerie blinked water out of her eyes.

He held her even tighter. Gentle waves brushed against him, soothing now, but he expected another attack at any moment.

"I had on a life jacket," she murmured, "but I do appreciate your effort."

He kept an arm around her stomach as he dragged her back toward the yacht. A ladder hung from the back of the vessel, and he threw out a hand, catching it. Griffin hauled them up, and water poured from their bodies.

Valerie was soaking wet and absolutely the most beautiful thing he'd ever seen. She sagged into one of the back seats.

He stared at her, his hands fisted at his sides. "I'm sorry."

She frowned at him.

"About Tomas."

Pain flashed on her face as lightning crackled overhead. "I don't want to go back there," she whispered.

He wasn't sure what she meant but... "You don't have to. You don't have to tell me a damn thing about him. I shouldn't have asked." He eased onto the seat next to her. She shivered, and he swore. Griffin shot from the seat and hurried to get her a towel. He didn't find one, but he did pull a blanket from the cabin. He took it back to her. Wrapped her up. "I'm a jealous bastard."

Her fingers gripped the edge of the blanket.

"I don't like knowing that others have been close to you, before me." He was not explaining this well. He sounded like a total jackass.

"I never expected you to be a virgin." Her flat voice. "Is that what you wanted of me? For me to be untouched? Different...from the woman I am now?"

"I don't want you to be different. I want you to be exactly as you are." That was truth. One he hadn't fully expected. "And I'm more fucking jealous because I think you loved Tomas." There, he'd said it. He was more jealous because she'd loved the guy and not because of the sex. Though, yeah, he didn't want to think about her having sex with someone else.

Her gaze held his. "You shouldn't be jealous of a dead man."

So...fuck. She hurt. She hurt remembering the man she'd loved and lost. "I'm sorry," he said again, wishing there was some way he could comfort her. Wishing he could just do *something* for her. Anything. He wanted to take away her pain.

"I'm sorry, too."

Griffin's brow furrowed. "Why are you apologizing?"

"Because I'm the one who bitch slapped us both with the wave." She winced. "I got a little stressed." She glanced toward Elliott, then lowered her voice—as if that would help with a shifter's enhanced hearing. "When I lose control of my emotions, I lose control of my magic, too. I went back to a dark place. A place with too much pain."

He'd done that to her. His fucking jealousy. *His* problem. He'd deal with it, and he would not hurt her again. "You don't ever need to tell me about him." Griffin wrapped his arm around her. Realized that she just fit him. Her body pressed perfectly to his.

"I never expected you to be a virgin." Her voice was musing. "But when I think about it, I believe I might like to use a few spells on the women who knew you before me."

He feathered a kiss over her temple. "Does that mean you're jealous?"

"I guess it does." She seemed surprised.

Griffin smiled. Good. If she was jealous, then that meant his witch might just be getting as lost as he was.

"You should probably keep those women very far away from me." Her voice was serious. "I'd hate for them to accidentally be turned into rats."

"Accidentally?"

He felt her shrug against his body. "Accidentally on purpose."

Would she do it? His fingers slid under her chin. He tipped back her head so that he could stare into her eyes. Stare into them. Lose his soul in them. He was starting to realize it was the same thing. "I'm not so sure you're as bad as everyone says."

"I'm not." She gave him an angelic smile. One of such pure innocence and— "I'm much worse." Soaking wet, hugging her towel, still wearing her life vest, she gave him a devilish wink.

Laughter boomed from him. Griffin couldn't help it. The woman might be dead serious, she might be the most dangerous witch to ever walk the earth...but, screw it.

She made him happy.

Maybe *he* was the crazy one.

***

Warren stared into the darkness. He could hear the roar of the boat's engine approaching. Finally. He'd wanted to go with Griffin to the drop, but the guy had insisted on Warren staying at the island.

Griffin had wanted protection at the island. Just in case...

In case of what?

The only trouble that Warren saw—that trouble was Valerie Storm. And Griffin was bringing the woman right to them.

But Griffin had worried, he'd been convinced that Carmichael might try to break into the mansion on the island. Griffin was certain that Carmichael wanted to hurt Valerie. Not just hurt her, kill her.

No one can kill the king's mate.

"He left you all alone?"

Warren's nostrils flared as he whirled around. A tall, blond male stood just a few feet away. The guy had a smirk on his face. "Who in the hell are you?" Warren demanded.

"Devon Vesiux. Council elder."

"Witch," Warren snapped.

Devon lifted a brow. "Shifter."

"Great. So we both know what we fucking are." Warren let his claws burst out. "Now you won't be surprised when I cut the skin off you." He took a menacing step forward. *Guess Griffin was right about this place needing protection.* "Because I doubt Griffin gave you an invitation to his home."

Devon shook his head. "This isn't his home. We both know Griffin barely tolerates the human world."

True enough.

"Just as he barely tolerates witches." Devon's expression was grim. "I can hardly blame him, given what happened to his parents. The guy doesn't have a good history with my kind."

Warren kept closing in on the fellow. He'd warned Devon. When the guy got cut, it would be his own damn fault.

"He didn't choose her, you know. Valerie. She wasn't the one who should have been his mate."

"Oh, you can see someone's destiny, huh? Didn't think witches could do that."

"Witches can do all manner of things. Like...love spells."

Warren stilled.

"Do you know Valerie's specialty? Have you been around her long enough to figure it out?" But before Warren could reply, Devon announced, "Illusions."

"Yeah, I know that." She'd used one hell of a spell on his niece.

Devon's eyes narrowed. "Used a spell on you, did she?"

Warren didn't answer.

"Or maybe she used one on someone you care about."

A muscle jerked in Warren's jaw.

"Illusions." Devon drew out the word. "She can make you think you're seeing heaven or that you're facing hell. Her gift. Never found anyone who can match her power."

"You should get out of here." He could still hear the boat's engine. Closer now.

"She's using her magic on your king. Making him see her in a different way. The image she shows him is nothing more than an illusion. It's the illusion he's fallen for—"

Warren's laughter cut off Devon's words.

The witch's expression tightened.

"You're a damn fool." Warren was still smiling. "Griffin hasn't fallen for her. It's just the mating bond. That's all. Lust. He wants to fuck her. He's not in love with her. He'll get his fill while the mating burns hot, and he'll control *her*."

Now Devon stared at him in pity. "I've known Valerie for centuries. No one controls her. Your king is the fool." He turned away.

Warren grabbed him. Whipped Devon back around. "He's a fool who put his mark on *you*." And he pointed to the still red lines on Devon's face. "You might have healing magic, but I know the marks left by a shifter's claws."

"I was trying to help him."

"Why don't I buy that?"

"Because you—like every other male who meets Valerie—you underestimate her power. You think it's just lust. You think it's just fucking. It's not. You'll blink, and she'll own him. He'll be willing to give up *everything* for her. He won't take her back to his realm like he promised. He'll keep her here, and Griffin will start a war between the witches and the shifters. The ground will be red with blood, and the air will be filled with magic."

The bastard was wrong. He was—

"I *gave* Griffin the tools to use against Valerie. If he wants to fuck her, if he wants to keep her, he can." Faint lines of tension bracketed his mouth. "I understand shifters can't ever let go of their mates. He can keep her forever. He just has to bind her magic."

"Bind her? How?"

"I gave him the tools." Devon's eyes began to brighten. He lifted his hands. "You need to convince your king to *use* them. Before it's too late."

"But—"

The witch snapped his fingers and vanished.

"Fucking witches," Warren spun around, searching the room around him. But Devon was long gone. Warren hated magic. *Hated* it.

The roar of the boat's engine was even louder now. He rushed out of the mansion and ran down to the pier. He waved his hands, wanting to warn Griffin that they had company. Company that might still be lingering close by. "Witches!" Warren yelled. "The sonofabitch was *here!*"

Devon. A guy who'd come to spread lies because there was no freaking way that Griffin was actually falling for Valerie. Couldn't happen.

The boat pulled into position near the dock. He tossed a line to Elliott, and his friend tied off the vessel. And Griffin—

Griffin had his arm wrapped tightly around Valerie. The shifter king carefully lifted her onto the dock, and once she was steady, he removed her life vest. When she shivered, Griffin tucked her against his side.

Every move was tender. Careful.

Valerie glanced up at Warren and gave him a wide smile. "Did I hear you calling for witches? Ta, da. Here I am."

She was soaking wet. Her dress clung to her like a second skin. A blanket had been wrapped around her upper body, but it blew in the breeze. The woman was absolute pure sex appeal. Too beautiful by far. And Griffin...

Griffin was staring at her as if he'd just glimpsed heaven.

Valerie. The mad witch.

Fuck.

Devon had been right.

She'd put Griffin under a spell, and Warren had to set his friend free.

CHAPTER SIXTEEN

"This will be your room." Griffin stood inside the bedroom doorway, looking unbearably cute yet uncomfortable as his gaze darted over her body, then away. "For as long as we're here." He rubbed a hand over his jaw—a jaw that was showing serious stubble signs. "Hope to hell that's not long."

His words brought up an interesting point. "You haven't tried to force me back to the other realm."

"No."

"Why not?" Not that he *could* do it. But...

"Because it should be your damn choice."

Warmth bloomed inside of her. "Won't that break the deal you had with the witches?"

"Already broke that deal. Told Devon to screw himself."

Devon. "That's how you knew about Tomas." She hugged the blanket a little tighter to herself. "He told you." *Thanks, asshole.*

Griffin nodded. "And I told him there was no deal. If he really wants a war with my kind, if he's going after my queen, then I'll give him a war. Shifters aren't afraid of anything."

No, but there had been a lot of young shifters in his realm. She'd seen plenty of them. And there were young witches, too. "When I take over, I won't let the witches ever hurt a shifter."

His eyes widened. "That's your plan? To take over? To rule?" He shut the door and slowly strode toward her.

She stiffened, a wee bit.

"Because you can already rule. You don't need the witches." He caught her hand, lifted it to his lips, and pressed a kiss to the back of her hand. "You're my queen."

Her breath was coming a little too fast. Her heart was pounding too quickly in her chest. Of course, he'd hear those sounds. He'd know the impact he was having on her. He'd know—

"Get some rest, Valerie. I'm not making any plans to leave, at least not until I see how that meeting goes with the vamp."

Enzo. Right. Her shoulders sagged as Griffin walked away. Wait. Hold up. *Walked away?* "You're leaving me?"

His shoulders stiffened. "Like I said, this is your room."

"But *you're* my mate." She bounded toward him. Let her blanket fall. "Don't you want to be with me?" Valerie put her body between him and the door.

"Hell, yes." An instant response. One she liked. "But after what happened...the way you *ran* from me, I didn't think you wanted back in my bed."

"Look me in the eyes. Tell me that you had nothing to do with the arrow that hit Rio. Swear that you weren't trying to kill me."

He stared straight into her eyes. His hands closed around her arms, and he pulled her close. "I swear that I had nothing to do with that arrow. After you left me, the first thing I did was destroy the poison that remained in the tower. It will *never* be used on you again."

Valerie only saw truth when she looked in his eyes. She wasn't some lie detector, though. She couldn't just look at him and know. But, oh, damn, she wanted to believe him. With every single fiber of her being. "We're real mates now. You can't kill your mate." Not if all the stories were true. "You do that, and you'd go crazy."

"Without you, I'd be freaking insane."

"That is so sweet." She stood on her toes and pressed her mouth to his. "Stay with me." The words came out almost as a plea. That wasn't what she'd meant. Valerie never pleaded for anything. Not since Tomas. Not since she'd begged Genevieve and Devon.

Tears pricked her eyes as she hurriedly pulled back from Griffin.

"What just happened?" His voice rumbled.

"You don't have to stay." She motioned to the door. "Do what you want." No begging. Not from her. No pleading. She didn't need Griffin. She didn't need anyone.

He picked her up. Scooped her into his arms, and Valerie let out a cry of surprise.

"You're what I want." He stalked to the bed. Dropped her. She bounced a little. "And you're most definitely what I want to *do*." He glowered at her. "Baby, you are still soaking wet. Why the hell haven't you magicked yourself dry?"

She crooked her index finger at him. "Can you keep a secret?"

"Yes."

So serious. She smiled. "I put a spell on my own blood. Made it so that any vamps who ever drank from me would become paralyzed. Well, that's what a few drops do. The idea is that I'd immobile the vamps long enough to get away. You know vamps...they love magic blood. I'm like their dream dinner." Stefan had actually been the inspiration for her brilliant idea, but she wasn't going into all of those specifics right then.

Griffin yanked off his shirt. He tossed it into the corner.

"If they take more than a few drops from me, they die." And, hopefully, she'd live. "But the spell has a downside." Most spells did. "There's a price for magic. Always."

His hands dropped to his sides. "What price did you pay?"

"I get weak when vamps drink from me. I power the spell *as* the vamp takes my blood. So I get lethargic. My power weakens. I'm almost...human." Talk about a killer secret. If the wrong person heard that, it could definitely be used against her.

She'd just trusted Griffin. Did he get that? She'd seriously trusted him with her life.

His eyes went wide. "Valerie." Her name came out as a curse. Or maybe a caress. Sometimes, it was hard to tell the difference.

"Let's keep that between us, okay?" She offered him a quick smile. "Long story short, I'm still wet because I don't have the magic to dry myself."

"But the giant wave, that monster wave that attacked—"

"I didn't do that deliberately." She swallowed the lump that had risen in her throat. "Pain did that. Pain that I try really hard to keep bottled up. Because if all of my pain ever escapes, I'm pretty sure I could wreck the world."

Griffin gave a low and vicious curse.

Welcome to my hell.

"Is pain all you know?" His voice was guttural.

Sometimes, it felt that way. "No." Her hand lifted. He'd leaned over, and her fingers trailed down his bare chest. His muscles were rock hard. Very impressive. "When I'm with you, I know more."

"You're about to know a whole fucking lot about pleasure."

She smiled at him. "Promises, promises, shifter."

His grin came slowly as he flashed his sharp canines and made her stomach do a little flip. Her shifter was so sexy. She absolutely loved his body.

Maybe she should show him just how much she loved it. Maybe—

"It can be a real bitch to get out of wet clothing. Let me help you." His claw slid down the front of her dress. He sliced into the material as Valerie gave a little gasp. The dress fell open, revealing her bra and panties because he cut the garment open from her chest to her thighs. But he didn't so much as scratch her.

Careful shifter.

He lifted her up. Shoved the dress off her. Threw it. Then his eyes were back on her. "Much better."

Valerie shivered.

"Cold, love? I can help warm you."

Her shiver hadn't been due to the cold. It had been due to the big, bad shifter who loomed over her and stared at her with ferocious lust glowing in his green eyes.

But he'd already bent over her. His mouth pressed to her neck. He licked, he sucked her tender skin, and then Griffin let her feel the edge of his teeth.

Her hips slammed up against him.

And he kissed his way down her body. His lips feathered over her collar bone. Down to her breast. Another slice of his claws, and her bra had been cut open. Her breasts thrust toward him. Her nipples were tight and aching, and when he took one into his mouth, Valerie's whole body flooded with desire. Her hands flew up, clamping around his shoulders, and she let out a ragged moan.

But down, down he went. Licking her stomach. Pressing a soft bite, then kissing away the wound. He caught the edge of her panties with his teeth. Valerie's breath panted out in a frantic rhythm. The pounding of her heartbeat filled her ears.

Using his teeth, he tugged her panties down. She kicked them away, and Griffin helped—then he was shoving her thighs wide. He'd opened her to him completely. He stared at her exposed sex a moment. Licked his lips.

"What are you waiting for?" Valerie whispered.

His smile was absolutely wicked.

His head lowered. He put his mouth on her. Valerie would have erupted off the bed if his hands hadn't been clamped so tightly around her hips. She cried out his name and pushed herself against his mouth. His lips. His tongue.

He was stroking her. Licking her. Tasting her like he'd been starved. And she couldn't hold off her orgasm. He'd promised her that she would know pleasure.

She did.

The climax poured through her. It rippled along every nerve and cell in her body, and she yelled his name.

Aftershocks flashed through her. Contractions fluttered in her sex. She opened the eyes she'd squeezed shut to find him staring down at her. His face was harder, rougher. And his teeth seemed even sharper.

Valerie swallowed. "That was a great...start." She tried to smile, but it was kind of hard to catch her breath.

"Want more?"

Yes, please.

He flipped her over. Rolled her in one of those fast shifter moves. In a blink, Valerie found herself up on her knees, with her hands clutching the headboard. He was behind her. Big, strong, *aroused.* His cock shoved at the entrance to her body, but he didn't plunge inside of her. Not yet.

Why not?

"Hold tight." His breath slid over her ear.

She shivered. Again, not from cold. Not even close. She was burning hot now. Her hands tightened around the top of the headboard.

"Good." His hand feathered around her hip. Dipped between her legs. His fingers slid over her clit.

Her head tipped back. She didn't want to be good. Didn't he get that? Good wasn't her deal.

Valerie pushed her hips back at him. *Bad.* That was what she wanted. To be very, very bad— with him. "Make me come again."

He growled. Her favorite sound. And he shoved into her. All the way inside. So deep that she lost her breath, and it was *awesome.* He withdrew, plunged deep, over and over, and his fingers kept strumming her clit. Her hands clamped around the wooden headboard as she drove her hips back against him. The slap of their bodies filled the air. She was moaning, and Valerie didn't care who heard her. Another climax was coming, one bearing down hard on her, and there was nothing that mattered to her beyond this moment.

His mouth locked around her shoulder. She felt the press of his teeth.

The climax hit her. Even stronger than the first. A storm of pleasure that swept over her as her body shuddered against him. But Griffin wasn't done. He kept thrusting into her. Holding her so tightly now with both of his hands on her hips. He lifted her whole body up. Plunged deep.

Then he was pouring into her on a hot tide of release. His body wrapped around her, and this time, the thundering heartbeat that she heard was his. She could feel the mad beat. And she could also feel her own heart struggling to match his rhythm.

He lowered her onto the bed. Curled around her. Her breath continued to pant out too fast, and even though he'd slid out of her, Valerie swore that she could still feel him inside of her body. She licked her lips, lips that had gone very dry, and she wondered just what all she'd been saying—or maybe screaming—there at the end.

"Don't run from me again." His voice was low. Deep.

Her head turned toward him. Her body was absolutely replete, and she wanted to snuggle down right there and just sleep. To let go of her worries and fears.

Right. Like that ever happened. "Don't try to lock me up. I don't do so well as anyone's prisoner."

He tucked a lock of her hair behind her ear. "What about as someone's partner? Could you do well as that?"

Valerie swallowed. "I don't know."

"Are you afraid to find out?"

Was he trying to taunt her? She wasn't in the mood for games. Not with him. "Yes." She held his stare. "I barely survived losing one man I cared about. I don't think...if it ever happened again, I wouldn't survive." She already didn't want to think of a world that didn't have the shifter king in it. And what did that say about her?

That it's already too late for us both.

She slid closer to him. Caught his arm and wrapped it around her body. "Remember, I'm a screamer."

"So I heard a moment ago." She could almost feel his smile.

Her own lips quirked. "I mean while I dream. Just wake me up if I start doing crazy shit." A yawn slipped from her.

His arm tightened around her. "Will you tell me why?"

Why. Why she screamed in her dreams. Why she levitated. Why it *hurt.* "I already told you. There's a price for magic. When you break the rules, when you make the rules, when you go dark..." Her eyes closed. "The price is higher than you can imagine."

He pressed a kiss to her cheek. "If you scream, I'll wake you."

Her breath slid out, nice and easy now. It was strange, but she felt safe in that moment. Of course, she *should* feel safe. She was in the shifter king's arms. He'd claimed her as his mate. To a shifter, there was nothing more sacred.

So as long as he kept thinking she was the one for him, that they'd just randomly wound up in that dungeon together, everything would be okay.

***

"She put a spell on him." Warren crossed his arms over his chest and glowered at Elliott. "I mean, isn't that shit obvious?" His gaze shot up, to the ceiling above them. A whole lot of noise had been coming from upstairs just a moment before, but now there was only silence. "She bewitched him. Made him think he was in love with her."

Elliott took a step back. "Hold the hell up." He shook his head. "I can see a lust spell working. The woman is sexy as sin. But love? Who said anything about love?"

"You *saw* him with her. I know you did. He's been frantic to get to her. Obsessed. It's more than just lust, and we both know it."

Elliott's hand scraped over his jaw. "They're mated. Of course, it's more than just lust now. It's the mating bond. He'll want her more than he ever wants anyone else, you know that. That's the way it works. Especially for a shifter of royal blood. Fate put the two of them together—"

"I don't think it was fate." Warren took an angry step forward. "I think it was Valerie Storm. I think she tricked him. I think she put him under a spell. For all we know, the mating bond might be total bullshit. She's manipulating him. Using her magic to make him think the connection is—"

"You can't fake a mating bond." Elliott's words were flat. His dark eyes gleamed. "You've never been mated, so you don't know this shit. But there is no faking. It's either there or it isn't, and if it *is* there, there's no fighting it. You're tied—body and soul—to the other person. Linked. Good or bad."

Valerie was *bad*. "You can mate someone," Warren picked his words carefully, "and not go mad for her. Not put her before everything else.

He's risking a war with the witches. For her. Because she's got him under a spell. She didn't want the mating bond to be the only thing between them. Valerie Storm is brilliant. She wasn't going to leave anything to chance. She was going to have him, all of him, and she used her magic to ensure she got exactly what she wanted."

"Why are you so certain of this?"

He released a slow breath. "Because right before you arrived, the witch council elder, Devon, he was here. He said she used her spell on Griffin. Devon said Griffin has to bind her, before it's too late."

Now Elliott's brows rose. "Bind her? How—"

They both stiffened. They'd heard the soft tread of steps on the stairs behind them. They also knew that the man coming toward them—he'd heard what they were saying.

He must have heard them, after all. No shifter had a better sense of hearing than the king.

Warren squared his shoulders as he turned to face Griffin. Lifting his chin, Warren deliberately answered Elliot's question as he said, "Griffin knows how to bind her."

Griffin didn't speak.

So Warren continued, speaking straight to him, "Devon said he'd already given you the tools that you needed." He waited a beat, but Griffin still didn't respond. So he pushed, "Can you bind her?"

Griffin's face was an angry mask. "Yes."

Okay, that was something. But... "*Will* you bind her?" Warren asked. "For the safety of the shifters, will you bind your mate's power?"

And Warren held his breath as he waited to see what Griffin's answer would be.

CHAPTER SEVENTEEN

Bind her? "That's not an option right now."

Warren's eyes doubled in size. "Why the hell not?"

"Because we're meeting with fucking hostile vamps at sunset. Because I want her to be at her full strength and because I'm not about to believe BS that *Devon* hands to me." He pointed at his friend. "And why the hell would you believe him?"

"You mean believe a council elder...over a convicted witch criminal?" Warren's face mottled. "They were going to put her to death! How could you have forgotten that? She was found guilty—"

"I haven't forgotten a damn thing." He stalked across the room. Stood toe-to-toe with Warren. "But I'm starting to think *you* have. You're conspiring against your king. With witches. You're meeting with them in secret and not telling me?"

"I didn't have a chance to tell you before," Warren snapped. "You burst back in here, looked at her like you were starving, then you ran upstairs to fu—"

Griffin's hand wrapped around his friend's throat in a lightning fast move. "She is your queen. You will speak of her with respect." Fury blasted through him, and he tried to rein in his dragon. The beast wanted to roar and rage with his fire.

Not now. Warren is pack.

Warren gave a jerky nod.

Elliott just watched them, his face tense. Worried.

Griffin forced himself to let go of Warren. Then Griffin took a step back and shoved his hands behind his body.

"We need to all take a really deep breath," Elliott announced into the silence.

Griffin glared at his friends. "She's my queen. That's all there is to it. I won't turn on her."

"Even if she's crazy?" Warren demanded. "Even if—"

Her scream broke through his words. Griffin immediately turned and raced up the stairs. He shouldn't have left her. He'd just wanted to check in and make sure the others knew to be watching for vampires—and unwanted witches. *Too late for that.*

He flew up the stairs and shoved open the bedroom door. Valerie was in the middle of the bed. Still naked. He'd just dragged on a pair of jeans before rushing downstairs. As he hurried toward her, he saw claw marks appear on her stomach. A red, angry line—blood welled, then vanished.

"What in the hell?" His bellow seemed to echo through the house.

Her scream died away. She jerked upright, staring straight at him with wide eyes.

He put his hand on her stomach. No wounds. Totally healed.

"Sorry," Valerie whispered. Her eyes seemed to be filled with tears. "Didn't mean to wake you."

She hadn't woken him because his dumb ass had been downstairs instead of in there, with his mate. "You're telling me *everything*."

Valerie shook her head. "I won't scream again." She winced. "Maybe. I'll try really hard. I'll—"

"You'll tell me *everything*." His voice was flat. "Because I'm your mate. And we won't have secrets. If I'm fighting the vampires and the witches for you, you'll tell me the truth. You'll tell me why you scream. Why you *bleed* in your dreams. You won't keep anything from me." His hand still pressed to her stomach. "I'll know if you lie."

"Shifter senses." Her chin notched up. "Just so you know, I'm good at lying, and I—"

"No more." Again, his voice was flat.

Her lips parted.

"No more lies. No more pretending. No more bravado. You show me every part of yourself, and I'll show you who I am."

Valerie gave a quick, negative shake of her head. "This is me. You might not like it, but—"

He kissed her. A deep, hard, claiming kiss. "There is nothing about you that I don't like." And it was true. Unsettling, but true. "Sweetheart, I even think your weird laugh is sexy."

Her eyes had flared wide. She blinked. "I-I don't have a weird laugh."

"You cackle. Like a cartoon witch."

Her cheeks flushed. "I absolutely do not."

"You absolutely do." He kissed her again. "And I like it. I like you. So I want to hear everything you've got. If we're in this together, *we are in*. You tell me your secrets, and I'll tell you mine."

"What secrets do you have?"

He slid onto the bed with her. Caged her with his body. "You're first."

She yanked up the covers, shielding her nakedness. A crime. "Fine. But when you freak the hell out, you only have yourself to blame."

He waited.

"Tomas. Okay? It all started with him."

He wouldn't let his jealousy break free. Griffin locked his teeth, chained down his beasts, and waited.

"He was a human. Sweet and kind and he loved me. *Me*. Not because he had to...there was no magic involved. It was just us. He made me laugh."

Griffin was fucking hating Tomas.

"But he got sick. Today, we'd probably say it was cancer. Back then...he was just sick." She swiped her tongue across her lower lip. "I wanted to heal him, but I couldn't do it alone. I needed help from my best friends."

A bad feeling swept over him.

"Genevieve and Devon," she whispered. "We had plans. Such fine plans. We were going to take over the council. Shake things up. I knew we were the strongest witches. I knew what we could do. Since the three of us were so strong, I thought it would be easy to heal Tomas. Easy to even make him immortal. We could be together forever."

He didn't like this story. But then, he'd known he wouldn't like it, even before he'd demanded that she tell him her secrets.

"I worked a spell to link me and Tomas together." She glanced away from him. "His pain was so intense, I just—I did it to ease his suffering. I would take the pain. Pain makes witches stronger. Mostly because we've had to endure so much damn pain." She gave a hard shake of her head. "I was linked to him. I went to Genevieve and Devon—they were my friends. I thought they'd help me. They were supposed to *help* me."

"They didn't."

"They used their magic to trap me." Her voice turned husky. "I was screaming at them. Raging. But they wouldn't let me go. And Tomas was *dying*. Because of the link, I could feel it. Every single second. I tried to make Devon and Genevieve listen, but they wouldn't. When Tomas died..." Her lashes swept down. "So did I."

"No." An instant denial. "You're not dead. You're right the fuck here." And his heart was racing too fast.

"I came back." Her smile was a brief flash, and it never touched her eyes. "Witches can work all kinds of magic, but they don't bring back the dead. They never try. And I always wondered...why not? Why does life have to end? We have so much power. Why not bring back those we love? If you could do it, wouldn't you?"

Shit. "You brought him back."

"Genevieve and Devon couldn't hold me forever. The minute I was free, I ran back to Tomas. His body was in our bedroom. He was cold when I touched him. I screamed for him." Her gaze seemed to look right through Griffin. "Pain and magic. A bad combination. I opened a doorway. One that no one had opened before me. I went in, and I got him. I brought him back."

The same way she'd brought Rio back.

"But Death didn't want me to leave. Souls can't come and go without a price being paid. I *died* when Tomas died, so that let me slip into the next world. I brought him back with me, and I thought everything would be okay."

"What price, Valerie?"

Her lashes fluttered. "When I'm awake, I'm strong enough to fight the demons that come for me. They know not to even try to get to me. But when I dream, they slip through my cracks. And they try to take their pound of flesh."

"You're telling me that you're tortured every night? Because you saved that human?" His claws were out. *This shit will end.* "He'd better have fucking been grateful to you. He'd better have kissed the ground you walked on for the rest of his life—"

"Didn't work out that way." Her lips pressed together, and her delicate shoulders straightened. "This was a long time ago. Right around the time of the Salem drama. Yeah, I'm a lot older than I look. A blood witch stays young forever. But with the years...well, age means power. There's a reason the ruling witches are called council *elders,* you know."

"Valerie."

"Tomas remembered everything. Dying. Me bringing him back. He decided I was evil. An abomination. You don't mess with nature. He would rather I have left him to death, and not shown him what a monster I was." Her voice turned soft, "I think the famous phrase might be, 'I will not suffer a witch to live.'"

No. *No.*

"He lit the first torch at my bonfire in Salem. He watched as the flames rose around me. I'd risked everything for him. I'd *suffered* for him, but he just backed up and watched me burn." Her mouth tightened. "Turns out, though, there are a few benefits to surviving death. Fire doesn't impact me the way it does other witches because I have demon fire inside me. That's the fire that erupted after—after Rio. You, um, probably remember it."

Her fire was rather unforgettable.

"So the flames don't hurt me. I got away from the bonfire that Tomas had set."

"Tell me you killed the bastard."

Her brow furrowed. "I'd given up so much to save him. I loved him. I couldn't just turn around and kill him. He was confused, scared."

"He was an ungrateful *bastard.*"

"I left him. Left him to live his life, and I never turned back. I loved him, and I had just wanted him to be healed. To be whole. His sickness was gone. He—"

Griffin caught her shoulders and hauled her forward. "He tried to *burn* you alive."

He'd also tried to drown her, along with some other Salem goons. But..."He did try to burn me. So did Genevieve, and so did Devon." She stared into Griffin's eyes. "They were with him that day. Did I forget to tell you that part? They were in the village, pretending to be humans, and chanting all the while for me to burn. *Burn, burn, burn.* See...they'd watched what I did to him. They knew I was the strongest witch to ever live. They also knew I'd be the witch in their way. Always in their way because I had more magic than they did. So they tried to get rid of me. They were the ones whispering in his ear. In the ears of everyone in that damn town. Using spells on the humans. They were the ones turning on their own kind. And I've fucking hated them ever since."

And he'd made a deal with them. Sonofabitch. "Valerie—"

"I scream when I dream because my guard is lowered. I've had centuries of that pain, but it will end."

He could only shake his head. "You saved Rio. You brought him back from the dead, knowing the cost it would be for you."

"I saved Rio." She nodded. "I'd do it again. No one dies in my place."

"Have you..." Dammit. "Have there been others that you've saved? People you've brought back from death?"

Her gaze slid from his. "Yes. Not many. But, sometimes, I couldn't look away."

"You *will* look away from now on."

Her stare whipped back toward him.

"You will never do this magic again. You will not raise the dead. You will not *hurt*."

She smiled. Her dimples winked. "That's so cute. You think you can control me." Her hand rose and patted his cheek. "It doesn't work that way. I feel like I've told you this before."

"I will do anything to protect you." She needed to understand this. "You can't keep raising the dead. I saw you while you slept—something was clawing open your stomach. You opened a freaking doorway, all right. And I think when you dream, whatever is on the other side of that door tries to get you back."

"That's why I'm going to take over the council. When I'm ruler, I'll have the whole witch nation behind me. I can use their power, and I can make a spell strong enough to never feel that pain again. Whatever is trying to get out, I'll stop him. I'll be free." Beneath Griffin's hold, she shrugged. "And I'll also be running the show. I'll be in charge. The witches won't know what hit them."

He sure as hell didn't know what had hit him. His hold on her was too tight. He should let go, but he didn't. In his mind, Griffin could still see the claw marks on her stomach. And that shit happened to her every night? "There are protection spells. You can work those now, to keep this sonofabitch from hurting you."

"You're worried about me." Her face softened. "That is so sweet. I don't think anyone has ever worried about me before."

"You're being attacked every fucking night. And this shit has gone on for how long?"

"A few centuries." She shrugged. "Don't tell all my haters. They'll say it's why I'm absolutely insane." Her face was tense. "But I'm not, you know. I'm not crazy. I might be a killer. I might be bad. But I'm not a psycho. Every attack is for a reason. Those I target deserve what they get."

"Protection spell," he gritted out. "You will *make* one that is—"

"I can't make one strong enough to shut him out."

Him?

"Not yet. I've tried. But when I'm ruling the council, I will. I can use the power from all the witches. I can do it."

She just had to survive a battle to the death with Genevieve and Devon. And their witch guards. And every single other paranormal who wanted her dead. "I'm not going to lose you." No matter what he had to do. He'd find a way. He would keep her safe.

"There you go again, being sweet. Careful, shifter, or I'll start to think you care."

"I do fucking care."

Her eyes widened, but Valerie didn't have one of her quick comebacks for him. In fact, she almost looked scared. "Why?"

"Why?" Griffin repeated, then he pushed her back onto the bed. Her hair spread out over the pillows as she stared up at him. "Because you are mine."

"Mates."

"More the hell than that." He caught her hands and pinned them above her head. "You are *mine*. I knew it from the first minute I saw you."

She laughed. He would never get tired of that beautiful sound. "You did not. You were a giant dragon, and you probably wanted to eat me."

"If I hadn't known you were mine, the dragon would have burned you on sight. Don't you get it? Don't you see? That's what Genevieve and Devon thought would happen."

Her lips parted. "What?"

"That's why they put you in the cell next to me. I was the assassin hired to kill you." He'd never get over that. Shit. "So they brought you to me. I should have used my flames on you."

"But you were wearing an enchanted collar. It controlled your fire."

He just stared at her.

"Didn't it?"

"Don't you remember? The collar broke when you were still in the cell next to me."

"That was because I helped you. I gave you my magic. You transformed back into the form of a man—"

"Or Genevieve and Devon broke the collar. They *were* the ones to make the spell. And isn't there a rule among witches that binding spells can only be broken by the ones who put the enchanted pieces in place?" The bastard Devon had been the one to snap the collar on him.

"Sonofabitch." She looked shocked for a moment. Finally, he'd caught her off guard. "It...it wouldn't have worked," Valerie said, voice halting. "I told you that fire won't—"

"Did *they* know that, though?"

Her lashes flickered. "Genevieve and Devon...they always asked me how I escaped the flames in Salem. I told them I used a spell to transport myself. I never told anyone—except you—that fire doesn't hurt me anymore."

"So they believed that by putting you in the cell next to me, they were bringing you to death. They didn't want the other witches to see you. Half of the witches are terrified of you and half are in awe of you. A quiet death was better."

Her lips pressed together for a moment, then she murmured, "But you didn't kill me. You just blew a little smoke my way."

"I mated you. And I knew *exactly* what I was doing." He pressed a kiss to her mouth. "Because you are mine. My dragon knows it. My wolf knows it—"

"What about the man?" Valerie cut in. "What does he think?"

He thought he was looking at the only woman he wanted to be with for the rest of his life. The woman he'd kill to possess. The woman who'd somehow found her way into his very soul. "He thinks he won't ever let you go."

"Even if I'm bad for him? Even if I bring a war to his door?"

"There will be no war. And you aren't bad for me."

Her eyes seemed to darken even more. "Don't be too sure of that." Then she twisted, catching him by surprise and rolling them both across the bed. "I can be very bad."

He thought she was fucking good.

"Let me show you." Her fingers slid over his chest, moving in a silken caress. "Maybe you'll start to like bad." Her head lowered. Her mouth pressed to his chest. Licked his nipple. Bit.

He groaned.

"See," she whispered, "I think you're starting to like it already." Her hands went to the snap of his jeans. She jerked them open, carefully eased down the zipper, then took his heavy length into her hands. Her soft, silken hands. His dick was hard and fully erect, and when she stroked him, pumping his erection from root to tip, Griffin's hands flew out and fisted around the sheets.

The sheets ripped beneath his claws.

"Going to ask you to use some of that legendary shifter control right now." She glanced at him with a sexy smile. "Think you can hold out?"

"Val—"

She took him into her mouth. Sucked him hard and deep, and his roar burst out, strong enough to shake the house. She didn't let up. She licked and kissed, she worked him with her mouth and tongue, and the sheets were in freaking shreds beneath his hands. He wanted to come. Wanted to erupt into her hot mouth. Wanted *her*.

So he was taking her.

He grabbed her hips as his control shattered. *Legendary, my ass.* When it came to Valerie, he had no control. He lifted her up, making her straddle his hips, and then he plunged into her. Her hands flattened on his chest, and she gave a long, low moan.

Then she was rising up, pushing down, building in a rhythm that would take them both to oblivion. Her fingers pressed to his chest, and he swore that they seemed to heat.

"Ready to be bad?"

He was about to *erupt*—

"Here goes."

Her fingers shot a pulse of magic straight into his chest. He looked down. Sparks danced around her hands. Pleasure drove through him. She gave a sharp cry as she climaxed, and her pleasure seemed to just surge into him, amping up his own release. Filling him, strengthening, going on and on in the most powerful orgasm of his life.

When it ended, he sucked in a deep breath. She'd collapsed on top of him, covering him with her body. Her breasts pressed into his chest, and her mouth was at his neck. She kissed him, right over his pulse point. "That was amazing. Let's do that like a million times."

He was still in her. And she was wrapped around him.

She *fit*.

His arms closed around her back. "A million." Because they had time. All the time in the world.

She gave a little moan and snuggled even closer. "Don't leave this time." Her voice was husky. A bit groggy. "Feel better...when you're near."

"I won't go anywhere." Leave her to be clawed? To be hurt? Never again. "It's okay, baby, I've got you."

"No." Her breath feathered over his neck. "I've got you."

CHAPTER EIGHTEEN

She felt warm. Not like...on fire, villagers-want-to-burn-me warm but...toasty.

Safe.

Valerie cracked open one eyelid and realized exactly why she felt so cozy. She was in the arms of her shifter. He was still sleeping, but even in sleep, he held her tight. She liked that. He held her so close, as if she mattered.

Maybe she *was* starting to matter to him. Wouldn't that be something? Her big, bad beast. Falling for someone like her.

"You're watching me sleep."

Surprise rippled through her. "No, I'm not," she instantly denied. "Because if you know I'm watching, then you can't be asleep."

His eyes opened. No sleepiness there. Absolute awareness.

For some reason, a blush stole across her cheeks. She could feel the heat filling her face. "Hi."

He smiled. "Hi."

"Um, you stayed." Which was awesome. "And I don't think I screamed again."

"You didn't. No levitations. No more claw marks." His fingers trailed over her shoulder.

"Maybe...maybe it doesn't happen if you aren't alone. Maybe I can keep you safe."

That was something to consider. To wish for. "Don't know." She rolled away from him. Rose from the bed. "I've never let a lover stay the night, so I don't know if I scream when someone is with me or not."

"You've...damn, you have a great ass."

She'd paced to the window, but she glanced back at him, smiling. "Glad you noticed."

He'd sat up in bed. "You've never spent the night with a lover?"

Not since Tomas, no. "When you sleep, you're vulnerable. It would be too easy for a lover to slit my neck with a knife. Or shoot me. Or—"

"You didn't trust your lovers."

She glanced back through the window. Sunset was coming. "No."

"My claws are sharper than any knife. You don't worry about me slitting your throat?"

Her brow furrowed. "You can't kill your own mate. You'd go crazy."

The bed covers rustled. He padded toward her.

Then he wrapped his arms around her. "Is it really so hard to just say that you trust me?"

It was. Yes, incredibly so. "I don't think you fired the arrow that hurt Rio."

"Good. Because I didn't."

"But I think a shifter did. If you want my top three suspect list, it's Goldilocks, Warren, and Elliott."

He'd gone tense behind her. "Why them?"

"Because Goldie, um, Lucinda hates me. If someone made me think half my hair fell out, I'd probably want to get some revenge, too." She kept her gaze on the water. The waves were really quite beautiful. "And while you told me that only you and Carmichael knew about the witch poison in your tower, it's obvious Warren and Elliott are your best friends. They're the top power after you, aren't they? I'm betting they both know your secrets."

"I *never* told them about where the poison was hidden."

"Maybe you didn't. Someone else could have told them. Like your brother." Now she glanced over her shoulder. "You'll notice, he wasn't in my top three, even though you banished him." That still didn't sit so well with her.

Griffin turned her in his arms. "Why don't you suspect him?"

"Because he's too obvious of a bad guy."

The faint lines near his eyes deepened. "You're underestimating him. Don't do that. Carmichael is dangerous. He hates witches. He knew about the poison."

"In case I'm wrong, I have Edgar tailing him." She smiled. "Didn't see that coming, did you? You just saw my gorgeous ass and overlooked my scheming mind."

He pressed a kiss to her forehead. "I love your scheming mind."

"Edgar is also there to protect Carmichael. Not just to spy on him."

Griffin's brow furrowed.

"Because if I die, and someone *does* want you to think it was Carmichael, then I suspect he'll be meeting a bad end before you can get to him."

"It's not Gold—I mean, Lucinda. She's not the one who shot the arrow. She was devastated when she realized Rio had been hit. The girl was crying hysterically."

"Could have been because she missed her target. I don't think the shooter ever wanted Rio hurt. The shooter didn't expect him to be brave enough to try saving me." The jerk had underestimated her henchman.

My friend. Wait, nope, she would not think of him that way.

His voice low, Griffin told her, "I've known Warren and Elliott since I was a child. They'd give their lives to protect me."

That was the point he seemed to be missing. "But would they protect me? Or would they try to protect you *from* me?"

And there it was. The faintest flicker in the depths of his eyes. "That's what I thought." She waved her fingers, instantly dressing herself. Tight jeans. White top. Some cute sandals. Why not look fab when she faced the vamps? Better for them to underestimate her. "And just because you've known someone since you were a kid, it doesn't mean that person can't turn on you. Speaking from absolute personal experience here. When we were little, Devon used to tell me that we were going to grow up and get married." Her chest ached a moment. "Instead, he spends most of his adult time trying to kill me." She eased away from Griffin and paced back toward the bed.

Silence. The uncomfortable kind. She could feel a new tension in his body. She turned and found him studying her. "What?"

"He wants to marry you?"

"No, I imagine that would be his worst nightmare now." She waved this away. "When we were kids—you know, little kids just imagining life. He wanted to marry me back then. Before everything went to shit."

"Before Tomas."

"Yes."

Griffin seemed to mull that over in his mind. "You never considered that he stopped you from saving Tomas because Devon wanted you for himself?"

She laughed. "No, he was way over me by that point. In case you didn't know, he and Genevieve have a big on-again, off-again thing happening."

Griffin's expression remained tense. She probably shouldn't have brought up Devon. Good thing she hadn't mentioned their brief span as lov—

"Did you ever sleep with him?"

She rocked forward onto the balls of her feet. "So, I'm trying to keep up the honesty thing with you, but I have a feeling my answer is just going to piss you off."

His lips thinned. "You slept with him."

"I may look like I'm twenty-five, but I've been around for a very long time. I've got a lot of lovers out there. So if you're going to be jealous—"

"I am." He stalked toward her. Totally naked. All muscle. All sexy. "Very jealous. Because I hate the idea of anyone else having you."

She was not supposed to find that sweet. And it wasn't. It was possessive. Growly. Shifter to the core. "You can't have my past." She lifted her hand and pressed it to his chest. "And I can't have yours." Did she dare say it? Would it reveal too much? *Don't say it. Don't say it, but...* "You can have my future."

Valerie wished she hadn't said that. He might laugh at her. Might throw out some mocking comment that made her feel like hell. "Forget it," she added quickly as she tried to sound dismissive. "That's not what I meant to say." She pulled her hand away.

He caught her wrist. Brought her hand right back to his chest. Pressed her palm over his heart. "You are my future. You think I don't know that?"

She hadn't realized... "That's good."

"No, I don't think 'good' is the word. 'Good' is too tame for us." He smiled at her. "But our future will be earth shattering. Epic. Incredible. And maybe even a little terrifying."

She found herself returning his smile.

"Now are you ready to face the vamps and find your missing witch?"

"Absolutely."

"Anything I need to know before the big meet up?"

"Enzo can't be trusted. He'll turn on us in an instant if he has the chance." She considered this. "And I think he and Calliope are sleeping together. Blood, sex, and magic are a dangerous mix."

His brow furrowed. "Tell me something I don't know."

"If he's drinking from her and having sex with her, Calliope will be his drug of choice. Vamps get addicted to witch blood. It's one of the reasons I made sure they wouldn't like *my* blood."

"A junkie denied his fix can be very dangerous."

She nodded.

"But not as dangerous as shifter who wants to protect his mate."

He seemed to be warning her. Well, no *seemed* about it. He was.

She could see the hard warning in his green eyes as he said, "Your life matters more to me than anything else. Remember that."

He turned away, giving her a very nice view of *his* ass. She admired it for a moment, then wiggled her fingers, sending clothes flying to cover him. "And you matter to me, shifter. Remember that."

He'd slipped his way past her guard. For the first time since Tomas, a man had started to make her wonder if there was more to the world than power and magic.

Maybe...maybe there was love out there.

Love for someone like her.

***

Griffin entered the study. He opened the safe and took out the golden bracelets that Devon had given to him. Elliott had been safeguarding them for Griffin, and then, when they'd gotten to the island, securing them in the safe had been Elliott's first job.

"What are they?" Warren spoke from behind him. Griffin had known the guy was there, of course. Not like another shifter could ever sneak up on him.

"A present for your witch?" Warren pressed. "I have heard that witches enjoy gold. Are they your attempt to buy her love? Because, hate to break it to you, but I don't think *love* is an emotion that Valerie Storm can feel."

Griffin pocketed the bracelets. He turned toward his friend. Valerie's words played in his mind. *"If you want my top three suspect list, it's Goldilocks, Warren, and Elliott."* His gaze swept over Warren's tense features. "Why do you hate her?"

"Uh, because she's a witch? Supposedly the most evil witch ever born? Do you want me to name all of her kills? All of the people she's cursed?"

Griffin stalked toward him. "How has she hurt you?"

Warren opened his mouth, then frowned. After a moment, he swallowed, then said, "Are you forgetting what she did to my niece? Working her illusions, terrifying Lucinda?"

"You talked to the other shifters there that day. You know what Lucinda and her friends were doing."

"So that made it *okay* for Valerie to torment her? Like two wrongs make some shit right?"

That wasn't what Griffin was saying. "Are you truly going to stand before me and act as if you've never done anything wrong in *your* life, my friend?"

The target hit. Warren stumbled back. "I'm fucking *sorry.*" Pain flashed on his face. "You think I don't regret what I did? Every single damn day? I know I cost them their lives. I know I screwed up and your parents died, I know—"

Griffin fisted his hands in Warren's shirt-front. "I wasn't talking about that." Now he could only shake his head. "You don't seriously still blame yourself for what happened to them, do you?"

"I let the witch into our world." Warren's gaze had turned stark. "I trusted her. I led her to our land. She couldn't get in without me. She needed a shifter. I *killed* your parents."

"You were a kid. Shit, man, you were—"

"I wasn't some kid. I was sixteen. I was old enough to shift. Old enough to make my way through the portal. I believed her lies. Believed her stories. I let that woman get in. I let—" He broke off.

Griffin could only shake his head. "Valerie isn't the witch who killed my parents."

"My witch put a spell on me," Warren whispered. "I thought she was the most perfect woman I'd ever seen. I didn't realize how dangerous she was. Not until it was too late."

"Valerie isn't—"

"Valerie isn't Lorena. You're right. Valerie is a hundred times more powerful. A hundred times more dangerous. And you don't see the threat that she is." Warren's eyes glittered with fury and fear. "Are you under her spell? Because I swear, I think you are. I wasn't free from Lorena's magic, not until she drew her last breath."

Griffin stiffened. "I'm not under a spell."

"I said the same damn thing. You don't *know* you're under a witch's spell. Not until you're free. And then suddenly you realize your witch isn't so perfect. Not so beautiful. Not the center of your world. That's the moment when you realize you've done terrible things, made terrible mistakes, and you'd give your soul to make things right again." Warren gave a jerky nod. "Listen to me. Just listen. What if you and Valerie aren't even mates? What if she's just screwed with your head? Used more of her magic to make you *think* that she's the one for you? You don't have any way of knowing for sure. Not unless you bind her magic. That's what Devon said. Devon—"

"Devon wants Valerie dead." And Griffin didn't have time for this. "You're going to trust him over her?"

"He's not the one with a kill list a mile long. He's not the one who was going to be executed by his own kind. Every single thing points to her being the enemy. But you're too blinded to see that." Warren's cheeks flushed. "She's going to destroy you. Do you really just expect me to stand by and watch it happen?"

"Valerie is my mate. Not my enemy." The weight of the bracelets seemed far too heavy in Griffin's pocket.

"Devon gave you a tool to use. He said you could stop—"

"I'm not using the fucking bracelets on her!"

Warren blinked. Then his gaze flew down to Griffin's pocket. A furrow appeared between his brows. "If you're not using them, why are you taking the bracelets with you?" His eyes widened. "You *are* starting to see the truth! You realize she could be screwing with you. Good, *good!* We can stop her together."

Griffin could hear the roar of the boat's engine. "Go home, Warren."

"What?"

"I don't want you around my mate. Go back home, to the shifter realm. Wait for me there."

"But you will need my help, you'll need—"

"Stop." A guttural command.

Warren swallowed.

Griffin studied his friend. "She thinks you're trying to kill her."

A frantic shake of Warren's head.

"She doesn't trust you," Griffin added.

"The witch is trying to turn you against me, she's—"

"You want me to bind my mate. You talk about her as if she's our enemy. You look at her with hate in your eyes." Was it any wonder Valerie was so hesitant around the other shifters? "She *saved* Rio. She saved my ass in that witch dungeon. She's not perfect, I'm not claiming that she is, but you know what? I don't want her to be perfect. I'm certainly not perfect. I'm a killer. I'm a beast. I'm absolutely savage. And *she* is the thing I want most. Screw any spell. I don't care about spells. I care about her."

Warren had gone statue-still.

"So either you accept my queen or you get your ass away from me." Griffin didn't want to lose his friend. But he would *not* lose Valerie. "If I have to choose, it will be her. Always her."

"You're under a spell," Warren whispered.

"I'm not you." He should have seen that Warren still carried the heavy weight of guilt. "Valerie isn't Lorena. She's not trying to destroy the shifters. Stop blaming her for something that another witch did. See her for who she is."

He shouldered around his friend, heading for the door.

"I do see Valerie for exactly who she is," Warren threw after him. "*Everyone* sees her that way. Everyone but you."

Griffin reached for the doorknob.

But Warren wasn't done. "Shouldn't that make you suspicious? Shouldn't that make you stop and think...*why in the hell do you see her differently?*"

He looked back. "I see her perfectly." And he knew why. "Go home, Warren. I don't need you."

"You don't need anyone but her, is that it? She's going to destroy—"

"Don't fucking talk about my queen again." They were done. Dammit.

He yanked open the door and stalked into the hallway, fury filling his body. He hadn't realized how much animosity Warren held for Valerie. All of the shifters had kept their distance from her when she'd been at his castle. Everyone but Rio. They'd whispered about her, stared at her with fear...and hate?

And he'd just let that shit happen. What in the hell had been wrong with him?

He marched from the mansion. Headed straight for the yacht. Valerie was already on board, her dark hair blowing in the breeze.

When she saw him, a wide smile slid across her face, and she hurried back onto the dock. "Starting to wonder if I'd have to hunt for you!"

He pulled her into his arms. Put his mouth on her. Tasted. Savored. Claimed.

"Hello to you, too," Valerie murmured against his mouth.

His head lifted. He didn't let her go.

A faint line appeared between her delicate brows. "Is everything okay?"

"It will be." He'd make it better than okay. He'd make up for every single slight she'd ever received.

"Sunset is coming," Elliott called out, his voice bland. "But, you know, if you two want to keep making out and just ignore the vamps waiting, we can do that. My schedule is wide open."

They jumped onto the boat. Griffin helped to cast off the lines.

"Is Warren coming?" Elliott asked, glancing toward the house.

Griffin locked his back teeth. "He's going home. I need someone there to keep an eye on things." A partial truth.

Elliott cut him a sharp glance.

"Take us to the vamps." Griffin felt his teeth sharpen. "And if things go to hell, be ready to claw your way through them."

Elliott steered the boat away from the dock. "Always love fighting with a vamp. Been too long since I kicked some undead ass."

Griffin looked back at his island. Warren had stepped outside. He stared after them.

"He doesn't appear happy," Valerie announced. She lifted her hand and gave Warren a cheery wave.

He didn't wave back.

"It's a pity he hates me." She waved once more. Sparks danced above her fingers.

Griffin caught her hand. "Don't."

She blinked innocently. "What? You think I was going to hurt him?" Another flutter of her lashes. "He looked so mopey and down. I was just going to give the man his own personal little raincloud. You know, so it could follow him around."

Elliott barked out a laugh.

"Do *not,*" Griffin warned her.

She nodded. "Right. I should save my energy for the vamps. Good plan." Though she did look longingly toward Warren. "*Someday.*"

"What's that?" Griffin asked, narrowing his eyes.

"Oh, nothing. I just feel like Elliott. Totally agree with him. Can't wait to kick vamp ass." Her smile was huge.

"And what happens *after* we kick that ass?" Griffin wondered what Valerie's next step would be.

Her smile dimmed. "We find Calliope. We get her help. And I take down the witch council. Easy."

It didn't sound easy.

But then, he'd learned that when Valerie was involved, *nothing* was easy.

***

"You bring Valerie to me, just Valerie." Calliope Briggs was absolutely sick of fear being a heavy weight in her stomach. "She's the one I trust. Only her."

Enzo cast a fast glance toward the window. "It's almost sunset."

"Then you need to go." *Valerie is back. That means I have a chance.* "She can help me. She can help us both. Bring her to me."

The vamp leader hesitated. "She wanted you to be on that beach—at the club, Daybreak."

Calliope shook her head. "I can't be out there. I'm not as strong as she is. If the wrong person sees me first, I'm dead." Just like Hurst and Fiona. "You lead her here. Only Valerie, understand?"

"That shifter isn't going to let her out of his sight."

He was a problem. Griffin Bastien. "Griffin was hired by the witch council. He's an assassin. He's just biding his time, trying to figure out a way to end Valerie. You have to get her away from him." She closed in on Enzo. She'd found that the vamp would do just about anything for her. "When you see him, before he even has a chance to speak, kill him."

Enzo whistled. "He's not going to be easy to kill."

She reached for his hand. Pressed two objects into his palm. "He will be if you use a little magic."

Enzo glanced down. "Silver bullets? Those aren't exactly magic."

Not normally. "These are magic. These bullets are enchanted. They *won't* miss their target. I don't care how fast he is. How big of a beast he can be. You aim these silver bullets at him, and you *won't* miss."

His tongue swiped over his lower lip. A dead giveaway to his nerves. "If I kill the shifter king, then I start a war."

Time to give Enzo some perspective. "If you don't kill him, then I'm as good as dead. And you don't want me to die, do you? If I die, you won't be able to have my blood any longer." Her fingers trailed down his chest. "You won't be able to have me."

His gaze fell on her throat. "I do like you. You're fucking delicious."

Wonderful. What every witch wanted to hear. "So kill him for me. And bring my friend to me."

Enzo nodded. His fingers closed around the bullets. "I'll be back as soon as I can."

Then he was gone. Marching out of the room as if he was heading to battle—which, well, he was. She hurried to the window and glanced down, watching as he filed out with a line of vamps. Vamps liked to live in dens. They thought there was safety in numbers. They were usually right.

They were—

Something hit her from behind. A sharp, stabbing pain. Her hand lifted, and she grabbed at her shoulder. Calliope's shaking fingers pulled out some kind of...dart?

"What in the hell?" Calliope whispered.

Her knees—her legs—gave way. She slammed onto the floor.

And she heard a man laughing.

Someone was in the room with her. Someone she hadn't even seen. She hadn't sensed anyone, hadn't felt the stir of magic in the air—

"One witch down..." His mocking voice drifted to her.

A heavy, numbing lethargy swept through her. Calliope couldn't even lift her lashes, much less her head. She couldn't see the man who stalked toward her.

"One down." His hand brushed over her cheek. "One to go."

CHAPTER NINETEEN

"I don't like this setup, man," Elliott muttered. "Two of us against how many vamps?"

Griffin didn't know. They'd just stepped onto the beach. He could see the outline of Stefan's club, Daybreak, in the distance.

"I don't see any humans around," Elliott continued grimly. "Maybe you should shift into your dragon. A little fire and those vamps will be ash. Only thing that burns faster than a vamp is, um, it's, uh—"

"Yes, please," Valerie entreated as she wrapped her hand around Griffin's arm. "Do finish that sentence. What is it that burns faster than a vampire? Is it, by any chance, a witch?"

Elliott scratched his chin. "I can't seem to remember what it is right now."

"Coward." She shook her head, then glanced up at Griffin. "You can change, if you want. I don't exactly trust vamps, either."

Griffin stiffened. "They're coming." He could hear their footsteps. "At least a dozen of them."

"Because you *always* bring a dozen buddies to a friendly talk," Elliott drawled.

Valerie bit her lower lip. "Is it just vamps? Or do you hear or smell a witch, too?"

The vamps were coming in fast. They were near Daybreak.

"Just the vamps," he told her.

"Dammit." She huffed out a breath. "Then let's go meet the bastards. Because I do *not* tolerate someone trying to screw me over." She straightened her shoulders. "Daybreak won't open until midnight, so the place should be deserted. Stefan will be around, though, in case we need him."

She started to walk forward, but he pulled her back.

"Griffin? What—"

He kissed her. "Few rules first."

Her eyes widened. "No, please, no. Tell me that we are *not* back to rules."

Elliott smothered what sounded like a laugh.

"Rule one..." Griffin began.

"You love your rules far too much," Valerie muttered. "It's positively unhealthy."

He ignored that comment. "You stay behind me. I'm the one with the super senses."

"Well, about that..."

He frowned.

She winced. "My senses may be a wee bit enhanced. Not as good as yours, of course, but..." Valerie cleared her throat. "Really good."

Yeah, he'd suspected. "I'm faster than you. I'm stronger."

He waited for her to argue.

"You've got me there." She nodded.

"So I stay between you and the threats." Protecting her was his job.

Valerie fired a quick glance toward Daybreak. "Any other rules?"

"You don't get hurt. That's rule two."

Now her gaze came back to him. "You don't get hurt, either. And that's my only rule for this little meet and greet."

"Careful, sweetheart," he rasped. "You keep talking like that, and I'll think you care about me." He deliberately threw back the words she'd given to him when they'd been on the island.

"I do." Her eyes widened, as if she'd just surprised herself. "I do."

"Damn straight. Glad you admitted it." He locked his fingers with hers. His claws were already out. "Now let's face the vamps."

Griffin, Elliott, and Valerie headed for Daybreak. They beat the vamps to the club, and when they walked inside, Stefan was waiting behind the bar.

Stefan raised a brow at Valerie. "You just had to use my place for your showdown, didn't you?"

"You heard, huh? Word spread on the paranormal grapevine?"

"It always does."

She shrugged. "Daybreak was convenient."

Stefan's fingers tapped on the bar. His snakes seemed to stretch. "You think you can trust the vamp?"

"I absolutely don't. But Enzo has Calliope. I need her."

Stefan's gaze slid to Griffin. Then to Elliott. "Two shifters against a den of vamps." He nodded. "Yeah, I'll take those odds. Should have opened a betting pool. Would have gone ten to one on the shifters."

"Nice to know," Griffin murmured.

Stefan saluted him. "When you want me to join in, just say the word."

Elliott advanced toward the bar. "What word is that?"

"Medusa," Valerie answered.

The snakes hissed.

Elliott stopped advancing. "Obviously, you two have played this game before."

The vamps were almost on them. Griffin pushed Valerie behind him.

The door flew open. Enzo was the first vamp into Daybreak. His men came in right after him. They fanned out. They didn't attack.

Enzo frowned as his stare slid to Elliott. "Just one shifter as backup? Seriously?" He was obviously insulted.

Griffin shrugged. "I know. It's overkill. If you jerks try to betray us, Elliott won't get to do anything but watch me kick your asses."

"Hardly fair," Elliott announced.

Enzo tensed. Then he was craning his neck. "Valerie, are you *hiding* behind this dumbass?" He laughed. "Didn't think you hid from anything."

A deliberate taunt. One designed to get Valerie to step away from Griffin.

But she didn't. In fact, Griffin didn't think she moved at all. Holy hell, the woman was actually following his rules. "Where's Calliope?" Griffin demanded.

Enzo scratched his chin. "Who?"

"You sonofabitch!" Valerie's sharp voice rang out. "My ally! I want her, right now! That was the deal, that was—"

"I'll take you to her," Enzo promised, his low words cutting through her cry. "Right after I kill the assassin. Don't worry, you'll thank me later."

Kill the assassin.

Fuck. Griffin lunged forward even as the vamp lifted a gun.

Enzo was smiling as he aimed the weapon at Griffin. Like Griffin was supposed to be afraid of a damn bullet. He could dodge anything that came at him. His teeth extended as his bones began to pop and stretch.

Bam. Bam.

Two bullets exploded from the gun. Two bullets that were rushing straight for Griffin. He jerked to the side—

The bullets froze in mid-air. Just stopped.

"What have you done?" Valerie's shaking voice.

Griffin glanced at her. Saw the sparks in the air around her. She'd obviously worked some kind of spell, and his crafty witch had just frozen the bullets in the air. A very impressive feat.

Enzo backed up. "Calliope wants *you*, Valerie. She said the shifter is an assassin. She wants him dead."

Great. Griffin stepped to the side, but the bullets, even though they were hanging in mid-air...they turned. Aimed at him.

"Did you just see that?" Elliott demanded, his voice holding shock.

Enzo let out a low laugh. "They won't miss. Calliope promised that they wouldn't. The bullets won't miss at what I aim for." He pointed at Valerie. "You stopped them, but it's just temporary. You can't hold them back forever. Calliope knows her shit. Those bullets are going to lodge in your shifter. He'll be dead, and then I'll take you to Calliope." A satisfied expression crossed his face. "See you in hell, shifter king. 'Cause those bullets are made of *silver*. And they are going straight for your heart."

Bullshit. Had to be.

Valerie stood in the middle of the club, her hands fisting at her sides. Her body trembled from strain. From the strain of holding those bullets back? Griffin ran toward the bullets. He'd just knock the bullets out of the air. But when he tried to touch them, a bolt of electricity threw him back.

"Stefan!" Valerie's voice was strained. "*Medusa*."

Snakes immediately flew across the room. Dozens of them raced for the vamps, biting and hissing, and when the snakes plunged their teeth into the vamps...

The vamps froze. Their bodies just locked down and only their eyes were alive with emotion—terror.

Griffin bounded for Enzo. He grabbed the vamp and put the SOB in front of his body. "The bullets are going to come for me, huh? Well, guess they'll have to go through you first."

Enzo struggled in his hold, but Griffin didn't let the bastard go.

"Griffin! It won't work!" Valerie yelled. Sweat dotted her face. "They'll just tear right through him. Transform! Change into the dragon. They might not penetrate your scales. *Shift*."

A snake waited at Enzo's feet. A big, thick, triangular-headed beast that stared up with cold, yellow eyes.

"Shift, Griffin!" Valerie ordered fiercely. "Shift right now!"

Griffin's gaze flew around the club. Elliott was fighting with two vamps, swiping out with his claws and sending their blood flying. Stefan was hurtling over the bar's counter, and the snake near Enzo had just curled back to strike.

While the bullets that *had* been frozen in mid-air...they were inching forward. Coming toward Griffin.

Valerie ran across the room.

The snake struck Enzo. The vamp immediately went statue-still, not even crying out.

The bullets were spinning, moving closer. Closer.

"I'm losing them!" Valerie cried. "Only chance...my blood...I can try to stop—" She shoved Enzo out of the way. He hit the floor—still frozen. Valerie launched herself at Griffin. She locked her arms around him. "It will be okay!"

He was changing. The shift rushing through his body. Scales slid over his skin.

"It's okay," Valerie said frantically. "I'm—"

She stiffened. She was staring up at him, and her eyes flared wide. He saw pain in the darkness of her gaze. He could smell her blood. Valerie's blood. No, *no*. He opened his mouth and roared.

"Got it," she whispered. Sparks danced around her, but her body was already slumping to the floor. "Stopped...them..."

He couldn't hold her. Couldn't lift her back up because he was transforming. The dragon had taken over, and the beast didn't have hands. He just had rage and fury. And his mate—*his mate* was bleeding on the ground. Vampires were all around her. He opened his mouth, feeling the smoke rise in his throat.

"Oh, shit," Stefan launched himself at Valerie. He covered her with his body.

And flames burst from the dragon's mouth.

***

Ash. Destruction. Death.

Griffin opened his eyes and found himself standing in hell. The club was a wreck. Blackened walls. Burning chunks of flame on the floor. Well, on what remained of the floor. Smoke was everywhere, billowing in the air.

The vampires were gone. Or maybe they were the ash drifting in the wind.

"Human cops and firefighters will be coming. We need to get the hell out of here."

Griffin jerked at the voice. His head turned, and he found himself staring at Elliott. Smoke drifted from the guy's shirt and pants, and Elliott slapped at his sleeve, smothering out a quick flame. Soot covered his cheeks. "We need to move."

Griffin shook his head. "What happened?"

Elliott grabbed his arm. "You happened. You went full-on, ballistic dragon. Toasted every vamp. Everything in your path."

He didn't remember that. He just remembered... "Valerie?" He didn't see her. Where was she?

"I'm sorry." Elliott's voice was strangled. "So fucking sorry."

What? "My flames wouldn't hurt her." He was certain of that. She'd told him the fire didn't hurt her.

"It wasn't the flames that got her. It was the vamp's bullets. She threw herself in front of them. Stefan told me they must've been bewitched. The guy said it took the blood of one witch to put the spell in place, so the blood of another was needed to cancel it out." Another flame sputtered near Elliott's shoulder. He let go of Griffin long enough to slap it out. "The bullets went into her back. She fell, and that's when you went full-on into dragon rage. I had to run freaking fast to make sure you didn't torch my ass. Those vamps...after the snakes got them, they couldn't move at all."

A snake slithered across the floor, dodging the flames.

Griffin watched the snake as it slipped out of the club's remains. He couldn't seem to look away. Everything felt distorted and slow. And all he could think was— "Valerie?"

Elliott cursed. "Don't shift again, okay? We have to get out of here. We can't have the humans finding us in this place." He pulled Griffin toward the door—well, toward the gaping hole in the wall.

"You can break down when we're gone. When we're far away from civilians."

Griffin dug in his heels. "Where. Is. Valerie?"

"Stefan took her, okay? He covered her with his body right before the flames went wild, and when the smoke cleared, they were gone."

No.

"She was...shit, I don't think she was alive. I'm so sorry."

Griffin shook his head. "No."

"She was bleeding so much. And...things were crazy, but I swear, I don't think I heard her heart beating. Stefan was yelling at her to come back, but it didn't make sense because she hadn't gone anywhere." He swiped at the soot on his cheek. "Then I realized...it made sense if she'd died. If she'd *gone*."

"No." It was all he could say because Valerie couldn't be dead. She couldn't be gone. Rule one...she stayed behind him. He'd told her to stay behind him.

Why would she jump in front of bullets?

And rule two...she didn't get hurt. It had been a rule. His rule. Valerie couldn't get hurt. He spun around, searching through the lingering flames.

"Dammit, we have to *go!*" Elliott yelled. "Don't you hear the sirens? The fire lit up the whole sky!"

Valerie wasn't dead. She wasn't. If she were dead...

He wouldn't have changed back. He would have stayed as a dragon. And he would have destroyed *everything*. Griffin shook off Elliott. He bounded after the snake he'd seen slithering away. The bastard snake was moving fast, but Griffin was faster. He shoved flaming debris out of his way and rushed down the beach. The snake left a perfect path to follow in the sand. Griffin's nostrils flared as he took in the scents around him. He could finally smell more than smoke and ash. He could smell blood.

Her blood.

The snake rushed toward a man who was hunched at the edge of the shore. The snake disappeared when he reached the figure. Stefan Medusa held something tightly against his body. The waves rushed up and hit him, but Stefan didn't seem to notice.

The scent of Valerie's blood grew stronger. "Give her to me!" Griffin's bellow echoed through the night.

Stefan rocked forward and back, holding her against his chest. "She knows I hate vampires. She brought them to my place tonight just because she knows I like to get payback against them. Wasn't because Daybreak was convenient. Such a lie. She did it as a gift to me."

Elliott's footsteps rushed up behind Griffin. "What in the hell? Is that Valerie?"

Griffin stalked forward. "She's not dead."

Stefan kept rocking her. "I was worried your flames would hurt her. I can't burn. I'm stone. Stone doesn't burn."

Stefan didn't know Valerie's secret? She hadn't told him?

"I can't make the bleeding stop," Stefan rasped.

When the waves retreated, Griffin saw that they were red.

Stefan tilted back his head. "She did that, for you." He seemed confused. "She let the bullets go into her own body. One severed her spine. I *heard* it. That's why she fell. The other tore through her back and went into her heart."

Griffin shuddered.

"Why did she do that? She's evil. Everyone says so." Stefan stroked back her hair. "Why did she save me so long ago? The vampires had cut my throat. Then they bit me...over and over again. I was dead. She brought me back. They turned on her when she grabbed for me. Even as she was using her magic to bring me back, those bastards were feeding on her."

Griffin felt his beasts clawing at his insides.

"She told me...said 'Never again.' She wasn't ever going to let a vamp get either of us. That if they tried, she'd kill them."

Now Griffin knew why she'd worked the spell on her own blood.

"She won't stop bleeding," Stefan whispered. "Help her. You're her mate. You *can* help her, can't you?" For a moment, he seemed lost. Scared.

Griffin took Valerie from Stefan. "How old were you when Valerie saved your life?"

"Ten."

Fuck.

"She raised me." Stefan's voice dropped. "Don't let her die. I will give you *anything*. Just don't let her die."

The Medusa didn't get it. Griffin would trade anything, offer *anything* he had if it meant keeping Valerie alive and safe. Griffin cradled her in his arms. The bullets were still in her. He knew that with certainty. He also knew that he couldn't get them out. He wasn't a doctor. He didn't know how to save her.

But he'd be damned if he let her die.

Griffin leaned over and pressed a kiss to her forehead. "You broke my rules." *Dammit, baby, you broke my rules!* She wasn't supposed to be lying there, bleeding and pale. She was supposed to be using her magic. Making the world kneel at her feet. Cackling and taking over. Making life hell for her enemies.

"Don't you do this," he whispered. "You die, and I will come right after you, do you understand? I'll fucking find you. I'll drag you back, and I don't care who I have to fight. I won't lose you."

The cry of the sirens was even louder.

"Griffin..." Elliott muttered. "You're holding a bleeding woman in your arms. It looks as if a bomb just went off in that club. We need to get out of here or we're going to wind up in a human jail. Shifters don't do well in cages, you know that."

"Dig the bullets out," Stefan told him quickly. "It might help. I don't have claws. I can't cut into her. You have to do it."

"What the fuck?" Elliott said, shocked. "No one is *cutting* her! Shit, don't be a freak!"

"She can't get better until the bullets are out." Stefan nodded quickly. "If they don't come out, she'll die. Do it. Help her."

Cut her?

Cut into Valerie?

"Her spine..." Griffin choked down the heavy lump in his throat. He shook his head. "No, no, I won't do that. I *can't* hurt her."

Stefan's shoulders slumped. "Then you kill her."

Griffin's wings erupted from his back. He gripped Valerie tight, held her against his heart, and he shot into the sky.

"You will *kill* her!" Stefan yelled after him. *"And I'll freaking kill you!"*

CHAPTER TWENTY

Griffin crashed down through the ceiling, sending shingles and boards falling in his wake. He landed on the floor, cradling his precious burden, and his knees didn't even buckle.

"For the love of...dammit, man, put on some clothes!" The outraged male voice demanded.

Griffin swung toward that voice and found Leo staring back at him. The Lord of the Dark looked pissed as he rushed across the room. But when the guy got closer, when he took a good look at Valerie's still form...

Leo staggered to a stop. "What happened to her?"

"She took bullets..." He had to struggle to speak as a man and not roar as a beast. "Meant for me."

Leo's eyes widened. "You're bullshitting me."

Fate—Mora—ran up behind him.

"Valerie Storm did not risk her life for you." Leo shook his head. "Something else happened. Don't play games. You tell me—"

"You fix her!" Griffin bellowed. "You fix her right now!"

Leo's jaw locked. "You'll want to speak a little more respectfully to me."

The hell he would. "Fix her..." He could feel the dragon getting ready to spit fire. To *destroy*.

"Calm down." Mora's soft voice. "Put her on the couch. Valerie isn't dying today."

He tried to lower her to the couch, but he couldn't let her go.

Mora's hand pressed to his shoulder. "She's not dying today, I promise."

If Fate said it, the words had to be true, didn't they?

Mora stared into Griffin's eyes. "This isn't the end I see for her. We just have to get the bullets out. Once the bullets are out, she'll recover."

Griffin sucked in one breath. Another. Slowly, he lowered Valerie onto the couch, positioning her on her stomach, then smoothing back her hair. He noticed that her blood was on his hands and his whole body shuddered.

"So..." Mora cleared her throat. "Call me squeamish, but I'm not exactly game for cutting into her body." A pause. "We should probably kidnap a doctor."

***

Valerie could hear a bird calling. Edgar? Was he coming back to report on Carmichael? She cracked open one eye and found herself staring at a white wall.

An unfamiliar wall.

She cracked open the other eye. Blinked. She could smell the ocean, and the bird call that she heard—not Edgar. Sounded more like a sea gull.

"Hey, sweetheart. It's about time you opened your eyes."

Griffin. Her gaze immediately jerked to the left. He was right beside her. In *bed,* with her. Staring at her tenderly. His stare was warm, his expression almost—"Oh, jeez. Did I die?"

Griffin shook his head. "No, you just scared the ever-loving hell out of me." He leaned closer and pressed a kiss to her cheek. "Don't do that shit again. Never again."

Valerie wasn't going to make a promise she couldn't keep. "Where are the vampires?"

"Ash."

Dammit. "Enzo, too?"

"Enzo most of all. His bullets shot you."

"Yes, well, they were intended to shoot you." She pushed herself up carefully, expecting pain to hit. But there wasn't any pain. Odd.

"You broke the rules. You weren't supposed to get hurt. You weren't supposed to protect *me.* You said you'd stand behind me."

"I don't stand behind anyone. You should have realized that about me by now." She didn't even feel tenderness in her back. Amazing. "And for the record, I'll never stand back and watch you get hurt. Those bullets were silver. They were bewitched. If I hadn't stopped them, you'd be dead." She considered the matter. "Nah. I would have brought you back. But that would have been harder—"

"You almost died." He pulled her toward him. His hands were tight and hard on her arms. "I can't bring you back if you die. I just *lose* you."

"And you lose your sanity. Right. Sorry. I was—"

"I won't lose *you*. Screw my sanity. I think I lost that the moment we met in that damn dungeon."

Her lips parted, but she didn't speak.

"You matter. *You*. You're the one in my blood. The one in my torn soul. You're the other part of me. You and your crazy laugh and your damn spells and your sparking fingers. *You*. And you can't die. You can't leave. Because if you leave, I'll fucking want to follow." He pressed a hot, hard kiss to her lips. "I love you."

Wait—what? She'd misheard. Misunderstood. There was no way he'd just said that to her. Valerie shoved at his chest, and he eased his hold, letting her go. She jumped from the bed. Jumped across the whole room. "What did you just say to me?" Her question sounded like a shriek.

He sat on the bed, his chest bare, the bed covers around his waist. He looked sexy and strong, and his gaze was still tender as it slid over her.

She was naked. She waved her fingers, seeing the little spark above them, and clothes appeared on her body. *I'm becoming as prudish as he is!* No, she just felt too vulnerable being naked in front of him in that moment.

"Since when are you modest?" Griffin rasped.

Since—*never*. But she was feeling weird. Her stomach was in knots. "You don't love me."

His head cocked. "Are you all right?"

"No, I was just shot—twice—and I have no idea where I am." Definitely not all right.

"We're at Leo's place."

"What? We need to get out of here!" Her hand slapped against her forehead. "Did he save me? Is that why I healed so well? Because if you made a deal with him, then we are screwed. He'll want our firstborn child or some Rumpelstiltskin crap like that."

Griffin's lips twitched. "No one is taking our firstborn child." His gaze dipped to her stomach. "She is gonna be a hell-raiser."

If she was like her mother and able to bring back the dead, yes, she literally could *be* a hell-raiser, but they'd cover that another time. "What deal did you make?"

"No deal. I kidnapped a doctor, brought him here, scared ten years of his life away when I showed him my claws, and the guy removed the bullets from your body."

That was...unexpected.

"You healed as soon as they were removed. Impressive. Didn't know you could do that."

She hadn't known that she could do that, either. Had her magic gotten stronger with their mating bond? It was possible. Shifters were incredible healers. Maybe the bond had given her some of his magic.

He rose from the bed. He wasn't naked, thank goodness, because when he was naked, thinking got a little hard for her. He wore a pair of low slung jeans, and his abs were absolutely lickable.

"How'd you heal so fast?" Griffin wanted to know.

"I have no idea."

His brow furrowed.

"I don't know. I should have died." Honest truth. "My healing rate is not normally like that at all."

Fury darkened Griffin's face. "You were willing to die for me?"

Yes. And that realization was unnerving.

"*Why?*"

She didn't want to examine the why part too deeply. "Why did you say you love me? You don't. You don't even like me. It's just physical. Lust because of the mating bond. A primitive response that you can't control. If you had your way, you wouldn't be with me." The words wouldn't stop. "I'm not the mate you would have chosen. I'm just the one you got stuck with. You don't want—"

He was stalking forward. His face had gone cold and hard. Deadly.

She kept talking. "You don't want someone like me. I will put hexes on people I don't like. I'll do magic even when you tell me not to cast spells. I will dance on the graves of my enemies because I think it's fun. I will—"

"I love you."

"No, you absolutely don't. You shouldn't say things like that. Sure, it might have looked scary when I was all bleeding and unconscious, but don't make some big, dramatic declaration that you don't mean. Don't *lie*. I don't like lies, unless I'm the person telling them, I don't—"

"I love you." He was right in front of her.

"*Stop* lying."

He caught her arms and pulled her close. "I'm not lying."

"You can't love me. You *shouldn't* love me. Don't do it. I'll hurt you. I'll make you wish you'd never met me."

"Impossible. Life didn't even get fun until I met you."

He wasn't being serious. "Let me go."

"No."

She twisted, trying to jerk free, but he held her tight. Didn't hurt her, he'd never physically hurt her, but he didn't let go. "*Why?*"

He smiled at her. "You don't need to be scared."

Her chin notched into the air. "I'm not scared of anything."

"Yes, you are." He stared into her eyes. "You're scared that I love you."

She wanted him to stop saying the *l-word*. To just stop.

"But when you're watching your mate bleed out, when her blood is on *your* hands and you're praying that she'll open her eyes, that she'll come back to you, that you'll hear her sweet cackle one more time—"

"I *don't* cackle."

"Things come into perspective for you. You realize you'd trade everything you had, you'd give up your kingdom, your beasts, *anything,* if it meant she'd be okay."

Her body stiffened. "Tell me you didn't."

"I would give anything for you."

"*Tell me* you didn't!" She'd healed too fast. Oh, no. "I'm not worth your kingdom. Or your beasts. I'm a witch who will turn on anyone and everyone near her. Some days, I'm not even sure I'm sane. So you tell me...tell me right now that you did not make a deal with Leo. You didn't give him your kingdom for me. You didn't give up your beasts for me. I can't let you give them up! I won't." She'd work magic. She'd get it all back for him. "I'll get it back," she promised before Griffin could respond. "I think I'm strong enough. I'll take out Leo. Never liked him anyway, I was more of a Luke fan. I'll get everything back for you. I can do this, I swear, I can!"

Silence.

Griffin kept staring at her. Watching her with a too intense gaze.

She clamped her lips together so she wouldn't yell at him to *say something!*

"I think you love me, too."

Her body iced. She wanted to deny his words. She had to deny his words. "I don't love anyone."

He smiled. Flashed his sharp canines. "You should be a better liar."

No. *No.* She would not love him. It would be a mistake. He'd turn on her, the same way that Tomas had turned. The way Devon had turned. She was the monster. Everyone turned on her. And she turned on them. She didn't want anyone close. Not Griffin. Especially not Griffin.

"I love you," he said again, and he sounded so sincere. He needed to stop that shit. "But I didn't trade anything for you. I didn't make a deal. Leo didn't offer me one. You healed on your own. If you hadn't, believe me, Leo would own my kingdom now. Because you are worth *everything*."

He hadn't traded—

She surged toward him. Rose onto her toes and put her mouth against his. He hadn't entered into some kind of devil's deal with Leo. Griffin was safe. He still had his beasts. He was alive.

Because, while she'd never admit it to him, Valerie had been utterly terrified. When she'd realized those bullets were touched by magic, that they wouldn't stop until they were inside of Griffin, she'd freaked.

Just *freaked*.

She didn't want to imagine a world without her shifter. Without his slow, sexy grin. Without his growl. She even liked his dragon. His green scales were gorgeous.

So she kissed Griffin right then, overwhelmed with relief. Her mouth opened against his, and he thrust his tongue past her lips. The kiss was hot, desperate, and oh, so good. Her Griffin. In her arms. Strong and warm. Alive.

I love you.

She didn't know why he kept saying those words. He didn't mean them. Of course, he didn't mean them.

But...

Deep inside, very, very deep, she rather liked hearing them.

He lifted her up. His hands curled around her hips, and he stepped forward, moving so that her back was against the wall. "Ditch the clothes," he growled against her mouth.

That sexy growl.

"I need *in* you," he told her.

Oh, yes, sounded delightful.

Her fingers did a little shimmy. She ditched *both* of their clothes.

He was kissing his way down her neck. Licking and sucking. Biting lightly at the curve of her shoulder. She shivered against him. Confession...she loved his bite. It turned her on so much that her toes were curling. Her legs had wrapped around his hips when he lifted her up, and now that their clothes were gone, his heavy cock pushed at the entrance to her body. Pushed, but didn't enter.

Why wasn't he entering? She sank her nails into him, clawing a bit because she knew what her shifter liked. He gave a guttural groan, but he still didn't thrust. The head of his erection lodged between her legs, rubbing over her clit, and she knew he could feel her getting wet for him, getting even more ready with every second that passed.

But he wasn't in. "Griffin!"

"Look at me."

He wasn't kissing her any longer. Wasn't giving her those delicious bites. He gazed into her eyes, and she couldn't look away.

"I love you." He thrust into her. Filled her completely. "Never doubt it."

She—oh, damn, she could only feel. Feel waves of need and desire as he withdrew and thrust deep. He lifted her up, brought her down, and drove them both to the very edge with an increasingly wild rhythm.

His mouth went back to her neck.

Her nails dug into his shoulders.

Faster, harder, deeper.

She didn't try to slow him down. Why slow down? She just wanted to go faster. "Harder!"

He spun her away from the wall. Carried her across the room while he was still inside of her. Then he was tumbling her onto the bed. Moving her legs, lifting them higher so that he could go even deeper inside of her.

The climax hit her with a burst of pleasure so strong she couldn't even cry out. Couldn't catch her breath. The pleasure rolled through her, sweeping Valerie off in a maelstrom of feeling. Every nerve. Every cell. And the waves of pleasure just kept going and going.

He was with her. He thrust into her again, filling her with the hot blast of his release as he emptied into her body, and he called her name, a rough, wonderful bellow.

In the aftermath, Valerie heard the thunder of her heartbeat. She realized that her nails were still biting into his shoulders, and she made herself release him. He was on top of her, in her, and she didn't want to move.

Wouldn't it be wonderful to just stay there with him? To go again? Maybe a time or twenty more?

But his head lifted. He stared at her with his gleaming, green eyes. His dragon eyes. "I will never have enough of you."

That was nice. She didn't think...oh, damn, she'd never have enough of him, either.

He gave her a half-smile. "Don't be afraid."

"I'm not afraid of anything." But the words were too husky.

"Liar." He kissed her. "You're afraid to love me. But that's okay. I'm patient. I can wait for you to come around." Another kiss. "I can wait forever, if that is what it takes."

Her heart seemed to skip a beat. "Griffin—"

He withdrew from her. Her greedy, happy sex clamped around him, trying to keep him inside. He smiled at her. Not a half-smile this time. A full smile. His heart melting smile.

Not that her heart melted. It didn't.

Maybe thawed a bit...

A bird cawed.

She ignored the sea gull. Griffin stood near the bed. Her gaze swept over him. She wanted more. So much more.

But the bird cawed again. Louder. And she realized it wasn't a sea gull. Not this time. "Edgar?" She grabbed for the bedding. "Seriously? Privacy! It's a thing! And you're not supposed to be here. You're supposed to be watching Carmichael."

"Uh, are you talking to your bird? *Now?* He's got shitty timing."

Edgar flew closer to her. His cries were louder, more frantic. And they were *not* what she wanted to hear. "We'll be right there." She conjured clothes for herself and Griffin. Valerie bounded out of the bed even as Edgar darted back through the open window. She grabbed Griffin's hand. "We have to go."

He didn't move. "You just woke up."

"No, I woke up a few minutes ago. We just had awesome, mind-blowing sex."

His eyes seemed to sparkle.

"But now we have to go. According to Edgar, your brother is with Calliope and my friend is *dead*." Her hands were shaking. "I didn't think he was the one we needed to fear. Dammit, this shouldn't have happened! Enzo was going to take me to her. Enzo was going to help me."

"Only I killed him." A muscle flexed in Griffin's jaw. "And I'd fucking do it again."

"We have to leave. *Now*." She'd been pulling him toward the door but, hell, if they went downstairs, she'd probably run into Leo. Or worse, Mora. She didn't feel like having a heart-to-heart with Fate right then. "Do you trust me?"

Because Edgar had told her where to go. He'd given her the location of Carmichael *and* Calliope. She could cast a spell and be there in moments.

Griffin didn't answer her. Right. She swallowed. He didn't trust her. He'd been just bullshitting about the love bit, so, of course, he didn't trust her, he—

"I trust you with my life."

Her breath heaved out. "You should not do that. Really, don't. Way too much responsibility for me." Her fingers threaded with his. "But hold tight for now, okay? I promise, I won't let anything happen to you."

He was smiling at her as sparks began to dance in the air around them. Wind whipped through the room. His smile dimmed a bit. "Uh, Valerie—"

"Keep holding my hand. In just a moment, this will be over."

The wind howled.

The bedroom door flew open. Leo stood there, glowering. "*Valerie! What in the hell?*"

"Later, Leo!" *See you in hell.*

She and Griffin vanished.

***

The wind stopped howling. The world stopped shaking. And Valerie opened her eyes to find herself standing in the middle of a luxury condo. The place was totally high end. Marble tile. Leather couches.

A dead witch on the floor.

Calliope. Valerie let go of Griffin's hand and raced across the room. Calliope was sprawled on her stomach, with her hands spread at her sides. And Calliope wasn't alone. Carmichael knelt beside her. His hands were fisted, and fury had etched deep lines onto his face.

"What did you do?" Valerie yelled at him.

But she knew, already. Edgar had come to her. He'd been following Carmichael. The shifter had led her bird right to this high-rise condo. And right to Calliope.

"Poison," Carmichael whispered. He opened his hand, and she saw the small dart that he held. "The same poison Griffin used on the witch who killed our parents." His gaze lifted, and he stared straight at Valerie. "She's dead. She's *gone.*"

CHAPTER TWENTY-ONE

Valerie lunged for Calliope's still form. Griffin knew what she intended, and he grabbed her, pulling her against his body and holding her tight. "You're not bringing her back."

"Let me *go!*"

He just held her tighter. "I won't let you do it. You went through hell when you pulled Rio back, and I can't let you do it again."

She jabbed her elbow into his chest. "It's Calliope! She's my *ally!*"

"An ally who sent vampires with fucking magical bullets after us. That's not the kind of ally you can trust." His arms wrapped around her stomach. "Baby, *no.* I can't watch you suffer. I can't."

Carmichael stared at them both, his head cocked to the side, a furrow between his brows. "Was that story true? She actually brought Rio back from the dead?" He rose to his feet. Threw the dart to the floor. "Thought that was just embellishment BS. Something to make her rep even stronger."

Sparks danced around Valerie's fingers. "Let me *go.*"

Griffin wasn't going to risk her, he wasn't—

She vanished from his arms. Reappeared right next to Calliope.

Fucking hell. "*Valerie!*"

She crouched and carefully rolled Calliope over onto her back. Valerie put her hand against Calliope's neck.

Griffin lunged for Valerie, but before he could get to Valerie, Carmichael had yanked her to her feet. "You can bring her back?"

She sent a bolt of electricity right at him. He flew across the room and slammed into a wall.

"If she hasn't been dead too long, I can damn well try. Then I'm going to kill you. I don't care if you are Griffin's brother. Shit, *shit*. I didn't even have you on my suspect list." She swiped a shaking hand over her cheek. "Why weren't you on my list?"

Griffin put his hand on Valerie's shoulder, fully expecting her to send a bolt of lightning through him, but she didn't. She shuddered. "She was my friend. I don't have a lot of those."

They needed to talk about the definition of friend. It *wasn't* someone who sent a vamp with magic bullets after you.

"I didn't kill her." Carmichael was on his feet. His hands were loose at his sides. "I love her. And if you can bring her back, please, do it. I will give you *anything* to bring her back."

Shock rolled through Griffin. "What?"

"You're not the only one who fell for a witch, brother." Carmichael didn't take his grief-stricken gaze off Calliope's still body. "I thought it was wrong. I tried to fight the attraction because of our parents. Dammit, she's the reason I came home. I thought if I stayed away from Calliope, I'd be safe. The need, the hunger I felt for her would go away." His claws burst out. "But I just left her unprotected. I let her *die*." Carmichael bounded across the room. Stopped right in front of Valerie. Didn't make the mistake of touching her this time. "I will give you *anything*, just bring her back. Please. I can't live without her. I have to get her back."

"No." Griffin's immediate denial. "Not happening. It hurts you too much, Valerie. You *aren't* bringing her back. You can't."

She glanced at him with a sad smile. "Don't remember asking permission."

"I *won't* let you do this. Her bullets almost killed you hours ago, and you're going to bring her back from death? Why? Why the hell would you do that?"

"Because when I escaped from Salem, when I had no one and nothing, Calliope hid me. She gave me food and shelter, and she made sure I survived the winter."

"She's gone. You'll hurt yourself if you try to bring her back." Frustrated fury twisted his guts. Valerie couldn't bring back everyone. Didn't she see that? "Monsters rip you apart while you sleep. Every time you bring someone back, it gets worse, doesn't it?" His suspicion, but when she flinched, Griffin knew that he was right. "Baby, *no*."

"I have to try. I need her. I can't defeat Devon and Genevieve without her."

"Fuck them." He meant that. "Come back to my world. You'll never need to know fear or pain again. I'll protect you. I swear it."

She shook her head. "You can't protect me from what's inside myself."

"Valerie—"

But she was staring at Carmichael. "If you really didn't poison her, if you want her back, then you have to keep Griffin away from me. Don't let him stop me."

No. This wasn't happening. "Nothing will keep me from you."

Her smile flashed and never lit her eyes. "I'm really hoping your brother can, at least for a few moments."

Before Griffin could say anything else, Carmichael attacked him. His brother slammed into him, and Carmichael's claws went straight for Griffin's throat. The sonofabitch had always fought dirty.

Too bad for Carmichael...Griffin fought *dirtier*.

***

Howls and snarls filled the air behind her, but Valerie didn't glance back at Griffin and his brother. If she did...*no. Don't.*

She had to focus on Calliope. She hunched over the other witch. Calliope's body wasn't moving at all. She was still and cold, just like stone.

Just like stone.

Valerie blinked. Something nagged at her mind, but her fear pushed her forward. She began to chant, calling up the dark power that would let her cross over and bring Calliope back. She could find her friend and get her out, she could—

Nothing happened.

The magic pulsed in the air, but nothing happened.

"Something is wrong!" Valerie screamed.

The howls and the snarls were silenced behind her.

"I just have to try harder." She pushed out a breath. Dug deeper. Grabbed onto the power resting so heavily inside of her. She'd cross this threshold. She'd find Calliope.

Flames burst over Valerie's skin. Pain knifed through her, and she screamed. Pain was part of dark magic. Pain was part of power. So she pushed through. She pushed—

"I'm sorry." Griffin's voice. And...

Something locked around her right wrist.

Then her left.

Something cold. Something...something that immediately had the flames dying and a cold chill sliding through her body.

Valerie blinked. She stared at her wrists. Two golden bracelets adorned with diamonds. One bracelet around each wrist. Beneath the diamonds, she could see the faint etchings. *Spell.* "No." Betrayal was there, gutting her. This couldn't happen. Griffin wouldn't do this. He *couldn't*. She shoved at the bracelets, but they bit into her skin, sinking deeper the more she struggled. "What have you *done?*"

"The only thing I could do! Dammit, *listen—*"

Wind whipped through the room. Too much wind. Too strong. Not her wind. Not her magic. Because Valerie's magic had been bound.

In a blink, Devon was there. Standing right beside Calliope's body. He had a satisfied smile on his face as his gaze fell to the bracelets circling Valerie's wrists. "Excellent job, assassin. I knew I could count on you."

No, no, this *wasn't* happening.

She spun to face Griffin. Valerie glared at him as betrayal raged and twisted inside of her. "Why did you do this?"

"Valerie—" Torment flashed on his face.

"Because I hired him," Devon announced. "Because he had to get past your guard. Because you had to trust *someone,* and with your track record, I knew it had to be a lover. You only let your lovers close. Close enough to kill."

Griffin shook his head. "I couldn't let you try to bring her back, Valerie. I was protecting—"

"Protecting the shifters," Devon cut in. "Because they are what matters most to him. Not some deranged witch. And, don't worry, Griffin, I'll stick to our deal. As soon as she's dead, I'll make sure the bond is severed. You'll stay sane, and you'll be able to find your real mate."

Behind Griffin, she saw Carmichael struggle to rise. Blood poured from the wounds on his body. Wounds made by Griffin's claws.

Devon snapped his fingers, and Valerie was at his side. Because *he* could work magic. He wasn't bound. "I've missed you," Devon whispered in her ear.

Griffin lunged forward.

Devon snapped his fingers again.

Griffin seemed to slam into an invisible wall. "What in the fuck?" His fist pounded against that wall. "*Valerie!*"

She had to blink away tears. "Do you know what you've done?'

Griffin's eyes were desperate. "*Valerie!*"

Griffin had put the binding bracelets on her. Only Griffin would be able to take them off. And she doubted that Devon would ever let him get close enough to do that. She swallowed the lump in her throat. "You killed me."

Giant, scaled wings burst from Griffin's back. "*Valerie!*"

"Say good-bye," Devon murmured.

Her gaze fell to Calliope's body. So still. A perfect statue. Statue! Valerie knew this poison. Hadn't she deliberately fashioned her blood to create a similar, paralyzing impact on vamps? And she'd gotten the inspiration for that poison from a very specific source. "Get Stefan!" Valerie yelled. "Carmichael, Stefan can help—"

The condo disappeared. Calliope's body disappeared. Griffin disappeared.

Her whole life disappeared.

***

"Valerie!" Griffin's bellow had cracks racing across the ceiling. One moment, Valerie was there, staring at him with her eyes too big and dark, with her skin a stark white, and the next, she was just gone.

"What did you do?" Carmichael's grim voice demanded.

Griffin couldn't move. He felt rooted to the spot. Valerie had just been there. She'd been standing right there.

"*What did you do?*"

"She was burning. The room was burning around her. I...I had to stop her." He'd been choking on fear. "She almost died on me hours before. I wasn't going to lose her." The damn bracelets had been in his pocket. He'd fought off Carmichael. Grabbed Valerie and—

"You sonofabitch. You were *working* with Devon?"

Griffin spun around to face Carmichael. "No. He...shit, he gave me the bracelets but—"

"You *bound* her magic. Do you know what that does to a witch? She's helpless. Human. Devon can do anything he wants to her. And guess what he's going to want to do?" Carmichael scooped Calliope into his arms. "He's going to kill her. Hell, she's probably already dead."

The fuck she was.

Carmichael turned for the door, holding his witch carefully in his arms. "I'm going for Stefan. I recognize his name. I met him at Daybreak shortly after you kicked my ass out of our home. Maybe he can help Calliope."

She's probably already dead.

More cracks spread across the ceiling. His heartbeat seemed to thunder in his ears. He'd been so desperate. Fire had been shooting from Valerie's fingers, from her whole body, and he'd seen claw marks slice open her back. She hadn't even seemed to be aware that *something* had been ripping her open. She'd kept chanting, her voice getting weaker and weaker, and he'd just wanted to protect her.

But Devon had been there. Devon had been waiting.

"A trap." His voice was guttural. "Calliope was a trap. Devon wanted Valerie to find her, to try and bring her back." Because when Valerie was weak and distracted, Devon could attack. "The fucking sonofabitch."

Valerie's flames had broken the glass in the condo. Shattered all of the windows. A black raven flew inside. Went right for Griffin's eyes.

"Stop it!" He swatted away the bird. "I'm getting her back! I'm—"

The bird flew for the window, only to then circle and rush back at Griffin.

Her familiar. A very pissed familiar.

Carmichael was gone. He'd taken his witch out. Held tight to his dead witch. *I should have held tight to my witch.*

Griffin could feel his mind starting to splinter. Valerie had stared at him as if he'd betrayed her. He had. He'd been fucking desperate, and he'd betrayed the woman he loved. Fuck!

The raven came for his eyes once again. Griffin dodged, and the raven flew toward the window once more. This time, the raven cawed. Loud. Long. Desperate.

Griffin's eyes widened. *He keeps coming for my eyes...because the little bastard either hates me or there is something he wants me to see.* "You know where he took her, don't you?"

A caw. That had damn well better be bird for yes.

"Take me to Valerie. *Now*."

The bird took to the sky. Griffin let his transformation sweep over him. It was dark outside. No moon hung in the cloud-filled sky, so maybe that would help. Maybe the humans below wouldn't notice the enraged dragon flying across the night sky.

But even if they did notice, he didn't give a damn. His mate was missing. His witch was gone. And if he had to tear apart the world in order to get her back, he would.

CHAPTER TWENTY-TWO

Another day, another dungeon.

Her luck was shit.

"If you want to kill me, you shouldn't lock me up. That's like...a fatal mistake."

Devon glowered at her words. "If I had my way, I would have slit your throat right in front of your shifter."

Well, wasn't he the bloodthirsty one? "And *I'm* supposed to be bad?"

"Genevieve wants to make an example of you. The other witches need to see that the council is the highest authority. That there *is* no one stronger. Certainly not a witch on her own."

"Ah...so that's why you killed Hurst, Fiona, and Calliope. You figured if I had my own coven, I'd be too strong to stop. Even with these beauties." She banged her bracelets together. "Probably right, by the way. My coven would have found a way to free me from these stupid bracelets."

He laughed. "Hard for the dead to help you."

Her lips curved. "Don't be too sure."

He stepped closer to the bars of her cell. "It didn't have to be this way."

She gave a disgusted sigh. "Okay, look, I'm in a dungeon, I'm really pissed at my shifter *ex,* and I am not in the mood to listen to some sob story about how everything could have been different. The whole world would have been different if I'd just—what? Not fallen in love with a human? Stayed in good witch line and followed orders?"

"*Loved me.*"

What?

"I was right in front of you, Valerie. And you never saw me."

He was right in front of her then, separated only by the bars of her cell. She could see him perfectly.

Devon's smile was pure evil. Damn him. "Guess you see me now." He held her gaze a moment longer. Then he vanished.

"Devon!" she screamed his name. "Get your sorry ass back here! *Devon!*"

But he didn't appear. And she was trapped in some dank, dark dungeon. She could smell death and rot all around her. It was hell. Or, well, close to it. Valerie had the feeling she'd be seeing the real deal very soon. Like as soon as Genevieve managed to organize a public enough execution. With the bracelets around her wrist, would fire take Valerie out this time? She didn't know, and she certainly didn't want to find out in a terrible, burning way.

She was so fucked.

And the thing about this whole situation that sucked the most...her heart hurt.

Valerie rubbed her hand over her chest. It *hurt.*

Because Griffin had said he loved her. Then he'd locked binding bracelets around her wrists.

***

"Stefan!"

When he heard the roar of his name, Stefan stiffened. His gaze was on the sad remains of his club. Not much left of the place now. Because of one angry ass dragon. "We're closed," he snapped. Humans were still buzzing around the scene. Like they were going to do something with their official looking uniforms and their red fire trucks. "Get lost."

"Valerie sent me."

Now he did turn around, and Stefan felt relief sweep through him. "She's alive? I knew she—" He was staring at a guy holding what looked to be a dead woman. A guy who'd visited his club before—*a shifter.* "Are you freaking insane?" He grabbed the fellow's arm and shoved him—and his dead chick—into the nearby shadows. "Human cops are everywhere! And you're going to bring me a dead woman? Go bury her and get the hell away from me."

But the man didn't move. Jaw locking, he gritted, "Valerie sent me to you. You can't turn me away."

Stefan's nostrils flared. "You smell like a shifter." He'd noticed that during the guy's first visit to Daybreak. The fellow smelled just like a too-familiar shifter. "Is the dragon with you?"

"No, I don't know where my dumbass of a brother is. He betrayed Valerie and then—dammit, stop!"

One of Stefan's snakes had just lunged for the fool. "Griffin betrayed Valerie?" He'd thought...no, he'd *hoped* the shifter loved her. Valerie needed someone to love her. She deserved for someone to love her.

Not that Stefan had ever made the mistake of telling her that.

"Griffin put some kind of magic bracelets on her wrists. She stopped being able to cast spells, and then that dick Devon took her away."

Not good. Stefan's snakes hissed. "One bite from a snake," Stefan warned him, "and you'll turn to stone. You won't be able to breathe. Won't be able to move. Your heart will stop. But you will feel *everything* that happens to you. My venom can take down anyone. It will take down you, your brother, it will—"

"A witch?" the shifter asked, voice tight. "Can it take down a witch?"

"Yes." He'd use his snakes on Devon. He'd track the fool, let his snakes attack, and he'd free Valerie.

"I think...I think someone used it on Calliope."

Calliope.

Finally, Stefan glanced at the witch in the man's arms. Hellfire, it *was* Calliope. Lying as still as death. As stone. She was as beautiful as always, her hair long and thick, her skin a smooth ebony, her cheek bones high and sharp. But there was no life to Calliope. No spark. "I...didn't do this."

"No, someone fired a dart at her. One laced with poison."

Someone had shot her with Medusa venom? Impossible. Yet...

"Can you heal her?"

He pulled the witch from the shifter's arms. With a hiss, Stefan let his fangs slide out.

"Fuck, man, are those *snake* fangs in your mouth? And what is up with your eyes?"

If Medusa venom was holding Calliope immobile—frozen, not dead but not quite alive, either—then a bite from Stefan would wake her up. Only he could heal those who'd been poisoned by the venom of his snakes. He put his mouth to Calliope's throat. Bit.

She moaned.

It *had* been Medusa venom that took her out. Oh, hell.

Calliope shivered. "Wh-where am I?"

Stefan lifted his head.

She blinked at him. "Stefan?" Her head turned. "Carmichael?" A smile came and went, lighting up her eyes. "You came back? I thought you weren't, I thought—"

The one she'd just called Carmichael pulled her away from Stefan. The shifter held her as tightly as he could. Stefan easily read the expressions crossing the face of the shifter called Carmichael. Relief. Love. Desperation.

He gave them a moment. After all, Stefan had a heart, even if legend said it was encased in stone. He tapped his foot, waited and then... "Ahem."

Carmichael lifted his head.

Stefan smiled. "Hi. Remember me? The one who just saved the day?" Dammit. He almost sounded like Valerie. Her traits had rubbed off on him over the decades.

Calliope gave a weak laugh. "That sounds like something Valerie would say."

Carmichael stiffened. And his expression went straight to—*Sorrow*.

Stefan tried to keep his snakes under control. "Where is my witch? Tell me everything again. Very slowly."

"Devon has her," Carmichael said, voice grim. "She...Valerie was trying to help Calliope. Trying to bring her back from the dead."

"She wasn't dead," Stefan cut in. "Obviously. Just petrified. Big difference."

Carmichael nodded. "One that Valerie eventually realized, but not before some crazy shit went down. Fire erupted from her, her skin was torn open as if invisible claws had sliced her—"

Yes, he'd seen that particular horror a time or two before. "She plays too hard with dark magic."

"My brother, Griffin, he was there. He went insane when he saw her pain, and he put these gold bracelets around her wrists."

Gold bracelets and a witch? Meant one thing... "He bound her?"

"Then Devon appeared. Did that witch vanishing thing and took her away, but not before Valerie told me to find you. I brought Calliope here as fast as I could."

In and out. In and out. Stefan tried to breathe and not go ballistic. "Where is your bastard of a brother right now?"

"Last I saw, he'd shifted into a dragon and was chasing after...um, a raven."

Stefan remembered a raven, one that had clung to the shoulder of Valerie's young henchman right before she'd whisked him away so he could stay with trolls.

"My brother *isn't* evil, so stop looking that way," Carmichael snapped. "He'd said something about Valerie nearly dying on him already, because of some magic bullets—"

Calliope gave a quick gasp, then muttered, "Oh, shit. My bad."

"So he might have overreacted with the bracelets," Carmichael continued doggedly, "but you didn't see the fire. Or the way her skin was *sliced* open. You didn't—"

"I've seen it before." And yeah, it was a nightmare to watch. His gaze darted to Calliope. "You know what Devon is going to do."

Her eyes were huge. "Public example. He'll want all of the other witches to see what happens when you try to overthrow the council."

Exactly. "Put word out with your witch contacts." He figured she had to have them. "Find out where the execution will take place." He spun around, heading for his car. He'd get reinforcements. Call in his own allies to help.

But Carmichael jumped in his path. "How'd you heal Calliope?"

He should probably answer that. "She'd been injected with venom from my snakes. My bite counteracted the venom. Simple."

"Devon is the one who injected her, right? I found a dart, like he'd shot it into her."

Probably exactly what he'd done.

"But my question..." Carmichael rolled back his shoulders as Calliope crept closer. "If it was *your* venom, then how did Devon get it?"

Stefan glanced between the increasingly angry shifter and the frowning witch. "Medusa venom has long been used on witches." He raised one brow. "It's what was used on the witch who killed your parents. Haven't you put the puzzle pieces together and realized the poisons are one and the same?"

Shock flashed on Carmichael's face. Okay. Obviously, he was not the puzzle type. Squaring his shoulders, Stefan informed him, "*I'm* not the one who gave Devon poison. I haven't given anyone so much as a drop of my blood since the day a band of vampires attacked me and tried to drain me." Since he'd been a kid. "Want to know who sent those bastards after me way back when?"

"Devon," Calliope answered.

He nodded. "So it stands to reason that one of them gave him the blood. I thought Valerie had killed them all, but one bloodsucker must have escaped. And knowing Devon as I do, I'm sure he'll be using that poison on Valerie, too. Just in case the bracelets don't work."

Hope lit Carmichael's eyes. "They might stop working?"

It was Calliope who answered. Carefully, she explained, "Valerie is the strongest witch I know. If anyone can break them, it would be her."

She was the strongest witch Stefan had ever met. "So that's why Devon will dose her. He'll wait as long as possible because he doesn't want the other witches to know he has the poison. That's witch 101—never use Medusa venom on your own kind."

"I didn't know there was a witch 101," Carmichael muttered.

"There is. I'll give you lessons." Calliope never glanced away from Stefan. "If the others realize he's got the venom, they'll turn on him."

Stefan could see the plan spinning in her devious mind. He smiled at her. "I knew there was a reason Valerie liked you."

"And you." She inclined her head. "Tell me what you need."

"First, get me the location of Valerie's execution." He'd *already* said that, and the woman showed no signs of getting the intel. She needed to hurry that shit up. "And second, I'm going to need you to bring in a few people for me."

"People?" Carmichael shook his head. "No way, man. Humans are off-limits. They can't handle this—"

"Rio," Stefan announced, ignoring the clueless shifter. "He's the first one I need. The shifter boy Valerie raised from the dead."

Calliope nodded.

"Then I'll need a vampire named Magnus. The angry Scottish bastard has to pay his debt."

Carmichael frowned. "A vamp? I thought you *hated* vamps."

"I do. So does Val—most days. But once, Magnus was dying, and a beautiful witch saved him."

Carmichael just shook his head. "Why?"

"Because that's what she does." Stefan tapped his chin as he figured out who else they should pull in for the battle. "We'll also need a djinn. Ellya is conniving as the day is long, so just get her here before she can trick you."

"Again...*why?*" Carmichael demanded.

Calliope smiled. "Valerie saved her life. She brought Ellya back from the dead."

Carmichael's worry was apparent. "It doesn't sound like she *should* have come back."

Maybe. Maybe not.

"You want them all here, don't you?" Calliope said. "Because Valerie would want them? For the end?"

She'd finally caught on. "Use a locator spell. Get them here. It's time for them to pay their debts." Because this was it. The end. Valerie wasn't going to die. Devon wasn't going to win.

Today was the day that the wicked, dark queen...well, it was his favorite witch's turn to rise.

***

"The only time he ever gave me jewelry," Valerie lamented as she glared at her wrists, "and it was to bind my ass." Not romantic. Not awesome.

And her chest still ached. She kept having to blink because her vision was all blurry. She was hunched on the floor, her head bowed like she'd suffered some great and tragic loss, and this was *not* her.

Her hands slapped against the stone floor. She wasn't the type to give up. She never gave up. So she needed to think shit through.

She couldn't pry the bracelets off her wrists. Only the person who'd put them on her could remove them, so the story went. That meant she had to find another way, another—

The ceiling caved in—no, it crashed in. Valerie gave a sharp cry and her hands flew over her head as she tried to protect herself from falling debris. From stone. From dust. From whatever hell else was raining down on her. Smoke seemed to fill the cell.

Smoke?

Heavy, oppressive silence settled around her. The place was as dark as a tomb. *Ha, so fitting.* Even with her enhanced vision, she couldn't see anything in the darkness. She couldn't see anything except—

Glowing, green eyes.

Her breath caught.

"My...my..." His voice came out of the darkness. Deep and gravelly, more beast than man. "What beautiful eyes you have..."

She scrambled back. She couldn't see him clearly, but he could obviously see her perfectly. Only she didn't know if he was there to help or...Valerie cleared her throat. "My eyes...they make it easy for me to see what a lying asshole you are."

She heard the faintest tread of his footsteps. Or was that the scrape of claws? *Crap*.

"My..." His voice rumbled. "What a gorgeous mouth you have."

Her mouth pressed into a thin line. Did he think she didn't know what he was doing? She'd teased him this exact same way the first time they'd been in a dungeon together. "This shit isn't funny." She swiped at the stupid wetness on her cheek. "My mouth—it's this way so that I can tell you to go to hell."

A rush of wind battered at her. Valerie gave a quick scream, but he was already in front of her. His hands—tipped with claws—grabbed her. "Already there," Griffin rasped. "Been there, will be there forever...if I'm without you." Then his mouth crashed onto hers. He tasted like paradise. Like her every wish.

And her every bad dream. Because he was what she couldn't have. A taunt. A joke. She'd wanted a lover, a mate, a man who'd have her back and *always* choose her, no matter what. Only he hadn't been that guy. He'd been the one to bind her. He'd been the one—

Something snapped.

Shit. Was it her heart? Did a broken heart actually *snap*?

Valerie wrenched her mouth away from him. "You're free."

The bracelets clanged against the stone floor. Valerie flexed her wrists, twisting them around, and making sure this was real.

"I'm so fucking sorry."

He was warm and strong and solid in front of her.

"I couldn't stand to see you in pain. You were bleeding and burning, and I lost my *mind*."

Sparks danced around her fingertips, lighting up his face. Hard planes. Square jaw. Bright eyes. Testing herself, she fluttered her fingers, and jeans appeared on Griffin's body.

"I love you. I would give my life for you in an instant. I would do *anything*. But, Valerie, I can't watch you hurt. Your pain tears me apart. I just want you to be safe."

Her hand lifted. Her fingers touched his cheek. "You can't protect me from everything. I don't *want* to be protected from everything. I have to be able to fight my own battles."

"You don't have to fight them alone. Can't you see that? You *never* have to fight alone again. I will always be at your side."

Footsteps were racing toward them. Guards coming in fast.

"I love you," Griffin told her, his voice so deep and hard. "And I'll love you until I die."

"*Griffin!*" Devon's snarling voice echoed around them. "Get the hell away from her!"

Griffin put his body in front of her. He was protecting her, again. Valerie stood on her toes and peeked over his shoulder.

"You obsessed sonofabitch." Devon stood on the other side of the bars. "You just couldn't let her go, could you? I gave you a chance. I told you I'd break the mating bond, but you still flew here, determined to get her. Determined to save a witch who should have burned years ago."

A team of witch guards stood just behind Devon's glowering form.

"She can't get out." Devon gave an evil grin. "You think I didn't consider that you might fly to her rescue, shifter king? Here's the thing...you could get in, but she *can't* get out. This cell is witch proof. You try to take her out, and lightning will hit her body, the volts pumping through her over and over again. That particular punishment will also happen if you sprout your wings and try flying through the fucking hole you left in the ceiling or if you use your enhanced strength to try and break these bars. I made sure Valerie *can't* leave, not until *I* give the command." He straightened his shoulders. "I have the power here."

"You have nothing." Valerie moved to Griffin's side. She stared at her enemy and crushed the golden bracelets beneath her feet. "Soon everyone will know it."

He smiled at her. "You're dying at sunrise. I'm getting everything ready. It's almost time. The witches will see you fall. Then no one will ever try to question the council again."

Valerie peered at the guards behind him, then glanced back at Devon's gloating face. "Where is Genevieve? Don't you need to find her, and you know, ask permission for every single thing that you do?" She fluttered her lashes at him.

Devon slammed his hand against the cell bars. *"You're dead!"*

"Not yet." Valerie smiled. "I'm not."

Devon lifted his right hand. At that command, every guard stepped forward and aimed their weapons.

Griffin immediately leapt in front of her.

"*Stop* doing that!" Valerie snapped. It was a fatal flaw far too many were exhibiting and—

"The silver bullets in these guns are for him, Valerie," Devon told her with a satisfied smirk on his fat face.

She grabbed Griffin, used an enhanced strength no one had known she possessed— *another secret I have and, yes, I did lie about that one*—and she shoved him behind her back.

Griffin snarled.

But Devon just grinned. "Won't do you any good to take the bullets this time, Valerie."

And Griffin—damn him—had already moved to her side.

"Too many of them." Devon shrugged. "And all the silver bullets are bewitched to find their target. You can't block them all." His laughter rang out. "You see, this scene was a trap. And, you, Valerie, were the bait."

Valerie glanced at Griffin, her stomach tensing.

"I couldn't kill him back at Calliope's place. Not when it was just me. He was too strong. But I did learn from Calliope and that now dead vamp Enzo. They gave me a great idea. I just had to get Griffin in a confined space. Draw him in. And he'd be a sitting duck."

"Because he came for me," Valerie whispered. Oh, this was not good.

"I was curious, though..." Devon tilted his head as he studied Griffin. "Would he still be as crazy for you when your powers were bound? Had you put a spell on him?"

Her shoulders stiffened. "*No.*"

"Right. Of course, not. Because you wanted him to love you for yourself, didn't you? I figured that out. You always wanted someone to see past your wicked ways."

Griffin's stare was on her. Heavy. Considering.

Her gaze cut back to Devon. "You didn't put shit together. You had someone feeding you intel all along. You think I don't know *that?*"

"You were caught far too easily the first time I had you." Devon nodded, as if he'd gone over all of this in his mind, numerous times. The guards kept all of their weapons trained on Griffin. "You *wanted* to get caught, didn't you? So once I figured that part out, it made me wonder...why? And then I realized—"

"You realized you were an asshole. Check." Valerie was seething. And getting desperate.

Griffin caught her hand in his. Brought it to his lips. Kissed her knuckles. "He's going to be a dead asshole," Griffin promised.

A warm glow spread through her. A glow that calmed some of her desperation. Griffin could say the nicest things.

Devon's eyes turned to slits. "You let yourself get caught the first time because you wanted to be close to Griffin."

She smiled. "Did I? And here I thought putting me in the cell next to the big, bad dragon was *your* idea. Because you thought he'd toast me."

Spittle flew from Devon's mouth. "You already knew you were his fated mate, didn't you? That's why you allowed yourself to get caught, why you wanted to be in the cell next to his. You were fucking two steps ahead of me!"

"Um…" She squeezed Griffin's hand. "*Fated* may be the right word." She gave her mortal enemy a wide grin. "Have you talked to Fate lately, by the way? Because she is a fountain of information. I bet if you talked to her, she'd say something like…oh, I don't know…you're going to die at sunrise, burned by flames that are hotter than hell."

Devon glared.

Valerie kept her smile in place.

Then Devon pointed at Griffin.

Her smile faltered.

"The dragon's scales may very well be strong enough to stop the bullets, but he won't have time to change before the silver hits him…so I guess we'll never know for sure."

Bastard. Bastard—

"I could shoot him now. Let him die right in front of you."

"I'd just bring him back." Her chin lifted. "*Your* mistake." She could feel the sparks rising from her fingertips. Those wonderful sparks wrapped around her hand and Griffin's. "I can't get out, but I can work my magic *inside* this cell. If Griffin dies in here, then I'll just bring him back."

"But you'll be weak, won't you? Weak and helpless…" Devon's eyes gleamed. "So very easy to kill."

And that was his plan. To kill Griffin. To make her watch him die. She would save him and by saving him…

Well, guess my number will be up.

"Of course, you don't *have* to save him," Devon murmured. Sly as the devil. "You could just let him die. That way, you keep your power. And if you're strong enough, then maybe you can find a way to defeat me. To take over. To win in the end with some crazy plan that you probably have spinning in your head."

Valerie glanced at Griffin. His gaze was on Devon. Griffin's profile was so strong.

"I mean...he *has* betrayed you," Devin pointed out in a helpful tone. "Griffin slapped the binding bracelets on you, and come on, we both know that he had plans to ditch you as soon as he could. Griffin didn't want a permanent mate. When he first took you to the realm of the shifters, he wasn't going to sleep with you. He was going to cast you aside—"

Griffin's head turned. He stared into Valerie's eyes. "Do not save me."

Oh, no, he had not just said those words to her.

But Griffin wasn't done. "Don't even think of bringing me back. If their bullets kill me, you let me die. Our mating bond will end. You won't be hurt because witches don't react the same way to the bond as shifters do." His smile was heartbreaking. If she'd...had a heart. "That's why I never expected you to love me."

"She *can't* love," Devon threw in. "Dumbass."

"Stay strong," Griffin urged her. "Don't you dare fucking save me."

Valerie licked her lips. "You have..." Now she turned her head to focus on Devon and his goons. "You have incredible intel. Intel that I suspect a traitor gave you." She pretended to think about it even as her nostrils flared. "Griffin, do you smell that? It's not just witches here any longer..."

The soft tread of footsteps came closer.

She felt Griffin stiffen. Then *he* was lunging for the cell bars. She jumped in front of him. "No, don't give them what they want."

Rage.

Pain.

Death.

Griffin's eyes were burning with emerald fury, and his canines sprang to razor-sharp points.

She schooled her features and turned to face another foe. "Ah...you *were* on my suspect list. My top three, in fact. It feels good to be right."

The traitor glared at her. Then he lifted his claws—and Elliott rushed toward the cell.

CHAPTER TWENTY-THREE

Griffin hauled Valerie away from the bars just as Elliott's claw-tipped hands reached for her. Elliott strained, but the fool couldn't reach either of them.

Griffin glared at the man he'd considered to be his friend. "You sonofabitch. I'm going to make your death slow and painful."

Elliott snarled. His bear was close to the surface. Not close enough, though. "You fucked her. I knew you would. You came in, spouting BS about it just being a temporary mating, but I could tell the truth just by hearing the way you said her *name*. You were going to bring the witch into your life, into our lives, and you were going to keep her."

Hell, yes, he intended to keep Valerie forever.

Elliott had jerked his hands back through the cell bars. His body vibrated with fury. "I was at your side. For *years*. I was waiting, biding my time. I knew I'd have the chance to take over. I just had to wait long enough. Then she appeared. My moment. Finally."

"Uh, yeah," Valerie cleared her throat. "I'm not your moment. I'm not your anything." Her hand went to Griffin's chest. "I'm his."

Damn right she was.

"Told you," Valerie muttered to Griffin. "In my top three. He was too flirty. I mean, I'm awesome, but not that awesome. He was obviously trying to seem *too* friendly."

Elliott's face was changing. His jaw hardening. His nose flattening. The guy could barely contain his shift.

"You never had any real control." Griffin glanced over him in disdain. "You think you can rule all the shifters the way you are? Chaos, that's all you'll bring."

"No." A frantic shake of Elliott's head—his hair was getting thicker. "Devon has promised to help me. He'll give me—"

"A spell?" Valerie supplied helpfully. "And then you'll be able to keep your control." She made a *tsk, tsk* sound. "Oh, Devon, must you lie to everyone?"

Valerie didn't sound afraid. They were facing really shitty odds. Guns were trained on them. They were trapped in the cell. But his witch sounded brave. She was all but laughing in the face of death. And he had never loved her more. "You own my heart, love," Griffin told her. "And you always will."

Her gaze slipped toward him. "Griffin?" Her eyes widened.

"How sweet," Devon drawled. "And that is the perfect note we should end on." A pause. Then, "Shoot him."

"No!" Valerie screamed. "Don't, don't you—"

The bullets fired. Griffin pulled up his beast, calling for the dragon because he knew that he needed his strongest monster. Scales burst onto his skin. The bullets were rushing toward him.

"*Stop!*" Valerie screamed. Sparks flew from her fingers, hitting the bullets, but they didn't stop. They were all trained right on him.

Valerie leapt toward Griffin, but he wasn't going to let her take bullets meant for him. Hell, no. Not again. Not ever again. He grabbed her in his arms and twisted, shielding her. Hunching his back—

His wings burst out.

The bullets tore through them. The bullets ripped through his wings. They slammed into his back. Into his sides. Into his legs.

The gunfire sounded like firecrackers exploding, over and over again.

Then there was only silence.

"He's still on his feet." A hushed announcement that came from one of the guards.

Another demanded, "How in the hell is the bastard on his feet?"

Blood poured from Griffin's wounds. He could feel the burn of the silver inside of him. Griffin couldn't lift his head. It had sagged forward, but he felt his witch's fingertips tracing over his cheeks.

"You own my heart, shifter," Valerie whispered.

He forced his eyes to open. He was still shielding her with his body.

"And you always will." A tear leaked down her cheek. "I will bring you *back*."

He wanted to speak. Wanted to tell her how much he loved her, but his legs wouldn't hold him up any longer. He fell to the side and crashed onto the stone floor. Valerie fell with him, scrambling to hold him in her arms.

Darkness grew around him.

"Well..." Devon's grating voice rang out. "Guess we have a new shifter king in town. Congratulations, Elliott."

Elliott. His friend. His enemy.

Since Griffin had banished Carmichael, Elliott *was* the next in line to rule.

"I'll bring you back," Valerie promised again. Her lips pressed to Griffin's.

Funny. He couldn't feel her kiss any longer. He couldn't feel her at all.

Don't bring me back, baby. Don't. That was the only rule that mattered.

***

Griffin was dead.

Elliott stared at his friend's body. So many bullets had torn into Griffin. Too many to count. And they had *stayed* in his body. He could see the smoke rising from the silver bullets buried within Griffin.

Valerie was crouched beside Griffin's broken body, and tears streamed down her cheeks. She was whispering to him. Kissing his face. And he'd never seen such pain before. It seemed to ravage her.

Devon clapped his hand on Elliott's shoulder. "Was it everything you wanted and more?"

What? It was—he shook his head. What was happening?

Soft laughter reached him. Taunting laughter. Familiar, female laughter. His head turned. The guards moved back, and there *she* was.

Genevieve. His Genevieve. The witch who'd come to him months before. Offering him his every desire. Offering him a kingdom. If he'd just take it.

But Griffin is bleeding. Griffin is dead. And he was my friend.

Genevieve seemed to glide toward him. A faint glow lit her features. She looked more like a perfect princess than a witch. So heartbreakingly beautiful.

But...

Griffin was my friend.

And Elliott found his gaze sliding back to the cell. His head pounded. Something was wrong. Very, very wrong. "Griffin?"

Valerie's head snapped up. "I am going to rip you apart." She swallowed. "*After* I get him back."

Elliott's hands locked around the bars. "Griffin!"

Valerie's hair whipped around her face. She grabbed for Griffin, held him tight, held him close. His blood covered her as she chanted.

Deep claw marks ripped into her arms. Into her face. Fire burst around her.

"Quite the show," Genevieve murmured. "Do we really have to watch it? Can't we just poison her now? I mean, we *have* the Medusa venom."

Her perfume seemed to fill the air. Elliott's temples throbbed harder. His chest ached.

"I told you already," Devon sighed, "we need her weak. She'll bring him back, she'll be weak, and *then* we can take her out."

"The Medusa venom *will* take her out. It takes out every witch." Annoyance snapped in Genevieve's voice as she stroked her hand over Elliott's arm. "We just need someone to go in that cell and dose her. She's distracted right now. It's the perfect opportunity." Her fingers slid to his cheek. "Elliott, darling..." She smiled at him. "Take this poisoned knife. Go in that cell and plunge it into Valerie's back. She's distracted, and she won't see you coming."

Valerie's body was being clawed by something, but she was still clinging tightly to Griffin. Holding him as if she'd never let go.

Because she loves him.

"Elliott, did you hear me?"

His gaze slid back to Genevieve.

"Plunge the knife into her back." She pushed the knife into his hands. "Devon and I can't go into the cell. If we do, the magic will trap us, too. No witch can enter. That's why it has to be you."

He shook his head. It hurt. Everything *hurt*.

But he was shuffling toward the cell. She'd opened the door for him. He stepped inside.

Blood. So much blood.

And why was he going to stab Valerie? Why?

"Do it for me," Genevieve called out. "Because you *love* me."

Right. He loved Genevieve. He stumbled forward. The flames around Valerie burned his arms, but Elliott didn't care. He had one goal. Valerie's back was to him. She was right there.

She was...

Fighting to bring back Griffin.

Because she...loved him?

What am I doing?

"I think your love spell is breaking," Devon's voice seemed overly loud. Worried.

"My spells don't break," Genevieve snapped back. "He's done everything I asked, hasn't he? And he'll put that knife in her back. He *will* do it."

Elliott was lifting the knife. He didn't want to lift the knife. He wanted to drop it. He wanted to help Griffin. He wanted to stop Genevieve.

Because he didn't love her. He'd...thought he did. He'd thought she was his mate. That they would have a life but—

Spell.

"V-Val..." Elliott tried to speak her name, even as his hand kept rising.

She didn't look back at him. She was too intent on Griffin. Far too intent.

"V-Val..." *Please, look at me.*

And she did. She whirled toward him, surged up—and the knife sank into her shoulder. Her lips parted as she gasped. As she shuddered. Then she fell. Just fell right there, her body as stiff as a board. Her eyes were wide open. She stared straight at Elliott's face.

And a tear slid from her eye.

"She's out!" Genevieve's voice shouted. "Get her!"

The witch guards rushed into the cell. Guards who'd shot a shifter with magic bullets. Guards who grabbed Valerie and dragged her stiff body out of the cell. Elliott turned to follow them, his body lurching as he thought...*I can get her. Stop*—

Genevieve slammed the cell door shut. "Darling, he might wake up."

Griffin was dead. Lying in a pool of his own blood.

My friend.

"I lied about no witch being able to enter the cell. Sorry. I was just afraid Valerie might kill whoever entered. You were expendable."

He'd stabbed Valerie. His shifter king was dead.

Genevieve gave him an admonishing glare. "I don't know if she finished the spell or not. You took your sweet time stabbing her."

Valerie.

Valerie cackled when she laughed. And when she looked at Griffin, when she thought no one was watching, her eyes would light up.

"Take this gun," Genevieve ordered as she shoved it through the cell doors. "It has bewitched silver bullets in it. When you aim at the target, it *will* sink into the prey, no matter what. Aim for Griffin's heart. Just in case, you know. Wait and see if he wakes up, and if he does...shoot."

He pushed against the cell door. It was locked.

She smiled. "I'll come back for you as soon as Valerie is gone. You haven't killed her, you see. You just paralyzed her. That's what Medusa venom does. It paralyzes the prey. I'll kill her in front of the assembled witches so they can all see that I was always stronger than she is. That *I* was always meant to rule."

"You…" Why was speaking so hard? "Spell…"

"Oh, right. Of course, I put a love spell on you. How else would I have gotten you to do my bidding? You were drunk one night, hanging out at some human bar in Vegas. The alcohol made you easy pickings."

"Hurry up, Genevieve," Devon urged.

She gave Elliott an encouraging nod. "Make sure the shifter king stays dead. And you know what? You won't get me because, well, I'm not really into the whole beast thing, but I'll let you keep the shifter kingdom. How about that? We'll both win."

She was lying.

She was also leaving him. Trapped in the cell. With witch guards watching him. Witch guards who were probably armed with silver bullets. If Griffin came back and Elliott didn't shoot him, those guards would.

They'll shoot us both.

In moments, Genevieve was gone. Devon was gone. Valerie was—well, about to die.

Elliott shuffled back to his friend. Fell to his knees. "I'm sorry." His hoarse whisper filled the cell. "So fucking sorry."

Elliott lifted the gun. Pressed it to Griffin's chest. Tried to make himself squeeze that trigger.

And then Griffin opened his eyes.

CHAPTER TWENTY-FOUR

Griffin sucked in a deep breath as he felt his heart lurch. The beat became frantic and fast the instant he realized that a gun was pointed dead center at his chest.

"I'm sorry." Elliott's gaze was desperate. His expression shattered. "I can't stop...she's got me...under a spell. Didn't freaking realize it."

"Valerie." Where was his witch? Where—

"Not...her. So f-fucking sorry..." The gun was shaking. "I can't stop. Got to...break the spell. If I don't sh-shoot, they will..." He jerked his head toward the bars.

To the guards who waited there. Witches.

But where was Valerie?

"They're going to...kill her. I'm supposed to k-kill you." The gun was shaking even harder now, and Griffin realized it was because Elliott was fighting himself. "I don't want to kill you." His voice was barely a whisper. "I sure as shit never w-wanted to be king. That's...not me."

The gun barrel pressed harder into Griffin's chest. Blood was on the stones all around him. Griffin realized the blood was his own.

Valerie had brought him back. The only explanation. That meant she'd made herself weak. He had to get to her.

"Help me," Elliott pleaded. "I can't st-stop. Don't know what...what to do...bullet always finds its t-target—"

In that case...Griffin lunged up. In one move, he ripped the gun right out of Elliott's hand. The guards rushed toward the cell. He fired.

Once.

Twice.

Three times.

"You're right," Griffin studied the guards who had hit the floor. "The bullets did find their targets."

Elliott grabbed the weapon, only instead of trying to pull it out of Griffin's hand, Elliott pushed it against his own chest. "Kill me. I-I can't fight her spell. Won't stop. *Kill*—"

Griffin slammed the gun into the side of Elliott's head. When that didn't knock the guy out, he just pounded Elliott with his fists until the shifter was unconscious. "I'll deal with you later."

Power pulsed through Griffin's body. More power than he'd ever felt before in his entire life. He smashed the gun in his bare hand, turning it into dust even as his dragon's wings burst from his back.

Bigger, stronger than before.

He hadn't just come back from the dead. Valerie had made him even...better.

Gods, he loved his witch.

"I'm coming, baby." He looked above him. The gaping hole he'd created before was still there. He shot straight up. He'd find his mate. He'd save her. And he'd *kill* the ones who'd made the mistake of fighting against her.

Nothing would come between him and his mate.

You own my heart.

Nothing.

***

"Valerie Storm is guilty, and she must die!"

Valerie stared at the mob around her. A mob of witches. Really, how fair was that? Hadn't they learned any lessons over time? They'd once been chased by mobs—more than once—and now they were all eagerly chanting for her death?

They'd regret that choice when she ruled them all.

"Tie her to the post!" Genevieve blasted as she stood in front of Valerie. "Tight! The fire will judge her!"

No, it wouldn't. Genevieve was going to be in for a really harsh surprise there. The fire wouldn't do a damn thing.

Devon stood to the side, watching all of this and looking all grim and subdued.

He was such a good actor. Unfortunately for him, that jackass was gonna be dying soon. Hadn't she promised him that he'd die before sunrise? The sun hadn't come up, not yet.

A raven let out a loud cry.

If she could have, Valerie would have smiled. But a smile wasn't allowed. Not then. No movement at all was allowed.

"She's one of us!" The faint cry came from the crowd. And it was a familiar voice. One she knew so well. Yet Valerie couldn't turn her head to look for the witch. "Why does she burn?" the witch demanded.

Fury flashed in Genevieve's eyes. "Bring out the witness!"

Ooh, a witness? Now this was just getting even better.

Wind blew against Valerie's skin. She would have shivered but—*can't*. Maybe she should have felt afraid right then, but she didn't. She'd worked her magic on Griffin. She knew that she had. And any minute, she expected to see him rushing to her rescue.

She'd let him save her. Just this once. It would be good for his self-esteem.

Genevieve leaned toward her. "I see hope in your eyes. You think the dragon is coming for you? Think the hell again. I left Elliott with him. Elliott, by the way, is under *my* love spell. You might not have felt like working that particular charm, but I've always found it beneficial. He'll do anything I say." Her voice carried only to Valerie. "And I told him to stay in that cell. If Griffin so much as twitches, Elliott will put a bullet in his heart." Genevieve leaned back. All satisfied and smirky. "Oh, sorry, are you *crying?*"

A tear had slipped down her cheek.

"I don't see any witness!" the witch from the crowd called out. "We shouldn't burn our own! That's not—"

"Here's the witness!" Devon's voice boomed. Devon approached Valerie, with a male at his side.

She couldn't turn her head to view the male but something about his scent was striking a chord in her memory.

Something—

The male moved in front of her. Glared. Glared at her with bright, blue eyes. *Bright eyes. Dark, chestnut hair. A face that hadn't aged at all, even though centuries had passed since she'd last seen...Tomas.*

"The witch cursed me!" Tomas yelled. His gaze blazed. "I was a human, but she turned me into a monster. I don't age! I don't die!"

Really? He was bitching because he'd somehow gotten immortality? She didn't remember giving him that particular bonus. If she hadn't given it to him, then someone else had. Her money was on Genevieve.

"I burned you once," Tomas told her as he jerked a torch from Devon's hands. "And I'll do it again." He lunged toward Valerie and shoved the torch against her shirt. It caught fire quickly, burning and—

More wind whipped against her. Fierce, angry wind. Wind that knocked that little flicker of fire right out. She heard a roar. Such a powerful, unearthly cry, and then angry balls of flame were shooting down from the sky. Red and orange flames that didn't come at her, but instead were directed at the enemies who'd wanted her dead.

"He's alive?" Genevieve ducked for cover. Cover that she took by hiding behind Valerie's body. "Kill the dragon! Kill him!"

Dragons weren't easy to kill.

Tomas hadn't jumped for cover. He stared at Valerie with eyes that glittered with hate. "You showed me magic. Then you went away." He still had the torch in his hands. Tomas bared his teeth at her, and Valerie saw that he now sported fangs.

Well, that explains the immortality. Only he was blaming her for something she'd never done. She hadn't made him into a vamp. That particular sin couldn't be placed at her door.

A knife pressed to Valerie's throat. "Shift, Griffin Bastien!" Genevieve screamed. "Shift back to human form or I will cut her throat. The blade is magic. She *will* die."

The dragon flew to the ground and landed with enough force to shake the earth. Then he began to transform.

"Attack him!" Genevieve yelled. "Kill the dragon—kill Griffin!"

Devon, of course, scrambled to do her bidding.

"And, you," Genevieve hissed in Valerie's ear, "you are—"

"*Now!*" Valerie bellowed as she stopped pretending.

Pretending to be paralyzed because of the venom.

Pretending to be helpless.

Valerie ripped through the ropes that bound her. She twisted her body and swiped the knife right out of Genevieve's hands.

"You...you're paralyzed!" Genevieve gasped.

"Of course, I'm not. I'm just a damn good actress." Valerie jerked her head toward the tall, tattooed man who'd snuck up behind Genevieve. "Medusa." That code word never got old.

Before Genevieve could turn to see her attacker, a snake sank its fangs into her throat.

She fell, her body as hard as stone.

"I'll deal with you soon enough." Valerie smiled down at her foe and—

Fangs sank into Valerie's throat. Not the fangs from a snake, but from a vamp. Tomas had bitten her. He savaged her neck, and she drove the knife back into his stomach. She stabbed him once, twice...

Tomas let her go.

He stumbled back, her blood dripping from his mouth. Horror widened his eyes.

Dizziness swept through her. "Bad move, Tomas. Very, very bad." Dammit, his bite was making her even weaker. She couldn't afford more weakness. She had to bluff her way through this shit. Bluff it when she felt human.

Tomas fell. His body jerked and shuddered.

He hadn't taken enough of her blood to die, not yet. But—

"Valerie!"

Her head whipped up. Griffin was there. Naked, sexy Griffin. He'd transformed from his dragon, and he was rushing toward her. As he shoved the crowd out of his way, Valerie caught sight of a familiar witch.

Calliope.

Calliope had been the one heckling Genevieve. As soon as she'd heard her friend's voice, Valerie had known there was still hope.

Calliope clapped her hands and clothing appeared on Griffin's body. A few foolish witches tried to attack him, but Carmichael lunged forward—Carmichael *and* Warren. They'd both been hiding in the crowd. They fought with claws and fangs, using their brute strength against magic.

The witches weren't used to fighting shifters and when the witches started to bleed, they also started to run.

"No!" Devon's guttural yell. One that echoed over the chaos. "You don't get to escape again."

Devon lunged toward Valerie. He'd grabbed the knife she'd used on Tomas. Valerie didn't even remember dropping it because so much shit had been going down. But he shoved toward her, and he plunged the knife into her chest. "You don't get to be happy with your shifter. You don't get to take away everything I've built."

The blade sank deep. She felt it slide into her. Devon stared at her with his enraged eyes, and she remembered another time. Another place.

When he'd held her back...When he'd stopped her from saving Tomas...When he'd changed all of their lives.

She could see his fury. His jealousy. He'd wanted her for himself, and he was one of those fucking twisted pricks. The kind that thought if he couldn't have a woman, then no one could.

"He'll never touch you again." Spittle flew from Devon's mouth. "You'll never have the power you wanted, you'll—"

A shifter's claws tore through Devon's chest. Ripped straight through it as his eyes widened in horror. Even though pain racked her body, Valerie smiled. "I could bring you back..." Her hand lifted. Touched his cheek. "But I fucking won't."

Griffin's claws jerked out of Devon's body. He fell, blood pumping from him. His body was jerking and twisting.

"H-help me!" Devon's pain-filled shouts drew everyone's attention. The leading council elder was dying.

Who would help him?

Valerie glanced down at her body. The knife was still in her. One that had been enchanted by Genevieve so it packed a deadly punch. If she pulled it out...*no, not going to think about that right now.* She knew what would happen when that knife left her. She'd seen Genevieve use this particular trick on other enemies. As soon as the blade stopped touching her body, Valerie would die.

"Baby?" Griffin reached for her. His claws were gone. His gaze was stark. Scared. His fingertips trailed over her cheek.

She turned her head and pressed a kiss to his hand. "I have to finish him." Did Griffin understand? It was her kill. Her time.

"Baby, you're...you're hurt badly."

She didn't want to think about how badly. "It's okay," Valerie lied. "If I die, I'll just bring myself back." Had he seen the vampire bite her? Did he realize how weak she truly was?

Don't show weakness. The witches watching wouldn't respect weakness. Only strength.

Her gaze slid around, searching for—

"Do you need this?" Rio's voice. Rio—her henchman was right there. He'd shoved through the crowd, and he bent to pick up the torch that Tomas had used to light Valerie on fire.

She took the torch from him. It wasn't lit any longer, and dammit, she didn't have enough power to even spark the flame. The first thing a witch learned was how to make fire, and she *couldn't*. If she couldn't make fire, the others would know—

Griffin opened his mouth and let out a breath of fire. The torch burned bright and hot.

She stepped toward Devon. Stumbled. But Griffin was right there. He caught her left arm. Rio took her right. They moved together until she was over Devon's body.

He glared up at her even as he put a hand to his gaping chest.

"How are you even still alive?" Valerie asked him. "Griffin should have taken your heart." She swallowed. "Guess you don't have one."

"Because...gave it to you...long ago. Only...y-you..."

Seriously? "Guess what? I don't want it."

He lunged up at her, but she shoved the torch down. The fire burst over him, taking him away, burning him in an instant until the only thing that remained of him was...ash.

"Was he supposed to burn that fast?" Rio whispered.

She still gripped the torch. Valerie wasn't sure she could let it go. "I...may have cursed him a long time ago. Made fire his weakness. If he ever got too close...bam."

Rio cocked his head. "How long ago?"

The day that Tomas had died. Well, his first death, anyway. Since he was a vamp, she knew he'd at least died twice.

"How long have you been planning all of this?" Rio's eyes were huge, as if he'd just realized that maybe...maybe everything that had happened had all been anticipated by her.

Almost everything had.

She eased out a hard breath. "Since the day my two *friends* stopped me from saving a human I loved."

Griffin stiffened.

Griffin was still at her side. Griffin was holding her up. Griffin had given her the fire she needed to destroy Devon. She turned her head and smiled at him. "It's always...you."

"Your neck is bleeding." Griffin's eyes were on her throat.

"Right. V-vampire bite."

His stare shot back to her face. "That knife is in you so deeply, baby."

Too deeply.

"R-remember what I told you...about vamp b-bites?" She was shaking.

Torment. Terror. She could so easily see what Griffin felt as he said, "You're as strong as a human."

Right then, yes, she was. She was living only because of sheer damn determination.

Stefan leaped from the crowd. Stood in front of her. "You're *not* dying." His words were a bellow.

Jeez, way *not* to keep a secret from the witches. From all the eyes that were watching and waiting to see who would come out as the winner in this battle.

"I brought your former henchmen." Stefan knelt before her. "I'm in your service. The helpless kid you saved when I was just ten years old."

The kid she'd saved...and the boy who'd helped her to become immune to Medusa venom so that she could fake her paralysis when the time came.

"And I'm in your service." A tall, golden skinned vampire flashed his fangs as he took his position near Stefan. Like Stefan, the vamp took a knee before her. Magnus. He'd never wanted to become a vampire, and he'd been half-mad from hunger when she found him. She'd helped him, given him her magic blood, made him stronger, and in turn, he'd helped her to eventually turn her blood toxic to vamps. Because Magnus had wanted to fight the bastards who'd made him. She'd been his weapon. Magnus had cut through the worst of the vampire dens, with her help.

"And I still owe you, witch." A woman with jet black hair and golden eyes appeared near Magnus. Whispers floated in the crowd because the witches could feel the magic pouring from her. A djinn. Ellya.

"It's been a...long time, Ellya," Valerie murmured. A murmur was kind of all she could manage.

Ellya didn't take a knee. The woman had never bowed to anyone or anything.

"A long time?" Ellya's smile was brilliant. "Yes, I guess it has been a long time...since you pulled a desperate djinn back from death, making her swear that she'd grant you one wish...any wish you wanted."

Yes.

"You planned this all, didn't you?" Ellya gave a quick nod. "I admire that. You knew you'd need me to heal you, if things went south in your big battle. Fine, I'll do it. I'll—"

"Cut the mating bond." There. She'd managed to do it. Managed to get out those desperate words.

Shock stiffened Griffin's body. "*What?*"

"I'm dying." She could feel Death clawing at her, from the inside out. "I've been dying for a very long time." A secret she'd kept. Now she made herself stare into Griffin's brilliant green eyes. Screw the audience watching. It was all over, and only he mattered. "From the first time I tried to trick Death. He's been trying to get me ever since. *That's* why I scream at night. *That's* why you see the claw marks that appear on my skin. A price has to be paid for the magic I used." She could barely talk. Her whole body was ice cold. "I'm the price."

"*No!*" Griffin thundered. "You are not dying! You're staying with me. If this woman can heal you—"

"The wicked ones don't get...happy endings." She'd always known that. "But you're...not like me. You shouldn't suffer when I'm g-gone."

"*Valerie.*"

She only had seconds left. She could feel it. Her head turned toward Ellya, and Valerie could have sworn the djinn had tears in her eyes. Impossible, of course.

Everyone knew the wicked didn't love. Didn't care.

But I love. I love Griffin.

"Cut the mating b-bond." If she didn't, Griffin would go mad when Valerie took her last breath. "I wish...to...*cut...*"

She didn't get to say anymore. Because the heart that had been struggling so very hard to beat, it just stopped.

When she fell, Griffin was still holding her.

And she could have sworn that she heard Death laugh with delight.

Yeah, bastard. Laugh it up while you can...I'm coming for you.

CHAPTER TWENTY-FIVE

He caught her as she fell. The knife clattered to the ground. Griffin scooped Valerie into his arms even as he bellowed his pain and anguish. Claws burst from his fingertips. Talon-tipped wings sprang from his back. Flames blew from his mouth—

"He's losing his mind," Carmichael yelled. "Cut the mating bond. *Cut it!*"

Griffin's head whipped to the right. He saw his brother staring at him with *pity* in his eyes. Carmichael clutched the hand of the witch, Calliope. *How was she alive?* And Calliope was crying as she stared at Valerie's still body.

"My debt will be paid..."

That was the other woman talking. The one Valerie had called Ellya. She lifted her hands into the air. Lightning crackled overhead.

Hell, no.

Griffin put his precious mate on the ground. Then he sprang for the woman who would try to sever their bond. "Don't even *think* it."

Thunder echoed.

"It was...her wish," Ellya snapped back.

"Screw that. You're not granting her wish." He could barely breathe. Pain was splitting him apart. "You're granting *mine*."

"I owe you no debt. I don't even *know* you."

"I'm her mate." His bones snapped. His muscles bulged. "And if you don't bring her back..."

"I *don't* respond well to threats!"

"I will destroy *everything!*" Didn't she see what was happening? He could barely keep his dragon contained. The beast was maddened. Suffering. Wild.

Ellya's smile was sad. "That's why she wanted the bond severed. To protect you. To protect everyone."

"I *need* her." There had to be a way. Had to be. He whirled back to Valerie. Her hair had fanned out beneath her. Her skin was too pale. Her body too still.

Devon had done that to her. He'd destroyed the most beautiful creature in the world. The strongest witch to ever walk the earth. The strongest. The most conniving—

His head whipped up. That was it. He just had to think like Valerie.

"I *have* to grant her wish," Ellya told him, voice tight. "I'm bound by my debt to her."

"She just said—the only words Valerie actually said were that she wished for you to *cut*." She hadn't finished her sentence. "So cut the tie—cut her tie to Death."

Rain fell down on them, erupting from the sky. A soaking wet raven flew down and landed on Griffin's shoulder. He lifted Valerie back into his arms, his desperate gaze on her face. "She's been linked to Death since Tomas died. He started it all. She said she *felt* him die."

Ellya bit her lower lip. "I'm not sure about—"

"I wish you'd cut her tie to Death! Cut the fucking tie!" It was a dragon's roar because he could not hold his control any longer. Valerie was gone. Cold and still in his arms. She was *gone*. And the world was going to suffer. There would be hell. He'd bring the fire and the destruction and—

"I cut her tie!" Ellya screamed.

The rain fell harder. Heavier.

Ellya ran forward, and she pressed her palm to Valerie's cheek. "I *cut* her tie with Death!"

A blast of lightning hit Valerie in the chest. Her body jerked. The force of the blast raced through Griffin's body, separating him from Valerie as it sent him flying back through the air and crashing into a crowd of gawking witches. The raven shot away from him.

Fire ignited from that blast, sweeping over Valerie's body. Consuming her.

"No!" Griffin heaved toward her.

But the flames had already died away.

Thick smoke filled the air.

Rio coughed.

"Witches burn so fast." Calliope's sad voice drifted to them.

Griffin's shoulders hunched. "Carmichael...lead our people." Each word was a struggle. "Get everyone else...out of here..."

Madness. The fate he'd always known he'd suffer without his mate. Because of one witch's curse so long ago. The witch who'd taken his parents. At just thirteen, he'd hunted her down. He'd used the poison on her, poison he now knew was Medusa venom. But before he'd given her the poison, she'd laughed and told him...

"When death takes your mate, you'll make this world into hell."

He was in hell. Without Valerie. Without her laugh, without her smile, without her incredible strength. Without *her*.

He had to get her back. Had to fight Death. Fight the witches. Fight anyone and everything. He'd find a way. He would not lose her. Not when he'd only just gotten her in his life. And he hadn't appreciated her enough when she'd been there. He wanted to go back, back to that first meeting in the dungeon. He wanted to tell her he'd love her forever. That she'd always be his queen, that she was—

All of the witches had lowered their heads. They weren't running away. They weren't whispering or even screaming. Everyone was dead silent.

"Hello, Griffin."

Shock rolled through him. Because the smoke had cleared away, and his witch stood there. She wore a fiery red dress, and she looked like the best sin in the world. Her dark eyes gleamed at him. A wide smile curved her lips as her dimples winked. "Did you miss me?" The raven on her shoulder let out a triumphant cry.

Griffin bounded toward her. He yanked her into his arms and held her tight.

"Guess what? I don't think Death liked having me around." Her arms curled around him. "Because he sent me back to you."

Griffin kissed her. His mouth slammed down on hers, and he kissed her like the absolutely desperate, delirious man that he was. He kissed her deep. He kissed her softly. He kissed her tenderly. He *kissed* her.

Valerie. Alive. Warm and soft. In his arms. With her wicked smile. Her dark and dangerous gaze. His mate.

His life.

He put his forehead against hers. "Ellya cut your tie with Death. That was the wish she made."

"Really? That was possible? Huh. I distinctly remember telling her to cut *our* bond."

"Don't ever pull that shit again."

Her smile faded. "I did it for you. I didn't want you to be in pain without me."

It hadn't just been pain. It had been hell. "You die, and you take my heart with you."

Her lower lip trembled. "You can say the sweetest things."

"I love you." There. Not sweet. Grim. Primal.

"And I love you."

Now there were murmurs from the crowd. Gasps of surprise. What? Like the baddest witch to live *couldn't* love? She did love. He knew it. He thought she might love more, and deeper, than anyone else.

"You've got a kingdom to rule," he whispered.

"The kingdom can wait." Her gaze was on him. "Something else is more important."

"Valerie—"

"*You* are." A pause. "But for the record, Ellya didn't cut my tie with Death."

Fear clawed into his heart.

Ellya stepped forward frowning.

"You are awesome, Ellya, and I totally consider your debt paid, but *I* cut the tie. I told that SOB if he didn't let me come back to Griffin, if he didn't give me the one man I needed more than anything else, then I would raise every single dead witch in his realm. I'd raise every dead shifter. I'd raise *everyone*. There would be no line between life and death. There would be no need for grim reapers to carry the souls to the other world. I'd freaking destroy *everything*." Her lashes fluttered. "But if he let me go, if he let me be with my mate, then maybe I wouldn't be quite so *bad*."

She'd scared Death into letting her go?

"You were worth fighting for. *We* are worth fighting for," Valerie added.

Hell, yes. *Yes.*

"Now, though, you have to promise me one thing..."

He'd promise her *anything*.

"Love me forever?"

"Forever is just the start." He kissed her again. When the witches cheered, he knew that Valerie had won. She'd be the council elder. She'd rule the witches *and* the shifters. She'd have everything that she wanted.

And as long as he had her—warm, alive and safe in his arms—Griffin would have everything, too.

His perfect ending. Not exactly a happily ever after.

But a life with Valerie—that life would be wicked and wild. *Everything* he'd ever wanted. Everything and more.

***

The dungeon was dank and dark, and it was the perfect place to trap an evil witch.

Valerie stalked toward the cell bars. She exhaled slowly and said, "Bet you didn't think it would end this way."

Genevieve lunged toward the bars. "*Get me out of here!*"

"I will, soon enough." She glanced down at Genevieve's wrists. "Love the new jewelry. Those bracelets are killer."

"You put them on me."

"I did."

"And only you can take them off!"

"That *is* how it works."

Genevieve was panting. "You'll never take them off."

"I don't know. *Never* is a very long time." Valerie tapped her chin. "I will say, though, that I don't plan on removing those lovely bracelets anytime soon."

Genevieve let out a high-pitched scream of frustration.

Someone was dramatic. Valerie put her hands on her hips. "At least you're still alive. That's more than I can say for Devon."

"*He's* the one who put me up to all of this! He was obsessed with you! He was—"

"Devon is gone. You're still here. Maybe try taking responsibility for your own shit." She glanced to the cell on the right and to the shifter imprisoned there. "You might want to start by apologizing to Elliott. After all, you did screw with his life."

Genevieve flinched.

Elliott growled and flashed very, very sharp teeth.

"I think your love spell is totally broken," Valerie announced in a too loud whisper. "And I think he's pissed." She waved at Elliott. "Good news for you, though, bear. You get to keep living, and I'm hopeful that you'll even be able to redeem yourself one of these days."

"*He* gets a second chance? And I don't?" Genevieve blasted. "He's an animal! I'm a witch!"

"No, you're human. Now." And that was the best possible punishment for Genevieve. "It's going to be hell trying to live without magic, isn't it?"

Genevieve's hands fisted around the bars. "I know what you are!"

Valerie let her brows rise. "The leader of the witch council? The strongest witch on earth? The—"

"They think you have a heart, under all of that fire. That you aren't as evil as you seemed to be. That you actually care about those fools who think they are your *friends*."

Valerie's shoulders tensed as her hands fell away from her hips. "You'll want to be very careful how you proceed."

"Why?" Genevieve shrieked. "What do I have to lose?"

Everything. Oh, wait. Valerie had already taken all of that.

"It was planned. From the very beginning, wasn't it? *Wasn't it?*" Genevieve's voice probably could have broken glass.

"If by beginning, you mean the moment when you and Devon stopped me from saving Tomas...?"

Genevieve gave a jerky nod. "Yes. Then. You learned what you could do. That you could raise the dead. A terrible magic that no one should use. It's unnatural."

Valerie gave a little wince. "I'm pretty sure most magic is."

"You didn't *save* anyone out of the goodness of your heart. There is no goodness there, despite what the fools think." Spittle flew from Genevieve's bow-shaped mouth. "You did it because you had a plan. An end game."

Valerie just waited. She was rather curious to see what all Genevieve had figured out.

Genevieve backed away from the bars. She lifted her right hand and raised her index finger. "First piece of the puzzle...you knew the only poison that could immobilize a witch was Medusa venom. So you needed venom and *that's* why you raised Stefan. Not because you saw some poor kid being attacked, but because you saw an opportunity. Hell, maybe you originally planned to use his venom against me and Devon or maybe—maybe you knew that, eventually, we'd use the venom on you. So you got Stefan to help you. Got him to give you small amounts of the poison so that you could develop an immunity to it. Fucking diabolical."

"Yes, I was. I mean...I could have been." Valerie waited to hear more.

"After Stefan, you raised that crazy Scot, Magnus. The witch who was turned into a vamp."

"You don't see those particular transformations every day."

"No, you don't." Genevieve's chest heaved. "You brought him back because you knew that someone with his particular skills—witch magic and vampire blood—someone like him could make *your* blood poison. That way, you could stop vampires."

What an interesting story. "Now why would I be interested in stopping vamps?"

"Because you knew I'd transformed Tomas!" A shriek.

Valerie blinked in surprise. "You did that? No."

"You *knew*. Just like you knew I was the one whispering in his ear, convincing him to burn you at the stake. Tomas was your weakness, and I wasn't going to let him age and die. Not when I could potentially use him in the future. I convinced a vamp to transform him. And then I fed Tomas's rage against you."

Valerie slanted a glance at an avidly watching Elliott. Then she focused on Genevieve once more. "Did you use a love spell on Tomas, too?"

"Yes." A hiss.

"Then if I were you, I'd be careful. I mean, that spell is broken. *And* he's still alive. Or, rather, undead. And you know what? I bet he's pissed at you."

Genevieve's mouth dropped. "You—you didn't kill him?"

Valerie shrugged. "I saved him from death once. Couldn't quite bring myself to kill him after all that effort. But, let's just say your story so far is right—and I knew he was a vamp—maybe I just wanted to protect myself in case Tomas got biting close. And that's why I turned my blood into vamp poison. A poison that was, of course, inspired by Medusa venom."

Genevieve shook her head. "What will you do with Tomas?"

"Magnus gets him." She wasn't going to say more, not then.

Genevieve's breath came faster, harder. "The djinn was your next *save*."

Valerie pressed a hand to her chest. "What? You think I didn't just feel sympathy for a woman who'd been tragically betrayed by those close to her? Who'd had her magic stolen and tainted? You didn't think I might feel a little connection with her?"

"Nothing can trump a djinn's wish. That was your ace in the hole in case everything else went to hell."

"Or in case I did," Valerie muttered.

Genevieve's face had mottled a terrible red. "The one I don't understand..." She pointed to

Elliott. "He told me that you raised that useless boy, Rio."

Now Valerie stiffened. *You don't call my henchman useless.*

"He can't help you. The boy can't even shift. Everyone else was brought back to serve your battle plan. The boy makes no damn sense." Genevieve glared. "You didn't save him to be kind. I *know* there has to be a reason. There is no kindness in you. There is no goodness. There is nothing but a dark void."

"Go ahead, tell me what you really think..."

"Why did you save the shifter kid?" Someone sounded hysterical.

"First of all, he's not a kid. He's an adult. A guy who was willing to risk his life to protect me."

"You don't care about that crap!"

She should put this in terms that Genevieve would understand. "Big picture. He's a late bloomer. One day, he'll shift into the strongest beast the world has ever seen."

Genevieve gulped. "I knew it..."

"A beast who can destroy witches. Vampires. Demons. You name it. He will be the best assassin the world has ever seen. And he'll swear his loyalty to me."

"How do you know? Who helped you? Who told you all of this?" Genevieve's eyes narrowed to slits. "It was Fate, wasn't it? She always liked you, hell if I know why."

"I'm likeable." Valerie winked at her.

Genevieve let out a primal scream. "She told you what would happen. Bits and pieces, and you figured out the rest, you figured—"

"I can see potential." Those words shut up Genevieve. "I can look at a person and feel the power inside. What might be. What *could* be. Under the right circumstances, mind you. Not like it happens with every single individual. It's a little gift I have. A gift that came in handy while I was planning my future."

"I was right. There is nothing good in you, there is—"

Valerie finally dropped her act. It was time. "There is darkness and there is evil. There is pain and there is retribution." She wasn't smiling any longer. "Never think there is anything else. I administered your punishment. Your powers are gone. Those bracelets—even if you someday get them off—you'll never work magic again. I ensured that. My magic has bound you, soul deep."

The mottled spots on Genevieve's face faded. Her skin turned far too pale.

But Valerie wasn't done. "If you ever come after me or anyone who belongs to me, I will burn you to ash. I won't hesitate. I won't stop. I will protect what is mine with a fury that you cannot comprehend."

Genevieve backed up a step.

"You're right about me," Valerie told her with a nod. "I'm not nice, and I'm certainly not good. Let the others believe I am. All of those witches who now want to embrace me? Let them think they misunderstood me all along." She leaned forward, as if imparting a deep, dark secret. "But you've always known who I truly am. Just as I've always known who you are."

"You...you..."

"I'll kill you, and I'll make sure you never rise again. You see, even Death fears me."

Genevieve didn't have a comeback.

Valerie's nostrils flared. She could smell the other woman's fear. "Good. I think we're done here." But before she left...her gaze cut to Elliott. He was watching her with wide eyes. "That warning goes for you, too, bear. Ever try and tell anyone the truth, and I'll rip your beast away. You can join Genevieve in the human world. Your second chance isn't being given because I'm weak. It's being given because now, I own you."

She held his gaze because she wanted to make sure he got that message.

Then she brought her hands together in a little clap. "Well, good talk. I've got to get back upstairs. There are parties waiting. Parades being planned. Lots of people want to tell me how amazing I am. You know... the usual." She turned her back on them. Headed forward with her head high and her shoulders back.

After all, she knew how to make an exit.

And she knew how to keep up appearances.

Her steps were confident and determined as she climbed the stairs. Up, up, she went—

And hard hands grabbed her. She was pulled into the shadows on the second flight of stairs. She opened her mouth, and Griffin kissed her.

Kissed her like a starving man.

Kissed her like a man in love.

Kissed her...as if she weren't wicked.

Her hands curled around his shoulders. She'd known he was there, of course. Waiting and watching, wanting to make sure she didn't need protecting.

Sweet shifter.

His head lifted. He stared at her. Just stared with his dragon's eyes. Then his hand twined with hers. They walked up the rest of the stairs. Headed away from the dark, dank dungeon and didn't speak until they were in the privacy of their bedroom. When the door shut behind them, he was still holding her hand. She glanced at their linked fingers.

He'd heard everything.

She wondered...what story would he believe?

That she'd planned every act, that she was cold and hard-hearted?

Or would he think that perhaps there was something more to her? That she had saved the others because there was a shred of goodness inside of herself? That she'd just been lying to her arch enemy?

Griffin brought their linked hands to his lips. He pressed a kiss to the back of her knuckles. "The first time we met..."

"When you were trapped in that dungeon and I *saved* you?" Just in case he needed the reminder.

His lips twitched. "You told me that you were a liar."

Her stomach knotted. "I am. I am a very, very good liar."

"I know, love. I know." He pulled her closer.

But did he think she'd lied to him? Or to Genevieve?

"You saved Rio because the kid wormed his way into your heart."

She would never admit that. Never. She had a reputation—

"I could see it in your eyes. You became his protector from the first moment you saw him. That's why you went crazy on Lucinda. You have a soft spot for the underdog."

Valerie neither confirmed nor denied his theory.

"You never expected him to get killed. When he died for you, you reacted instinctively. I was there, baby. I *saw* you. I always see you. The real you."

She caught her lower lip between her teeth.

"I wasn't there when you saved Stefan, but I can imagine the scene. A kid getting attacked by vamps? That would have pissed you off. You don't like it when the weak are threatened. It's kind of your thing."

She bit down harder on her lip.

"And a witch who'd been forced to become a vampire? Of course, you would have felt bad for Magnus."

Yes...maybe.

"Then there's the djinn. She reminds me a lot of you. I wonder...did you know her before she died?"

Her lashes lowered. "I did."

"And she was your friend, wasn't she? Rather like Calliope? I don't think you like to give up the friends you have."

She made herself look into his eyes. "Genevieve was my friend once."

"And I think that is the only reason she is still breathing." He moved closer. Lifted their joined hands and pressed them over her heart. "I see you, love. All of you."

"Don't make me into some kind of do-gooder. I'm not. Never will be."

Griffin laughed. "I wouldn't dare." His laughter faded, but his eyes continued to hold a faint glow. "You dance on the graves of your enemies."

"Damn straight." If Devon had a grave, she'd be dancing on it right then. But his ashes had blown away.

"You seek vengeance for the wrongs done to you."

"Always." She had a list of revenge plans a mile long.

"You curse and you hex, and you have one hell of a good time."

"Only every single day." Life was about having fun.

"And you hold my heart..." He unfurled her hand. "In the palm of your hand." He brought her palm to his mouth. Kissed her skin. "You're my witch. And I love you, every single part of you. Good, bad, and all of the stuff in between."

Valerie shot onto her tip-toes. Kissed him. Kissed his sexy, delectable mouth. Kissed the shifter who'd chosen her. *Her*. With no magic involved. With no love spell. With nothing to blind him to her dark nature. He'd still chosen her.

And she'd always choose him. "I love you, too." Her perfect match. Her sexy beast. "Every single bit of you." Strong. Smart. Powerful.

His head lifted. "What do you want to do first, my queen?"

A laugh slipped from her.

And she could *see* the love in his eyes.

Her gaze darted to the bed. Then back to Griffin. "First?" Valerie murmured. "I'd like to do you."

He picked her up and carried her to the bed. She wound her hands behind his neck and lost herself in his kiss. She finally had what she wanted, and, no, it wasn't her new position as ruler of the witch nation. It wasn't all of the power that was suddenly at her command.

What she wanted...

Griffin. Someone who loved her, someone who wanted her...the good parts and the bad.

Her true mate.

***

The raven's echoing cry flooded through the dungeon. He perched on his master's shoulder, and they closed in on their prey.

The vampire glanced up, flashing his fangs.

"Am I supposed to be afraid?" Griffin bared his own sharp teeth. "Dumbass, think again."

Tomas swallowed. His eyes were the size of saucers.

"As a general rule, I don't like vampires." Griffin ran his claws over the bars of the cell. "And I especially don't like *you*."

"You're going to kill me."

"I would like nothing more." He could picture it so easily. In his mind, Griffin opened the cell. Swiped out with his claws. And the fool's head hit the stones. "You hurt the woman I love."

The raven gave a rough gurgle.

Griffin stroked the bird's head. "Easy." He smiled at Tomas. "Edgar wants your eyes."

"You're as fucking crazy as she is!"

"No." And he lost his smile. "I'm crazier. Because I had to be in this world *without* her. I know what it is like when she isn't here, and I will *never* let that happen again. Valerie is mine, and I will always protect her."

"I didn't want to be a vampire! Didn't want any of this! That other witch—Genevieve—she had me under a spell. She forced a vamp to transform me—"

"Bitch and moan. Bitch and moan. Is that all you can do? Try being a man. Try owning your shit." Griffin snapped his teeth together. "Valerie is giving you to a vamp named Magnus. She's trying to form an alliance with the vamps, and she believes she's showing some kind of good faith gesture. At least, that's the story Valerie is circulating. I think she just doesn't want to get her hands dirty by killing you herself."

Tomas flinched. "I'm sorry...for what I did. It was like...it wasn't me, it was like—"

"It's fucking *you* now. So you listen to me, and you hear me clearly." He held Tomas's gaze. "If you ever threaten her in any way again, I will burn the flesh from your body. I will make you suffer before the gates of hell finally open up and claim your ashes." He waited a beat. "Are we clear?"

"V-very."

The raven flapped his wings.

"Right," Griffin added, because he thought he knew exactly what Edgar wanted him to say. "And my pal here will make sure he takes out your eyes before the fire gets them."

Tomas backed up a step. For a moment, it looked as if the vamp might vomit.

"Valerie is not being weak by allowing you to live. She's showing how strong she truly is. Never forget that." If Tomas did forget...

The dragon would be ready.

Griffin spun on his heel. He was done there.

"I won't come after her! I-I swear, I'm different now...I'm me...and I loved her. I loved Valerie once. I—"

In a flash, Griffin was back at the cell. "Don't think about that shit again, got me? She's over you. She's taken. And she deserves far more than some weak ass fool who never appreciated what he had."

"What did I have?" Tomas whispered.

"The whole fucking world." Griffin could almost pity the vamp. Almost. "Valerie is giving you a second chance, but that chance *isn't* with her. Do exactly what Magnus orders, don't hurt humans, and, most importantly, stay away from my witch—or you'll find a dragon hunting you down."

Now he was done. Griffin and Edgar headed for the stairs. He marched up, thinking he'd showed incredible restraint. After all, he hadn't ripped out the fool's spine.

Valerie was waiting on the stairs. Hidden in the shadows. Much like he'd hidden and waited while she faced Genevieve.

He glanced at Edgar. "Did you tell her I was going down to the dungeon?"

The raven flew away.

Valerie wrapped her arms around Griffin. "You've got such a wonderfully wicked side."

He pulled her closer. She'd cloaked her scent from him. Hadn't made a sound. Sneaky witch.

"Just another thing I love about you," Valerie added.

Griffin lowered his head.

"But you need to know something..."

He stared into her eyes.

"I didn't love him. Not the way I love you. Nothing has ever felt like this. You *are* my world, Griffin. And I'm better, I'm stronger, with you at my side."

"Good." He feathered a kiss over her lips. "Because that's where I'll always be."

Her smile took his breath away. But then her eyes narrowed. Suspicion slid onto her face. "You know...I've been wondering about exactly what your third beast is. I mean, I know you turn into a dragon and a wolf..."

He'd been keeping some of his own secrets.

"You and Edgar seemed awfully chummy," Valerie added. He saw the moment the truth clicked into her eyes. "You're a raven!"

"Guilty." And only *some* of those many times had she actually been stroking Edgar's chest. The times the guy had been talking trash to her. The rest of the time, Griffin had gone to her. He had perched on her shoulder. He'd flown overhead, wanting to make sure she was okay. He'd stayed near her, just because he liked to be close.

He knew something special when he saw it.

"Sweetheart, let's get the hell out of here," Griffin murmured. They'd spent enough time in dungeons. The world was waiting.

Their world. Their life.

Wicked. Wild.

And everything in between.

EPILOGUE

The witch had tamed a dragon.

Leo, the newly minted Lord of the Dark, stared out at the blue ocean waves. He tapped his fingers against his thigh. He was still getting used to being in charge of the "bad" paranormals. They sure as hell did things he didn't expect.

Mora strolled to his side. She pressed a kiss to his shoulder. His beautiful Fate.

"Should I be worried?" Leo had to ask her the question. "I mean, she came back from the dead."

"Valerie is stronger than Death. She always was."

Again...not good. "She's got a dragon at her beck and call."

"The better to keep her enemies at bay."

His gaze jerked to her. There had just been something about the way she said that particular phrase...*The better to...* "Love, did *you* set her up with the dragon?"

She smiled. "Me? You think I guided her to the dungeon where they first met?"

Shit, she had. "You do realize that—together—they could be strong enough to take me down."

"They aren't your enemies. In fact, you play your cards right, and they might just be your best allies."

He wasn't sure he liked the sound of that. But, a close ally was better than a sworn enemy so...

"Besides, Valerie and I are besties." She gave him a wide grin. "Didn't I mention that to you?"

His temples were going to explode. "No."

"We've been friends...forever."

"You helped her. All along. You told her what was going to happen—"

"That would be cheating."

Only if they were all playing some insane game.

"Besides, I didn't need to tell her. Valerie always had great instincts." She kissed his shoulder again. "And she'll help you, when you need her."

He shouldn't ask. He should *not* ask. "Why am I going to need her?"

Her gaze lifted upward, as she stared at the clouds. "I'm afraid things aren't looking so good up there. In fact, you may just never know when someone will fall."

A fallen angel? Hell. "I need a drink."

"You should probably have two...and maybe we should invite Valerie and Griffin over for dinner."

Not good. Not...

"You know the old saying, 'Keep your friends close, and your enemies closer.'" She turned and headed back for the house.

He stared after her. "I thought you said they were our friends."

She kept walking.

"They *are* friends, right?"

She glanced over her shoulder. "How about we just see what happens next?"

Shit. Maybe he'd get three drinks.

But Mora laughed. "Got you."

He scooped her into his arms and held her tight. "Baby..."

"Witches can have mates, you know. They don't form the bond quite like shifters, and it's rare, but when a witch finds her true soul mate...legend says that nothing can separate them. That together, they can even beat Death."

So that was what they'd done.

"And when I use the word 'legend'—I mean, of course, myself. I'm the one who knew that a true bonding couldn't be stopped."

Sometimes, she was scary. And sexy as all hell. He kissed her. "Let's go be bad, love," Leo murmured against her mouth. "Very, very bad..."

"Thought you'd never ask."

THE END

A NOTE FROM THE AUTHOR

Thank you so much for reading WICKED AND WILD!

I had so much fun writing this book. Valerie may just be my favorite heroine. She says what she thinks, she does what she wants, and the witch has one hell of a good time. As I wrote this story, my fingers were flying over the keyboard. I loved having the opportunity to revisit my "Bad Things" world—and if you'd like to see more of these paranormal stories, shoot me an email at info@cynthiaeden.com and let me know!

If you'd like to stay updated on my releases and sales, please join my newsletter list.

https://cynthiaeden.com/newsletter/

Again, thank you for reading WICKED AND WILD.

Best,
Cynthia Eden
cynthiaeden.com

ABOUT THE AUTHOR

Cynthia Eden is a *New York Times*, *USA Today*, *Digital Book World*, and *IndieReader* best-seller.

Cynthia writes sexy tales of contemporary romance, romantic suspense, and paranormal romance. Since she began writing full-time in 2005, Cynthia has written over one hundred novels and novellas.

Cynthia lives along the Alabama Gulf Coast. She loves romance novels, horror movies, and chocolate.

For More Information
- *cynthiaeden.com*
- *facebook.com/cynthiaedenfanpage*

HER OTHER WORKS

Death and Moonlight Mystery
- Step Into My Web (Book 1)
- Save Me From The Dark (Book 2)

Wilde Ways
- Protecting Piper (Book 1)
- Guarding Gwen (Book 2)
- Before Ben (Book 3)
- The Heart You Break (Book 4)
- Fighting For Her (Book 5)
- Ghost Of A Chance (Book 6)
- Crossing The Line (Book 7)
- Counting On Cole (Book 8)
- Chase After Me (Book 9)
- Say I Do (Book 10)
- Roman Will Fall (Book 11)
- The One Who Got Away (Book 12)

Dark Sins
- Don't Trust A Killer (Book 1)
- Don't Love A Liar (Book 2)

Lazarus Rising
- Never Let Go (Book One)
- Keep Me Close (Book Two)

- Stay With Me (Book Three)
- Run To Me (Book Four)
- Lie Close To Me (Book Five)
- Hold On Tight (Book Six)
- Lazarus Rising Volume One (Books 1 to 3)
- Lazarus Rising Volume Two (Books 4 to 6)

Dark Obsession Series

- Watch Me (Book 1)
- Want Me (Book 2)
- Need Me (Book 3)
- Beware Of Me (Book 4)
- Only For Me (Books 1 to 4)

Mine Series

- Mine To Take (Book 1)
- Mine To Keep (Book 2)
- Mine To Hold (Book 3)
- Mine To Crave (Book 4)
- Mine To Have (Book 5)
- Mine To Protect (Book 6)
- Mine Box Set Volume 1 (Books 1-3)
- Mine Box Set Volume 2 (Books 4-6)

Bad Things

- The Devil In Disguise (Book 1)
- On The Prowl (Book 2)
- Undead Or Alive (Book 3)
- Broken Angel (Book 4)
- Heart Of Stone (Book 5)
- Tempted By Fate (Book 6)
- Wicked And Wild (Book 7)

- Saint Or Sinner (Book 8)
- Bad Things Volume One (Books 1 to 3)
- Bad Things Volume Two (Books 4 to 6)
- Bad Things Deluxe Box Set (Books 1 to 6)

Bite Series

- Forbidden Bite (Bite Book 1)
- Mating Bite (Bite Book 2)

Blood and Moonlight Series

- Bite The Dust (Book 1)
- Better Off Undead (Book 2)
- Bitter Blood (Book 3)
- Blood and Moonlight (The Complete Series)

Purgatory Series

- The Wolf Within (Book 1)
- Marked By The Vampire (Book 2)
- Charming The Beast (Book 3)
- Deal with the Devil (Book 4)
- The Beasts Inside (Books 1 to 4)

Bound Series

- Bound By Blood (Book 1)
- Bound In Darkness (Book 2)
- Bound In Sin (Book 3)
- Bound By The Night (Book 4)
- Bound in Death (Book 5)
- Forever Bound (Books 1 to 4)

Stand-Alone Romantic Suspense

- Never Gonna Happen

- One Hot Holiday
- Secret Admirer
- First Taste of Darkness
- Sinful Secrets
- Until Death
- Christmas With A Spy